NO MERE MORTALS

Seeing all the cliques grouped according to ancestral god makes me wonder about Nicole. Seems like she doesn't hang out with anyone but herself—and now me. But she's part immortal, too.

"So, which god are you—"

She suddenly jerks me across the hall toward an open door, almost sending me sprawling on the floor.

"What the—"

"The Hades harem," she explains. "You do *not* want to mess with them."

And, peeking out the doorway, boy can I see why.

The group just rounding the corner look like your average Goths—black hair, black clothes, black eyeliner—but with an edge. Pretty fitting for the god of the underworld's descendants.

Shoulder-to-shoulder, they stride down the hall, daring anyone to get in their way. The Zeus set stares them down, but most of the other students scamper out of their path. As they pass the doorway, a tall, thin girl with pale blue eyes stares at me with intimidating intensity. I know I must be a novelty and all, but she really doesn't need to look like she wants to melt me with her eyes.

"Who is that?" I ask, my voice barely a whisper.

"That," she says, grabbing my shoulder and dragging me into the classroom, "is Kassandra. Trouble on a cosmic scale."

ℯℯℯℯℯℯ

OTHER BOOKS YOU MAY ENJOY

Chicks with Sticks: It's a Purl Thing	Elizabeth Lenhard
Geek Magnet	Kieran Scott
Hope Was Here	Joan Bauer
I Was a Non-Blonde Cheerleader	Kieran Scott
S.A.S.S.: Westminster Abby	Micol Ostow
S.A.S.S.: Girl Overboard	Aimee Ferris
Scrambled Eggs at Midnight	Brad Barker and Heather Hepler
Sorority 101: Zeta or Omega?	Kate Harmon
Sorority 101: The New Sisters	Kate Harmon
This Lullaby	Sarah Dessen
The Truth About Forever	Sarah Dessen
24 Girls in 7 Days	Alex Bradley

oh. my. gods.

Tera Lynn Childs

speak
An Imprint of Penguin Group (USA) Inc.

SPEAK
Published by the Penguin Group
Penguin Group (USA) Inc., 345 Hudson Street, New York, New York 10014, U.S.A.
Penguin Group (Canada), 90 Eglinton Avenue East, Suite 700,
Toronto, Ontario, Canada M4P 2Y3, (a division of Pearson Penguin Canada Inc.)
Penguin Books Ltd, 80 Strand, London WC2R 0RL, England
Penguin Ireland, 25 St Stephen's Green, Dublin 2, Ireland (a division of Penguin Books Ltd)
Penguin Group (Australia), 250 Camberwell Road, Camberwell, Victoria 3124, Australia
(a division of Pearson Australia Group Pty Ltd)
Penguin Books India Pvt Ltd, 11 Community Centre,
Panchsheel Park, New Delhi - 110 017, India
Penguin Group (NZ), 67 Apollo Drive, Rosedale, North Shore 0632, New Zealand
(a division of Pearson New Zealand Ltd.)
Penguin Books (South Africa) (Pty) Ltd, 24 Sturdee Avenue,
Rosebank, Johannesburg 2196, South Africa

Registered Offices: Penguin Books Ltd, 80 Strand, London WC2R 0RL, England

First published in the United States of America by Dutton Children's Books,
a division of Penguin Young Readers Group, 2008
Published by Speak, an imprint of Penguin Group (USA) Inc., 2009

5 7 9 10 8 6

CIP Data is available.

Speak ISBN 978-0-14-241420-0

Designed by Irene Vandervoort.

Printed in the United States of America

For Mom and Dad, because they got it right on the first try

oh.
my.
gods.

CHAPTER I

WHEN I'M RUNNING I can almost feel my dad at my side.

He's been gone for nearly six years, but every time I lace up and slap sole to pavement I feel like he's right there. I can feel him talking about my inner strength and how I will be a world-class athlete when I grow up. That's part of why I love running—why I'm running right now, pushing myself a little harder than usual to win this race.

This isn't just any race—it's the final race of the USC cross-country summer camp. Every winner of this race for the last seven years has wound up with a full scholarship offer. Since USC is the only college I've ever considered attending, I plan on winning this race.

With the nearest runner almost fifty yards back, I'm not worried.

The finish line comes into sight. Dozens of people are waiting—coaches and trainers from the camp, campers who competed in the shorter races, parents, and friends. As I get closer I see Nola and Cesca—my two best friends—cheering like crazy. They've never missed one of my races.

I'm closing in on thirty yards.

Twenty yards.

Victory is guaranteed. I pull up a little bit, not really slowing down but relaxing enough to let my body begin its recovery.

That's when I see Mom.

She's standing with Nola and Cesca, smiling like I've never seen her smile—at least not in the last six years.

Why is she here?

It's not that Mom doesn't come to my races, but she wasn't supposed to be at this race. She's supposed to be in Greece, getting to know Dad's extended family at a gigantic family reunion while I'm at cross-country camp. Trust me, the choice between running eight hours a day and spending a week with creepy cousin Bemus was not a hard decision. Meeting him once was more than enough.

I wonder why she's home two days early.

Then, suddenly, I'm across the finish line and everyone surrounds me, cheering and congratulating me. Nola and Cesca push through the crowd and pull me into a group hug.

"You are such a superstar," Cesca shouts.

Everyone is so loud I barely hear her.

"Is there anything you can't do?" Nola asks. "You just beat the best in the country."

"You *are* the best in the country!" Cesca adds.

I just smile. Could a girl ask for better best friends?

The next runner crosses the finish line, and some of the crowd goes to congratulate her. Now that I'm not fully surrounded I see Coach Jack waiting to talk to me. Since he's my ticket to USC I pull out of our group hug.

"Hey, Coach," I say, my breathing starting to return to normal.

“Congratulations, Phoebe,” he says in his gruff tone. “I’ve never seen anyone win so decisively. Or so easily.”

He shakes his head, like he can’t quite figure out how I did it.

“Thanks.”

My cheeks blush. Sure, I’ve been told my whole life that I have a special talent for running—from my dad, my mom, my friends—but it feels a lot more real coming from the head coach of the USC cross-country team. There’s a rumor that he’s going to coach the next Olympic team.

“I’m putting you at the top of the list for next year,” he says. “If you keep up with your classes and continue to perform well in races, the scholarship is yours.”

“Wow, I—” I shake my head, beyond excited to be within reach of everything I’ve ever wanted. “Thanks, Coach. I won’t let you down.”

Then he’s gone, off to talk to the other racers who are now piling across the finish line. Turning, I look for Mom. She’s right behind me, still smiling, and I dive into her arms.

“Mom,” I cry as she pulls me into a hug. “I thought you weren’t coming back until Tuesday.”

She squeezes me tight. “We decided to come back early.”

“We?” I ask, leaning back to look at her.

Mom blushes—actually blushes, with pink cheeks and everything—and releases me. She reaches out her hand to the side, like she’s grabbing for something.

I stare blankly as another, clearly male, hand meets hers.

“Phoebe,” she says, her voice full of girlish excitement, “there’s someone I want you to meet.”

My heart plummets. I suddenly have a very bad feeling about what she's going to say. All the signs are there: blushes, smiles, and a male hand. But still, I shouldn't jump to conclusions. I mean, Mom's just not the type to date. She's . . . Mom.

She spends her Friday nights either watching movies with me or poring over client files from her therapy practice. All she cares about are me and her work. In that order. She doesn't have time for guys.

The guy connected to the male hand steps to Mom's side.

"This is Damian."

He's not a bad looking guy, if you like the older type with dark hair that's salt-and-peppering at the temples. His skin is tan, making his smile much brighter in contrast. In fact, he looks like a nice guy. So really, I would probably like him if not for the fact that he's glued to my mom's side.

"He and I are . . ." Mom giggles—actually *giggles*! "We're going to be married."

"What?" I demand.

"A pleasure to meet you, Phoebe," Damian says with a subtle accent, releasing Mom's hand and reaching out to shake mine.

I stare at his hand.

This can't be happening. I mean, I want to see Mom happy and all, but how can she go off to Greece and come back six days later with a fiancé? How mature is that?

"You're what?" I repeat.

When he sees I'm not about to shake hands, Damian puts his arm around Mom's shoulder. She practically melts into his side.

"We're getting married," she says again, bubbling over with

excitement. "The wedding will be in Greece in December, but we're having a civil ceremony at City Hall next weekend so Aunt Megan and Yia Yia Minta can be there."

"Next weekend?" I am so shocked I almost don't realize the bigger implication. "Wait. How can you get married out of the country in December? I'll be in school."

Mom slips her arm around Damian's waist, like she needs to get even closer to him. Next she'll be sliding her hand into the back pocket of his pants. No girl should have to watch her mother revert to teenage behavior.

"That's the most exciting part," Mom says, her voice edging on near-hysteria with excitement. I know instantly that I'm not going to like what she says. "We're moving to Greece."

"Be reasonable, Phoebola," Mom says—like using my nickname will make me suddenly okay with all of this. "This isn't the end of the world."

"Isn't it?" I ask, shoving the contents of my dresser drawer into my duffel bag.

Mom sits on the twin bed in the dorm room that has been my home for the last seven days. Twenty minutes ago my life was perfect. . . . right on track.

Now I'm just supposed to pack up my life and move halfway around the world so Mom can shack up with some guy she's only known for a week?

Sounds like the end of the world to me.

“I know you were looking forward to spending your senior year at Pacific Park,” she says, entering therapist mode. “But I think that the move will be good for you. Broaden your horizons.”

“I don’t need broader horizons,” I say, grabbing the pillow off my bed and tugging at my striped pillowcase.

“Honey, you’ve never lived anywhere but Southern California. You’ve gone to school with the same kids your entire life.” She places her hand on my shoulder when I lean past her to grab my blanket. “I worry that when you go off to USC next year you’ll be in for a shock.”

“I won’t,” I insist. “Nola and Cesca will be there.”

“So will thousands of other students from across the country. From around the world.”

“That doesn’t mean I need to be from around the world, too.”

Turning away from Mom, I quickly fold my blanket and drop it on top of my duffel. All my things are packed, but I’m not ready to go yet. Not when I know *he’s* out there somewhere. Not when my whole world is being pulled out from under me.

“Come,” she says quietly. “Sit down.”

I look over my shoulder to see her patting the bed.

I tell myself to remain calm. This is still Mom, after all. She’s usually very reasonable. . . . maybe she’ll listen to my argument. Prepared to discuss this like adults, I plop down next to her.

“Mom,” I say, trying to sound as mature as possible, “there has to be some other way. Can’t he move here?”

“No,” she says with a sad laugh, “he definitely cannot.”

“Why not?” I ask. “Is he wanted by the law or something?”

Mom gives me an of-course-not look. "His work demands he remain in Greece."

Work! There's something I can use.

"What about your work? Your practice?" I inch closer. "Won't you miss your daily dose of crazies?" Not a PC term, I know, but I'm operating in desperation mode.

"Yes. I will."

"Then why are you—"

She looks me straight in the eyes and says, "Because I love him."

For what feels like forever, we just stare at each other.

"Well I don't see why I have to go," I say. "I could stay with Yia Yia Minta and finish off my year—"

"Absolutely not," Mom interrupts. "I love your grandmother like my own mother, but she is in no position to care for you for an entire year. She's nearly eighty. Besides,"—she nudges me in the ribs—"you hate goat cheese."

"I know, but—"

"You're my baby girl." Her voice is determined. "I refuse to lose you a year early."

Great, Mom has separation anxiety, so I have to leave the hemisphere.

"Are you trying to ruin my life?" I demand, jumping up and pacing back and forth on the bare linoleum floor. "What, was everything going too smoothly? Worried that I didn't have enough teen angst to work with? That I wouldn't need therapy when I hit thirty?"

"Don't be ridiculous."

"Me? I'm not the one who flew off to a family reunion and came back with a fiancé—wait, he's not family is he? That would be beyond *ew*, Mom."

"Phoebe." Her voice is laced with warning, but I'm building up steam.

"I've heard about these spur-of-the-moment European marriages. Are you sure he's not just using you to get his green card?"

"Enough!" she shouts.

I stop cold and stare at her. Therapist Mom does *not* shout. I'm in serious trouble.

"Damian and I love each other." She stands up, tucks my blanket under her arm, and hangs the strap on my duffel over my shoulder. "We will be married next weekend. He will return to Greece. At the end of the month you and I will move to Serfopoula."

"Who's ever even heard of Serfopoula anyway?" I ask as I pace back and forth at the foot of my bed where my bright yellow rug used to be.

"Just think, Phoebe," Cesca says. "You'll be basking on the pristine white shores of the turquoise Aegean."

Okay, she has me there. Beach runs are kind of my weakness, but that is *so* not enough to make moving worthwhile. There are plenty of beaches in California.

Cesca gazes dreamily up at my cloud-painted ceiling, like she's picturing frilly umbrella drinks and hot cabana boys. Her sigh is positively envious. Fine. She can take my seat on the flight to Athens tomorrow.

“I don’t know,” Nola says. “A practically uninhabited Greek island with nothing on it but a private school and a tiny village? Suspicious, Phoebe.”

Nola—short for *Gra*nola, if you can believe it—is our resident conspiracy theorist. Her parents are hippies. Not *were* hippies . . . *are* hippies. As in they believe in free love, protest our school’s nonvegetarian lunches, and think the Cubans, the Mafia, and the CIA all conspired to kill Kennedy.

“Sounds like that tiny island in the Caribbean where the navy was bombing goats.” She flops onto my bed—sending three furry pillows bouncing to the floor—and folds herself into a yoga position. “Or maybe that was the island off the coast of California.”

“Either way,”—I snatch the pillows off the floor and stuff them into the nearest box—“tomorrow I’m going to be on a plane flying halfway around the world to live with a guy I barely met and now I’m supposed to call him Dad and pretend like we’re a big happy family.”

I realize I’m shoving the pillows so hard into Box Four of Six that I’m crushing the cardboard. Not smart, considering I don’t have any more boxes. Better that I take my frustrations out somewhere else than end up with one less box of necessities.

I stalk over to the desk and carve *3 Furry Pillows—Pink* onto the contents list. It’s no fun having to account for everything I’m packing. Not when I can picture grimy customs officers pawing through my belongings to compare the list to the stuff in the box.

Cesca spins in my hot pink desk chair, her mind still on the turquoise Aegean fantasy. “I wonder if it’s near where they filmed *Troy*. Do you know which part of the Aegean Snarfopoly is in?”

"Serfopoula," I correct, because Mom has drilled it into me. "And I don't care how close it is to anything. It's miles and miles away from here. A world away from you guys."

My two best friends in the whole world—since the first day of kindergarten when Nola gave Cesca and me hemp friendship bracelets and Cesca taught me how to tie my shoes the *cool* way. We've been inseparable for the last twelve years and now there's going to be an entire ocean and most of two continents between us.

How can I make it through my senior year without them?

Okay, now I'm close to tears. We've been locked in my room all afternoon, packing the last of my possessions into the six boxes I'm allowed to take. Six! Can you believe it? How am I supposed to condense a lifetime of living in the same house into just six boxes?

I understand leaving my furniture—my canopy bed, my dresser covered in bumper stickers, my antique desk with "I luv JM" carved into the bottom drawer and then scratched out—but six boxes will only hold about one-quarter of everything else. That means that for every one thing I put in a box, three get given to charity.

That makes a girl reevaluate her possessions.

The pink fur sticking out of Box Four catches my eye. I scowl at the offending pillows. Do I really want to waste space on pillows? Stalking back to the box, I jerk them out and fling them into the charity pile.

"Are you taking your curtains?" Cesca asks.

"Crap!" I swear, I'm going to forget something important—like those white gauzy panels covered with big, shiny sequins that reflect little dots of color all over my room when the sun hits them just right—and it's not like I can buzz back home to pick up a few things.

My eyes are watering as I pull down the curtain rod and slide the curtains off one end. Although their gauzy quality didn't do much to block out light, I now have an undiluted view of our neighbor's house. More precisely, Jerky Justin's bedroom window.

He's probably in there with Mitzi Busch right now.

That's the one, singular benefit of moving to the other side of the world. I won't have to see his smug face in the halls of Pacific Park anymore. There is no downside to being thousands of miles from the ex-boyfriend who delights in making my life miserable.

Like it's my fault I won't put out. Well, actually it is, but that doesn't mean he needed to break up with me at junior prom and make a big show of sucking Mitzi's tonsils whenever I'm around.

I turn from the window in a huff, inspired by the thought of never seeing him again. Nola and Cesca are standing right behind me, eyes wet and arms outstretched.

"Damn, we're going to miss you," Cesca says.

Nola nods. "Won't be the same without your energy."

I step into their arms for a group hug.

The thrill of leaving Justin behind evaporates and all I can think is how I'm never going to see my two best friends ever again. At least not until college—when we will all be together at USC.

No more holding back the tears. They stream down my cheeks, dripping off my chin onto my DISTANCE RUNNERS DO IT LONGER T-shirt, Cesca's silk ruffled halter top, and Nola's unbleached organic cotton peasant blouse.

Trying to salvage some degree of cool, I wipe at my tear-puffed eyes and say, "At least we get Internet on the island."

That would have been a deal breaker.

No Internet, no Phoebe.

Cesca wipes at her own tears, usually only called upon when she had to convince her dad she needed something really expensive. "Then you have to e-mail every day."

"Maybe," Nola says, her face glowing as she embraces the raw emotion of her tears, "we can have a regular IM meet."

"As if," I say. "There's a ten-hour time difference."

"We'll just have to work something out," she persists.

Nola is nothing if not persistent.

"You're right," I manage, if only because I want to put on a brave face until they're gone, when I can cry my eyes out on my stripped-to-the-mattress bed.

"Okay, enough blubbering," Cesca says. "Let's get your junk packed so we can watch *The Bold and the Beautiful* before I have to head home."

"Yeah," I say, tossing the curtain panels into Box Four, "it'll have to sustain me for the next year. You'd think we could at least get satellite on that stupid island."

There's not much to do on a ten-and-a-half-hour flight from L.A. to Paris while your mom is sleeping in the next row of a nearly empty plane. The movie selections were repulsive at best and the line at

LAX security was so long I didn't have time to buy the latest *Runner's World.*

"Ladies and gentlemen," a French-accented male voice announces, "we have begun our final descent into Charles de Gaulle airport and should be on the ground in approximately thirty minutes."

That was another thing. Our flight to Athens routed through Paris, but did I get to hop out and see the city of lights? No. We have forty-five minutes to get to our connecting flight and I'll be lucky if I have time to look out the window at the clouds over Paris.

"*Madame.*" A flight attendant gently shakes Mom awake. "We are landing, you must sit up."

Mom stretches in a big yawn and manages a sleepy, "*Merci.*"

The flight attendant throws me a skeptical look—like I can help it if Mom sleeps like the dead—but moves on to wake the other sleeping passengers.

I go back to scanning the clouds below for a peek at the Eiffel Tower or the Louvre or something monumental. Even a beret would be acceptable at this point.

"Did you sleep, Phoebe?" Mom asks as she slips back into the seat next to mine.

No, I want to say, *I didn't sleep.* How can I be expected to sleep when I'm crossing an ocean for the first time? Or starting at a new school for the first time since kindergarten? Or landing on foreign soil knowing it will be months, if not longer, before I get back to the land of shopping malls and French fries—and don't even try to trick me with the whole there-are-McDonald's-everywhere argument because I know it just won't be the same. Not when I'm eating the fries alone and not splitting my large order with Nola and Cesca over a big pile of ketchup.

But, since fighting never got me a new pair of Air Pegasus Nikes, I'm more content to pout than fight. Pouting leads to guilt-induced presents—some of my best gear came from dedicated pouting sessions. I just shrug and keep my eyes on the clouds.

Maybe I shouldn't be proud of manipulating Mom this way, but it's not like she *asked* me if I wanted to move to the opposite side of the planet. I deserve a little questionable behavior.

"Look, Phoebola."

Mom nudges my ribs and points to the other side of the plane.

I want to ignore her, but there is some serious excitement in her voice and I can't help following the direction of her finger. Through the tiny oval Plexiglas I can see an expansive city divided by a meandering river.

Ignoring the illuminated FASTEN SEAT BELTS sign, I climb over Mom's knees and slide into the window seat across the aisle.

The flight attendant walks up just as I land and gives me a serious frown. I make a big show of buckling my seat belt, pressing the tab into the slot just like she showed us before takeoff.

Appeased, she moves on to the next row.

I press my nose to the window, eyes following the meandering Seine. Even though we weren't staying in Paris even an hour, I had studied a map in the Air France magazine just in case the miraculous happens and we miss our connection, forcing an overnight layover. Knowing Mom, she'd probably find us a train to Athens. Anyway, a short distance up the river I see it. Though it should be practically invisible from however many thousand feet and however many miles away, the lacy iron structure of the Eiffel Tower stands out against the sea of grassy, tree-filled parks and old stone buildings. In my dreams I imagine running the 1665 steps from ground level to the observation deck at the top, hitting the wall halfway up and pushing through, finding my second wind and bounding onto the third level like Rocky running up the steps in front of the Philadelphia Museum of Art. I imagine I'm like Dad tucking the football into his elbow and leaping over a bunch of defensive backs to run forty yards to the end zone in the AFC playoffs.

"We'll come back one day," Mom whispers. "I promise."

I hadn't even noticed her take the seat next to me. Running fantasies almost always leave me oblivious. Especially ones that lead to thinking about Dad. The only time I'm less aware of the world around me is when I'm actually running.

I blink up at her, envying her beautiful green eyes that look so much more striking against our chestnut hair than my brown ones. Her eyes are glowing more than ever and I know it's because of Damian.

Turning back to the window, I find the Eiffel Tower gone and all I see is the rapidly rising asphalt of the runway.

Great, one step closer to stupid Serfopoula.

The only thing remotely exciting on the flight to Athens—if you don't count the woman trying to smuggle a hedgehog onto the plane—is actually catching it. We run through the airport like we have Cerberus biting at our heels, managing to get directions to the wrong gate twice—sometimes I think the French *try* to be unhelpful—and have to go through security again before sliding into the gate seconds before they close the door.

I consider slowing us down—maybe playing the bathroom card or the cramps card—but I have a feeling I would lose all my pouting points for a stunt like that. Besides, better to get it over with rather than draw out the inevitable.

By the time we land in Athens—after three and a half hours of listening to the two women in my row chattering nonstop in enthusiastic, rapid-fire Greek—I am almost happy to be on Grecian soil. Until we find him waiting for us at baggage claim.

Damian Petrolas, my new stepdad.

If not for the fact that he married my mom and dragged us halfway around the world and is making me go to his stupid school, I'm sure I wouldn't think he was such a bad guy. He's charming, the kind of guy that makes you feel like a princess, even when you want to hate him—which I do. He's tall, like over six feet, and with his black hair dotted around the temples with gray, he looks wise and powerful. Not bad characteristics for the headmaster of a private school, I guess.

Mom, forgetting all sense of decorum and public decency, drops her not-insubstantial carry-on and runs for him, practically throwing herself in his arms. I am left to lug her ninety pound—or I should say kilos since I'm in a metric country now—briefcase the rest of the way to the carousel.

My backpack weighs nothing in comparison.

"I've missed you so much," Mom says between the stream of kisses she's laying on his face.

"And I, too," he says, "have missed you."

Then, with no consideration for my sensitive stomach, he takes her face in his hands and plants a big, open-mouthed kiss on her lips. And Mom opens her mouth right back.

I am looking around for a trash can to lose my airplane pretzels in when he speaks to me.

"Phoebe," he says in the disgustingly charming accent, "I am so happy to welcome you to my country. To my home."

And then, with no warning whatsoever—and it's not like I'm sending out approach-me vibes—he steps forward and puts his arms around me. In a hug.

Ewww!

I stand there like I'm waiting at the starting line, frozen and not sure what to do as he's squeezing me and patting me on the back. Mom catches my eye over his shoulder and gives me a pleading look, which I ignore. Then she scowls her I'm-your-mother-*and*-a-therapist scowl.

The one I have long since learned never to ignore.

So, with all the courage I can find deep down in my toes, I lift one hand and pat Damian on the shoulder in a show of returning the hug. Mom looks not quite happy, but he doesn't seem to notice my hug is half-assed.

He releases me, then—to my continued horror—grabs my head and presses two kisses alternately to my cheeks. Cesca told me all Europeans do this, though different cultures do different numbers of kisses. I guess Greeks do two. I can't stop the impulse to wipe his kisses off my flesh. Thankfully he has already turned away, taking Mom by the hand and leading her over to baggage claim. Leaving me with the ninety-kilo briefcase.

Our bags—two really big ones for each of us because most of our clothes had to come in the suitcases since the movers aren't scheduled to deliver our boxes for nearly a week—are already circling the carousel by the time we get there with a rented cart. At least I don't have to lug the briefcase all the way to the car.

Damian, leading the way with the cart, asks, "Would you prefer the bus or the metro?"

Whoa! Bus? Metro? As in public transport?

"I don't know," Mom says. "Which do you think, Phoebola?"

I stop moving, but nobody else seems to notice. They keep on walking, even though I'm getting farther and farther behind with every step. Then I have to run to catch up because as much as I don't want to be in Greece, I want to be lost in Greece even less.

As I run up, he explains, "The bus system is quite a confusing adventure, so perhaps we should take the metro and save that for another trip."

Nice. Another decision made without me. Not like it's my life or anything.

"Hmmph," I say as I shrug my backpack higher up on my shoulder.

Damian pulls the suitcases off the cart, handing one each to me and Mom and taking two himself, and heads off in the direction of signs that look like the Adidas stripes next to a golf ball. Mom follows blissfully behind, oblivious to my irritation.

This is a picture of my life for the next year—no, make that nine months because no matter what Mom says I'm moving in with Yia Yia Minta for the summer before college. Nine months of Mom in blissville and not even caring what her only child wants is going to be a nightmare.

"Where's Stella?" Mom asks.

Crap. I forgot about the evil stepsister.

Okay, I have not actually met her yet because she didn't bother to come to the wedding in America, but aren't all stepsisters evil? (Myself not included, of course.)

Damian looks at Mom, embarrassed. "She had other commitments."

Yeah right. What he really means is she doesn't approve of this any more than I do. Only he couldn't make her come to the airport like Mom had made me move to Greece. Score one for Stella. Maybe I should take lessons.

"Oh," Mom says quietly. "I guess we'll just meet her when we get . . . home."

It's very hard not to puke on my shoes. Home? Like his house will ever be home. Like any house except the burgundy and cream bungalow we'd lived in since I was born will ever be home. Mom must be seriously twisted by love hormones.

"Here we go." Damian leads us down an escalator and onto a train waiting at the platform.

We file onto the train, Mom and I sitting while he stands in front of us. I watch out the opposite window as the train starts out of the station.

This is not my first time on a train—we rode the subway in New York once on vacation—but it takes me a few stops to get used to the stop-and-go motion. Then, as we pull into the third—or fourth or fifth, I kinda lost track—station I actually notice something besides the rolling in my stomach.

The station has a display, like a museum exhibit, on the wall behind the platform. There is some old stuff, like pots and plates and scraps of fabric, and a bunch of plaques with bits of history and timelines and stuff. A sign above it all reads, "Domestic Life in Ancient Greece" in really big English letters, with the Greek ones right below.

Hmm. Pretty cool, I guess.

If you're into Greek history and all.

The train pulls out and I manage to both keep my balance and control the motion sickness. When we pull into the next station I'm looking for the display.

This time, the sign says, "The Cradle of Democracy." A huge mosaic fills up most of the wall, showing a huge crowd of men staring at one guy standing on a platform. The one guy looks like he might be making a speech or something. There are no women in the crowd. Or, for that matter, anything but old white guys. Typical.

As the doors glide shut, I flop back against the bench and cross my arms over my chest. I hope this country has evolved from the stone age. I'm not a feminist or anything, but I like my rights and I'd like to keep them. The ancient world was not very equal opportunity.

We slide into the next station and I'm almost dreading what this display will be about. Gladiators getting mauled to death? The horrific slave trade? Thousands being slaughtered at some huge, *Troy*-like siege? I glance out the window panel, prepared for the worst, and my eyes zero in on one word: "Marathon." Before I even think about it, I'm off the train and running to the exhibit. It's all about the marathon, as in the ancient one run by Pheidippides in 490 BC. The original cross-country race. There are pictures of Marathon, the site of the battle victory that Pheidippides ran to Athens to announce, and of the spot in Athens where he supposedly dropped dead after making the announcement. There are actual spearheads from that time like the ones that might have been used in the battle. There are ancient sandals like the ones he may have worn for his famous run.

Thank goodness for Nike. I could never run in sandals.

"Here she is," I hear Damian say.

I turn just as Mom rushes up and throws her arms around me. "Never run off like that again," she shouts.

Practically the whole station turns to stare at us.

"Sorry," I say. But looking back over my shoulder at the marathon display, I'm not at all sorry. I've just come within inches of the ancient origins of distance running. What do I have to be sorry about?

"The city of Athens installed archaeological displays such as this in many of our metro stations for the 2004 Olympics," Damian says. He's lugging all four suitcases and the ninety-kilo briefcase behind him, but doesn't even look unhappy.

"Oh wow," Mom says softly and with a touch of awe in her voice, stepping up to the display for a closer look, analyzing every detail like she always does. "This says the modern Athens marathon follows the same path that Pheidippides ran in 490 BC. Phoebe, this is amazing."

Like I want to share my visit to the shrine of distance running with them? Hardly. "Whatever," I say as I turn away and head back to wait for the approaching train. "It's not that great."

When the next train pulls up we climb back on—Mom has taken her two suitcases from Damian and he is stuck pulling mine, which makes me smile. I'm torn between not wanting them to know how much seeing that exhibit means to me and wanting to see as much of the exhibit as I can before the train chugs away.

In the end, I twist in my seat and watch out the window as the shoes of Pheidippides race out of sight.

Someday I'll come to this station again and take my time memorizing every little detail of the exhibit. Maybe when I'm breezing through Athens on my way to college back in civilization.

After the fourteen hours in a cramped plane seat and an hour on a packed metro train, I'm actually looking forward to the three-hour ferry ride to Serifos, an island *near* Serfopoula. Of course there are no direct ferry routes *to* Serfopoula.

Still, I can imagine myself gazing out over the turquoise Aegean—the salty sea breeze drowning out Mom and Damian's repulsive lovey-dovey talk and blowing my stick-straight hair into beach-hewn waves. At least we aren't moving somewhere with no major body of water. Heck, there probably isn't anywhere on Serfopoula that isn't within running distance of the beach. Beach runs are my favorite. Salty sea air rushing in and out of my lungs. Sand shifting under my feet, making my calves burn with extra effort. Collapsing in exhaustion and watching the waves crash the shore while restoring my energy. Pure bliss.

The actual ferry ride is nowhere near the peaceful boat trip I'm hoping for. Thank goodness my Dramamine kicks in because we aren't on a slow boat to Serifos, we are on a hydrofoil—a super high-speed ferry that bounces me off the deck when it hits even the tiniest wave. It's named Dolphin something-or-other, but it feels more like riding a really angry bull. One that can't wait to shake every last human off its back.

Riding the bucking bull is bad enough, but one more second of watching goo-goo eyes and I'm going to lose the contents of my stomach over the side of the boat. Mom and Damian don't seem to notice. They are busy standing close and batting their eyes at each other. Every so often he whispers something in her ear and she laughs like a little girl.

"I have to pee," I announce, more crudely than normal. I fully intend on actually using the facility until I get in there and am about to unzip my jeans when the bull hits a ripple and sends me sidelong into the door. I can only imagine what will happen if I actually squat in hover position and we hit a real wave. Instead of tempting fate I decide I can hold it until we find land.

We get to Serifos and spend a few glorious steps on an unmoving surface while Damian leads us to the chauffeured—*is a private boat driver a chauffeur?*—private yacht—*yes, yacht*—that will take us the rest of the way to the stupid, ferry-less island.

Does that mean there's no way off the island unless I have my own boat? Great, I'm going to be stuck on this stupid island until I get paroled. Or until I make friends with someone who has a boat.

Now there's a plan.

When I step onto the boat I'm smiling at the thought of befriending someone with transport.

Damian leads Mom to a bench seat on one side of the rear deck and I head for the opposite bench. Hopefully this boat ride will be less earthquake-like than the last, and I don't want my potential calm disturbed by disgusting baby talk or anything.

I think I'm out of hearing distance.

Not that Damian respects my isolation.

I rest my head against the back of the bench and start to close my eyes when he moves into the seat next to me. Prying one eye open to glare at him, I ask, "Yeah?"

Mom is sitting on the other side of him.

"Phoebe, there is something you need to know before we arrive at Serfopoula." He folds his hands carefully in his lap. "Are you familiar with Plato's Academy?"

The big philosophy school where a bunch of old Greek guys got together to talk about intense stuff like the origin of life and what kind of poison worked best? "Yeah."

"Well," Damian continues, "there is more to the Academy's history than most textbooks contain. In the sixth century, the Roman emperor Justinian issued an edict demanding the Academy be closed and forbade formal philosophical education. The . . . *ah-hem* . . . benefactors of the school were not prepared to see it closed so they moved it here. To Serfopoula."

I don't know Damian real well, but I think it's not typical for him to *ah-hem* in the middle of a sentence. He seems like a very formal guy who keeps his speech squeaky clean. Still, I think I should just ignore this observation and instead say, "Justinian must have been pissed when he found out they disobeyed his orders."

"He never found out." Damian swallows hard. "The . . . *ah-hem* . . . benefactors kept the knowledge from him."

There is something strange in the way he says this. Something ominous.

It must have been hard to keep a Roman emperor and every tattletale who would rush to tell him from finding out. Maybe these benefactors murdered anyone who found out and buried them in the school basement. I get shivers at the thought and I have to ask, "How?"

"Well, Phoebe." Damian looks over his shoulder at Mom, who nods in encouragement. "There is little the Greek gods can*not* do when they choose to act."

CHAPTER 2

MY FIRST THOUGHT IS, *Damian is insane*. Like crazy, nuts, messed-up-in-the-head insane. As if Greek gods really exist.

They are myth. Myth, as in the kind of stuff you read about in sophomore English with guys killing their dads and marrying their moms—*ew*, and I think my life is gross. As in, the kind of stuff you see Brad and Orlando duking it out over on the big screen—yum. *Not* the kind of stuff the man my mom married fully believes in.

I look at Mom, ready to express my sympathies and assure her I am ready to head back to America and that we can sort the divorce out once we get there. But she's not freaking out.

She's nodding.

Sympathetically.

At *me*.

As if I'm the one who just found out my new husband is delusional.

That's when I first know I'm in trouble. Mom is professionally trained in the art of delusional psychopaths. She told me once she never goes along with their fantasies—it only makes things worse—and if she's staying calm then that means she believes him. Which means she believes the Greek gods exist, too.

And while I might doubt her judgment when it comes to major life changes like marriage and moving out of the country, Mom is usually completely sane when it comes to discerning reality from fantasy.

As if she can sense my shock, she reaches out and places a hand on my knee. "I know this is difficult to digest—"

"Difficult?" I shout. "Difficult? Algebra is difficult. The Ironman is difficult. *This* is insane."

"I thought so, too," Mom says. "At first."

"So you believe this?" What happened to rational Mom? "You believe him?"

She nods. "I've seen proof."

"You've seen—" I shake my head. This is not happening. "What kind of proof?"

"It's a little hard to explain," she says, blushing. "He made roses . . . materialize."

"Roses?" Ha! I've got him now. "He's just a magician. He pulled them out of his sleeve."

Mom blushes even more. "He wasn't wearing sleeves at the time."

Ewww! Therapy is definitely in my future.

All right, so the rational, that's-not-really-possible approach isn't working. I've got more tactics in my arsenal. I just need a minute to regroup. While I'm trying to come up with my next move I realize that, since I haven't seen any roses around since we landed in Greece, Mom must have known before we took off from LAX.

Even if she's being totally played, she should have said something.

She's had plenty of opportunities, including fourteen hours in the confined space of an airplane cabin where I would have been a captive audience. And who knows how many times before the move—

"Wait a minute!" My voice rises to an accusatory scream. "How long have you known?"

At least she has the decency to look ashamed. "Since shortly after Damian and I met." She glances at him and smiles. "As soon as we realized we were in love."

What!? I cannot believe this. What has Mom married me into?

"There's something else. . . ." Mom says.

Oh no. I can tell from the way she trailed off at the end that I am not going to like this.

She nudges Damian. "Go ahead. Tell her."

He clears his throat before saying, "The students at the Academy are not your average schoolchildren."

Like I couldn't have guessed that. At least this isn't more earth-shattering news.

"We have an acceptance rate of less than one percent. Our admission standards are far more stringent than even the most elite universities," he says, "and are extremely specific."

Should I be overjoyed? I throw Mom a look that says I'm not thanking her for the favor. She knows I would rather be back in L.A. than accepted into some snotty school any day.

"Really," he says, "we have only one criterion."

Uber-popularity? Unfathomable wealth? Genius-level IQ? Great, I'm going to be a dunce at a school of Einsteins.

"All the students at the Academy . . ." He tugs at his navy blue tie—my first clue that he's a little nervous about telling me this—but it doesn't really look tousled. ". . . Are, *ah-hem*, descendants of the gods."

My world starts to go black around the edges as I stare at Damian's negligibly loosened tie and hear Mom say, "Oh no, I think she's fainting."

The next thing I know, Damian is kneeling over me and Mom is frantically waving her purse over my face. I think she's trying to fan me back to my senses, but all I can think is it would really hurt if she drops it on my nose. Her purse is like Mary Poppins's bag—it holds way more than should be possible.

I hear Damian say, "She is regaining consciousness. Zenos, send out the gangplank and bring the gurney."

Xena?

Mom's purse comes darn close to clipping me on the cheek.

Wait. A gurney?

The last thing I need is to make my arrival strapped to a gurney pushed by a fictional warrior princess. That is not the way to make a good impression—if this stupid school is anything like Pacific Park, gossip makes the rounds faster than the flu.

Not that I have any hope of making a good impression. It must be pretty hard to impress someone who sits across the dinner table from Zeus.

Wait, what am I saying? I must be in shock. This is ridiculous. Damian must be having some elaborate twisted joke on me. And on Mom.

But she says she's seen proof.

The black edges come back just as Mom finally swipes me across the nose. And ouch, does it hurt. That shakes me out of it and I bolt up, ignoring the tingling dizziness in my brain.

"I'm fine, really." I bat away a few of the bright yellow bugs swarming around my head before I realize these are only in my mind. Knowing Mom and Damian and the gurney-pushing warrior princess would have a field day with this, I close my eyes and take three deep breaths before saying, "I don't need a gurney, you can call Xena off."

"Who?" Mom asks, clearly not up on her TV culture.

"Not Xena," Damian explains. "Zenos. Our yacht captain."

Somehow, it is only a minor relief to find out that he knows some fictional characters are actually not real.

"Sorry," I say. "My bad." For the time being, I think it's better to just play along. I can talk some sense into Mom later—when we're alone. "I've got it now." I open my eyes, relatively certain I can maintain consciousness for the moment. "Xena, not real. Zeus, real. Check."

Mom and Damian exchange one of those I-don't-think-the-poor-child-is-buying-it looks. They're not far off. Who can blame me, what with the idea that the Greek gods really exist still ricocheting through my brain? I deserve at least a little wiggle room when it comes to confusing reality with fiction. Maybe if I approach it with a little scientific logic, Mom will see how crazy all of this is.

"So, what does this mean?" I ask, rubbing my temple to make it look like I'm really considering believing all this. "Are the students all immortal?"

"No, no, of course not. Immortality is reserved for the gods," he says with a little laugh. As if *that's* the most absurd idea floating around. "We descendants are more like the heroes of ancient legend. Like Achilles and Prometheus, we have some, *ah-hem*, supernatural—"

"Whoa," I interrupt. "We?"

"Damian is a descendant, as well," Mom says.

I close my eyes and take a deep, deep breath. This just keeps getting better. "All right." I wave my hands at myself as if to say, *Bring it on*. "You're like heroes. . . ?"

"Yes," he continues. "Like those you may have read about, we have varying degrees of supernatural powers. In most descendants the powers manifest pre-adolescence, though there are cases in which they remain dormant until after puberty."

"It's really quite amazing," Mom says, bubbling with enthusiasm. "There are apparently built-in controls to protect the rest of the world, with the gods monitoring all use of—"

I tune out. I mean, Mom seems honestly convinced and, until recently, I've always trusted her judgment, but this isn't exactly the kind of thing that's easy to accept. Like I can suddenly decide that everything I've ever learned about the Greek gods is not just some fluff story English teachers make you learn. No, it'll take more than Damian's say-so to move the Greek gods from the fairy-tale land of Santa Claus, werewolves, and Cinderella into everyday reality. But even if I'm not a believer in "alternative realities," as Nola calls them, I'm willing to keep an open mind. Sure, I'll believe they're real. Just as soon as I see one. . . .

"Well, well," the girl who just appeared next to Damian says. "I see the barbarians have arrived." When I say appeared, I don't mean she walked up and there she was by his side. No, she appeared. As in out of nowhere. As in she wasn't there and then she was. She, like, shimmered into place.

That's the kind of proof that's hard to ignore.

"Stella," Damian says, a serious hint of warning in his tone. "What have I told you about materializing?"

"Please, Daddy," she coos. "I just had to see them for myself. They're like a new exhibit of rare animals at the zoo."

Her voice is sickly sweet, like those sirens in *The Odyssey* who used their beautiful singing to attract men to their deaths. There isn't a trace of sincerity in her. Not from the brown roots of her overhighlighted hair to her bright red painted toes. And I don't think it's a simple case of overenthusiastic tweezing that makes her look like a bi'atch with a capital B-I-A-T-C-H.

"We will speak about this later," Damian says. And he does not sound happy. "I apologize for my daughter's . . . rude behavior. Barbarian is a term applied to non-Greeks." He shoots her a sharp look. "It is not meant in a derogatory manner. Not only is it misapplied, since Phoebe is half-Greek and Valerie is now Greek twice by marriages, but, as Plato once said, the term is absurd. Dividing the world into Greek and non-Greek tells us little about the first group and nothing about the second."

Stella looks completely unfazed, like she pisses him off every day. Why do I think she excels at getting herself out of trouble with her dad? I have a gut feeling that she's going to enjoy making my life miserable—and probably won't get in any trouble at all.

"I never thought of it that way," Mom says, taking Damian's hand, "but that's also true in modern psychoanalytic theory. If one defines their world in terms of 'object' and 'other' then one only knows what the object is and what the other is not."

Stella rolls her eyes. Damian nods. I have learned—after many years of theoretical nonsense talk—to ignore the psychobabble. Trying to follow along only ends in headache.

"Besides," Damian says, giving Stella one last disapproving look before smiling at me, "you are not the only non-Greek to attend the Academy. We are primarily a boarding school and many, if not most, of our students are from abroad. Our ancestors were not, shall we say, confined to a particular geographical area."

Right. I remember all those stories about Zeus and Apollo and the other gods jumping around from one seduction to the next. There are probably little mini-gods all over the world.

Stella smiles tightly, as if saying, *Whatever*.

"You must be Phoebe," she says, stepping forward and offering me a hand. "I'm Stella . . . your new sister."

Now, I've always wanted a sister, but not one like this. In my mind I picture a little girl with ringlets and dimples who follows me everywhere and copies my every move to the point of driving me crazy. Stella is not a follower. That much I can see in the icy gray shallows of her eyes. She crushes those foolish enough not to fall into place behind her. I am not that foolish.

"Yeah," I say, taking her hand and letting her pull me up. I'm shocked when she doesn't let go halfway and send me falling back on my butt. "Nice to meet you." The words choke out around the gagging sensation in my throat.

Then she shocks the living crap out of me by pulling me into a hug. Over her shoulder I see Mom take Damian's hand and look at me with pride, like they can already see us having sleepovers and sharing secrets and painting each other's toenails. She thinks we're halfway sisters already.

Only she doesn't hear what Stella whispers in my ear.

"I hope you're ready for a living nightmare, *kako,* because this school will chew you up, spit you out, and smite the tiny pieces of whatever's left all the way to Hades."

Mom smiles at me.

I whisper back, "I've survived beach bunny cheerleaders, a slut-hunting ex-boyfriend, and five years of cross-country camp. I'm not afraid of some throwback to ancient myth with atrocious highlights and a Barbra Streisand nose."

Catching Mom's eye I smile big, even as Stella squeezes me way too tight around the ribs. One stomp on her pedicured toes and I'm free.

"All ready," I say, snatching my backpack off the deck.

As I sling my pack onto my shoulder I see a spark out of the corner of my eye, just before the strap breaks, sending the bag flying right into Stella's nose. Sure, it was an accident—you can't exactly anticipate strap failure—but I couldn't have aimed better if I tried.

Too bad, though. This is a brand-new backpack.

Hand cupped over her injured nose, Stella's face turns bright red. She growls and lifts her other hand like she's going to point at me—way rude, by the way.

"Stella," Damian warns as he points a finger at my broken strap. The torn fabric glows for a second before magically repairing itself.

I grab my backpack off the ground and check the strap. It's perfect, like it never broke in the first place.

Stella jerks her hand back to her side before turning in a huff and stalking off the boat. I glance back and forth between Damian's steaming look and Stella's retreating back.

Wait a second. . . . Did she do that to my strap? That must have been the flash of light. Serves her right getting bonked in the nose.

Next time she'll think twice about zapping my stuff.

Dinner at the Petrolas house is unusual, to say the least.

Mom and I usually set up a pair of TV trays in the living room so we can watch the latest reality show while we eat. Not the best idea with some of the ubergross stunts they pull, but it was our nightly ritual.

Not only do we not even have TV on Serfopoula, but Damian and Stella actually eat at a dining table. In a dining room. Weird, huh?

"There is a small village on the far side of the campus," Damian explains while a servant—yes, an actual servant—serves the food. "It mainly consists of housing for Academy staff and faculty, but there are a few commercial establishments. There is a bookstore, a small grocery that sells locally produced fruits, vegetables, and dairy items, and, a favorite among the students, an ice-cream parlor."

That's it? No CVS or Foot Locker? What if I need Band-Aids or new Nikes? "What about that other island?" I ask. "Where we caught the yacht."

"Unfortunately," Damian says, "only Level 13s are permitted to visit Serifos during the semester."

I'm about to ask what a Level 13 is and why they're so special, when Stella says, "I'm a Level 13."

Of course she is.

"Yes," Damian says. "Because she plans to attend university in England, Stella must study for an additional year beyond your American twelve."

Across the table—a massive piece of dark wood furniture worn so smooth it must date back to the original Academy—Stella smirks.

"Yes," she coos. "British academic standards are much higher."

"Yeah, well," I say. It is on the tip of my tongue to say she must need remedial school only her dad's too nice to say so, but Mom kicks me under the table. Ouch! Clutching my throbbing shin, I cover by saying, "I'm going to USC, so I don't need another year."

"If you need anything at all," Damian says, "please let me know and we will make arrangements. There is very little we cannot get here on Serfopoula."

Yeah, except TV.

The servant, an older woman with wrinkled leather skin and a loose cotton dress decorated with embroidered blue flowers, sets a plate in front of me. There is some kind of salad, with recognizable cucumbers, tomatoes, olives, and stinky goat cheese that would be edible assuming I can pick around the onions. Next to the salad are two big slimy things that look like green sea slugs.

Damian must be able to guess what I'm thinking because he says, "Those are *dolmades*, traditional grape leaves stuffed with a rice mixture."

Stella laughs at me and pops one in her mouth.

"Yia Yia Minta makes these," I say, poking at one with my fork. "They're just not usually so . . . wet looking."

"Ah," Damian says, smiling at the old servant woman. "That is part of Hesper's secret recipe. She drizzles them with olive oil before serving."

"Shhh." The old woman, Hesper, bats at him. "You talk too much."

"But, Hesper," he replies, "they are family now."

The hairs on the back of my neck stand up. At first I think it's because of Damian's mushy comment—I don't think one little City Hall marriage ceremony makes a whole new family—but then I catch Stella's eye and she's staring at my plate and looking, well, constipated.

Light from somewhere reflects off my plate, shining up at me.

I look down and—

"Aaaack!"

Jumping up, I knock over my chair, trip when my laces get caught on one of the legs, and wind up face-first on the floor.

"Phoebe," Mom cries. "What's wrong?"

She rushes to my side, but by then I've twisted around and leaped to my feet. I point at my plate—now looking like a completely normal dinner salad—and scream, "M-m-my food!" I glare at Stella, who is looking way too proud of herself. "It was alive!"

Those green sea slug *dolmades* had come to life and were wriggling around in my salad with the olives and stinky goat cheese.

Any other day in the history of my life I would have checked myself into the nuthouse for seeing things, but after seeing Stella shimmer onto the boat—and zap my backpack—and my plate glowing, I know I'm not crazy.

So does Damian.

"Stella Omega Petrolas!" he yells.

Two throbbing veins pop out on his forehead and his face turns bright, bright red. Wow, he looks like he's going to explode. Crossing my arms over my gray RUN LIKE A GIRL T-shirt, I smirk at Stella. Let's see her shimmer her way out of this one.

Damian takes a deep breath and says a little calmer, "You know the rules about using your powers against another."

"But, Daddy," she whines, the fake tears starting. She's even got the poor pitiful me pout.

I watch with great admiration. I've never been able to actually produce tears. Maybe if I pay attention I can pick up some pointers.

"No buts," he says. He points at her with his right hand and a bright light shoots from his fingertip and suddenly all of Stella is glowing. "Your powers are grounded for one week."

"A week!" she shrieks as the glow subsides. "That's not fair. I only—"

"One week. Next time it will be a month."

Stella tries to stare him down—like that has ever in the history of the world worked to change a parent's mind. If it did then I'd be in Cali right now, and not on some stupid island trapped with a supernatural teenager clearly intent on making my life miserable. I can only hope that the rest of the kids at this school aren't this bad.

"Please," Damian says, oblivious to his daughter's angry eyes, "continue the meal."

I pull my chair upright, but hesitate before sitting back down.

I don't plan on eating anything that was crawling across my plate two minutes ago.

Sensing a searing glare, I glance up at Stella. Her gray eyes burn with undisguised fury. In comparison, the *dolmades* are much more inviting.

Besides, I need to eat all I can before she gets her powers back.

"So what is this school like?" I ask, forking a piece of cucumber. "I mean, if everyone is from all different places, then how do they take all the same classes?"

"For many centuries," Damian explains, "all classes at the Academy were taught in Greek. The gods felt that their descendants should learn their native language."

Oh great. How am I ever going to pull that B average I need for USC if I can't even understand the instructor? This is like one of those social experiments where they drop kids off in a foreign country and they have to either learn the language or be stuck there forever.

"When the British Empire rose to power in the early 1800s, the headmaster lobbied the gods to change the official school language to English." He takes a drink of water. "This turned out to be an extremely wise decision since many of our students go on to study at Oxford, Cambridge, and Ivy League universities."

Whew! Though, in the great grand scheme of things, the language barrier would be a minor problem.

"And if everyone but me has superpowers," I say carefully, building up the courage to ask what's really bothering me, "am I going to get zapped like a zillion times a day? Am I going to get . . ." I glance nervously at Stella, only mildly secure in the idea that her powers are grounded. "Smoted?"

Damian gives Stella a disapproving look, like he knows she threatened to smote me. "Certainly not," he says, his voice clipped. "The students have been made aware of your arrival and know better than to use their powers against you. If *anyone* . . ." The word hangs there, but I think we all know he's talking about Stella. ". . . disobeys my instructions you are to report them to me immediately."

"Sure." I push my plate away. But what if I can't tell him because I've been turned into a sea slug?

"I assure you, Phoebe," he says, smiling like I said something silly, "no student has been smoted from the Academy in generations."

Yeah, like that makes me feel better. That just means they're out of practice. They'll probably do it wrong and I'll end up on Mars or something.

"I know this is a little . . ." Mom sits down on my bed while I unpack my suitcases. ". . . hard to absorb."

"Hard to absorb?" I cry, flinging my good Nikes onto the floor and wheeling around to gape at her. "Hard to absorb? Finding out that Ben & Jerry's had discontinued White Russian was hard to absorb. This is . . ." I wave my hands in the air, trying to find the words to actually describe how I feel. ". . . freaking unbelievable."

She starts taking T-shirts out of the suitcase and folds them into neat piles according to color family.

"I'm sorry," she says, setting a red RUN HARD OR RUN HOME T-shirt on the red, orange, and yellow pile. "I should have told you sooner, but I thought you had enough on your mind already with all the major changes in our lives. I didn't want to overburden you with this additional worry."

So instead she waits until we're almost here. When I can't get away.

I snatch the T-shirts off the bed before she can restack them in order of shade and hue. Color coding is so not my thing.

"Whatever," I say, not really meaning it—I mean, she did keep this a secret for over a month. A month! "I'm over it."

There is a tall dresser in the corner of my room, and I try to pull open one of the middle drawers while balancing the enormous stack of T-shirts in my left hand. The drawer does not cooperate and it takes a monumental tug to pull it open, sending the T-shirts tumbling.

After I pick the T-shirts up off the floor I proceed with putting them away.

The dresser is the closest thing my room has to a closet. Other than that I actually kind of like the room. Like the rest of the house, the furniture is seriously old—the sturdy, made-to-last kind—and the floor is age-worn tile in the same dark brown as the furniture. The walls are bright white plaster and they feel cold when I touch them. I can't wait for our boxes to get here so I can add some of my own color.

"Phoebe," Mom says like she's disappointed that I'm not spilling my feelings all over the tile floor. "You can't bottle up your emotions inside. Talk to me. Are you worried about fitting in?"

"Look," I say—fine, I shout—as I slam the drawer shut, "drop the shrink act. I'm fine. I don't need psychotherapy or a Rorschach test or an open dialogue. Just point me to the computer so I can e-mail home."

She looks like she really wants to say something shrinklike, but thinks better of it. Good thing, too. I grew up on her therapist approach. It so doesn't work on me anymore.

The computer—something from the dark ages of technology if the dingy gray plastic is any sign—is in Damian's office. You'd think a guy with Greek gods on his PTA could afford to upgrade.

He is in his office when we get there, filling out some paperwork at his desk. Looking up, he smiles and asks, "Are you here to use the computer, Phoebe?"

I nod, thinking that's enough of a response. Until Mom pokes me in the ribs.

"Yeah. I want to e-mail my friends back home."

"Oh." His face falls and he looks to Mom for support.

Great. Another secret? Another reality-shattering headline?

"Honey," she begins. Her voice is quiet and way too hesitant, but it's the hand on my shoulder that tips me off to the really bad news. "We don't want to say you can't stay in touch with your friends, but—"

"What? I can't even e-mail my two best friends?" I shake her hand off my shoulder. "I thought being stuck on this stupid prison-of-an-island was going to be bad, but I can't believe this! Why don't you just put me in solitary and slide bread and water under my door twice a day?"

"It's not that," she insists.

"Phoebe," Damian says, using what I know must be his patient principal voice, "you are entirely free to e-mail whomever you choose. But we must ask you not to reveal the truth about Serfopoula and the Academy. We trust you to act responsibly."

Is that all?

"Fine," I say, sounding like it's a major concession when I'm actually thinking, *As if they'd believe me.*

I mean, Nola and Cesca are my best friends and all, but there are limits to every trust. Their faith in me would be seriously depleted if I drop an e-mail saying, *Safe in Serfopoula. It's hot, the evil stepsister has already struck, and, oh yeah, my new school is run by Greek gods.* Not in this lifetime.

"If you click on the envelope icon at the top of the screen it will lead you through the setup process for your Academy e-mail. I suggest using that program since messages sent from outside e-mail addresses are delayed through our screening software." Damian looks pleased when I nod. "Well, then we will leave you to your e-mail in private."

Good. I was afraid they'd stay and watch over my shoulder to make sure I didn't slip up. Mom doesn't look as pacified as Damian, but she lets him take her hand and lead her out the door anyway. As soon as they're gone I slip into the chair in front of the computer and log on to create my new Academy e-mail.

After entering my entire life history, the program finally prompts me to select my alias. I stare at it for a while before I realize it means I get to choose my own screen name. Nice.

Normally I use PhoebeRuns. That's what I had at Pacific Park and on IM.

Here, though, that seems too much like home. And this is definitely not home. This is more like a detour. Like I got lost on my way to USC.

That's it! I quickly type LostPhoebe for my alias.

Finally, I am in the actual e-mail program and click on compose.

To: granolagrrl@pacificpark.us,
princesscesca@pacificpark.us

From: lostphoebe@theacademy.gr

Subject: On the Island of Dr. Demento

Hi Girls,

Mom and I got here. Finally. You would not believe what we had to go through just to get to this stupid island. Planes, trains, hydrofoil ferries. You name it, we were on it. And the stepdad was there to meet us at the airport. I seriously considered losing myself in Athens. Really, what could they do if I just disappeared?

Then as soon as we got to the island the evil stepsister showed up. Boy is she a trip. She could give Mitzi Busch a run for her attitude. How am I going to make it through an entire year without you guys?

I start school first thing tomorrow, without even a get-used-to-the-time-change day off. Apparently this school is uber-exclusive. I bet it's full of snobs and rich brats who think their parents' money gives them the right to act all superior. Don't you wish you were me?

E-mail me soon!

Love,

Phoebe

I click send and log off. Bed is calling me. After all, it is ten hours later in Serfopoula and that means I haven't slept in, like, thirty-six hours. And I have to go to the Academy with Damian at seven-thirty to fill out paperwork and finalize my class schedule.

The only good thing about this whole catastrophe so far is Damian says the track coach is world class and so is the team. And tryouts are tomorrow after school. At least I'll get a good year of training in to prep me for the USC team.

Barely dragging up the energy to change out of my traveling clothes, I pull on a clean T-shirt and a pair of smiley face boxers and collapse onto my bed. At least the bed is comfy—all white and just soft enough. Still, I think I'm going to dream about green sea slugs and shimmering stepsisters tonight.

When my alarm clock goes off at six I'm tempted to fling it against the wall. I'm suffering serious jet lag in the form of whole-body muscle weakness and a headache that makes brain freeze feel like a pinprick. Tugging the white fluffy comforter up over my head to muffle the deafening alarm, I consider my two options.

Either I stay in bed, shut out the outside world, and hope that by the time seven-thirty rolls around—when I have to meet Damian—all my pain has faded away.

Or . . . I can toss off the covers, pull on my sneakers, and go for a good long run that might not erase the jet lag, but will at least replace this sluggish feeling with familiar physical exhaustion.

To snooze or not to snooze?

From beneath the covers I hear my room door burst open and smack against the wall.

"Turn that awful thing off!" Stella shouts.

Flopping a corner of the comforter back, I force one eye open and squint at her. I don't say anything at first—partly because I'm surprised that she could hear my alarm all the way down in the slimy dungeon I've pictured her sleeping in and partly because I'm trying not to laugh. She looks like a pint of mint chocolate chip exploded on her face.

"Did you fall asleep in a bowl of pistachio pudding?"

She scowls and jabs her finger at the still-blaring clock.

Nothing happens.

"Aargh!"

I smile. Maybe I can get Stella grounded for the entire year—at least then I'd be safe.

If her face weren't covered in green I know she would be turning red.

When she stomps in my direction, I fling my arm out and smack the top of the clock. I don't want her getting any of the green goop on my fluffy white comforter. "Forget it," I say, sitting up and swinging my legs out of bed. "I'm getting up anyway."

For a moment she looks like she wants to continue her attack, but then turns and stomps back to her room.

My brain is waking up—no turning back now.

I grab a pair of track pants, a T-shirt, and a pair of white socks out of the dresser, pull them on in a matter of seconds, splash some water on my face in the bathroom, lace up my sneakers, and am heading out the door when the snoozing alarm clock starts blaring again. Smiling at the thought of Stella having to hunt it out from under my bed, I start down the path to the dock where we arrived last night. Where there's water there must be a beach.

The dock is in a little lagoon, nicely protected from the open sea, with rocky cliffs on one side and a narrow strip of sand on the other. Even though I'm not going to push my worn-out body too hard, I sit on the dock and do ten minutes of stretches. Pulling a hamstring is the last thing I need.

The sun is just starting to rise and casts a pale pink over everything. I take deep, filling breaths as I reach for my toes, taking in the salty clean smell of the sea. A different smell from the California beaches I'm used to. Purer, maybe.

I twist my upper body to the one side, going for that extra oblique stretch, and notice a cluster of little white buildings on top of the cliffs. Bathed in the early morning twilight, it looks just as pink as the rest of the island. That must be the village. It seems so strange that there are people that live up there in that little village, a world away from L.A., with whole lives that go on whether I'm here to see them or not. I guess that's true of everywhere—the cars you pass on the freeway, the towns you fly over at thirty thousand feet, and those little white buildings. Suddenly, L.A. feels even farther away.

Surrounded by pink and silence, except for gently lapping waves, I embrace the inner and outer peace. Leaving the dock for the thin strip of sand, I kick into a moderate run. If my entire year here were just like this moment then things might not be so bad. But I know that this feeling only exists when I run. It's why I run. That, and to feel closer to Dad.

As the sand squishes beneath my Nikes, I lose myself in the memory of our early-morning training runs. When Dad was training in the off-season we would run almost every morning. Almost always on Santa Monica beach. We would park near the pier, run the three miles down to Marina del Rey, and then race back to the pier for ice cream. If I beat him, I got a double scoop.

I don't even realize I'm crying until I taste my tears. Not slowing my pace, I wipe at my eyes. Why was I even thinking about Dad? Usually I don't think about anything when I run. I'm too focused on the sensation of running.

Clearing my mind, I notice the burning in my quads. How long have I been running? The world around me is no longer bathed in pink. A quick glance over my shoulder confirms my suspicion. The dock is nowhere in sight and the sun has cleared the horizon.

I need to get back.

Dropping to a walk, I'm about to turn around and head back when I notice another person running on the beach. He's less than two hundred yards away from me, close enough for me to appreciate the loose, easy movement of his gait. I can tell his body is made for running, and somehow I know that his soul lives for it. I guess I recognize a kindred spirit.

Before I know it—because I'm mesmerized by watching him run—he's jogging to a stop right in front of me. I practically melt into a puddle of girl drool.

He looks around my age and he is beyond beautiful. It isn't just his hypnotic blue eyes or his perfect, sloped nose, or his sculpted high cheekbones. His lips are full and soft and yummily pink. The kind that just make you want to grab him by the hair with both hands—even though I can't see his hair under the blue bandanna—and make out until you can't think anymore.

"Hi," he says, his voice just low enough and smooth enough to send shivers down my spine.

"Hi," I say back.

Brilliant. Normally, speaking is not a problem for me, but I'm hypnotized.

His mouth lifts up at one side, like he finds it funny that I'm staring and incapable of speech. "Where did you run from?"

"Um," I say, continuing my display of brilliance. A large portion of my brain is distracted by the faint accent that makes his question sound like a melody. I manage to gesture vaguely over my shoulder. "The dock."

His eyebrows shoot up. "That's nearly eight kilometers."

"What?" That's like five miles. I've been running for over half an hour. Even if I keep my same pace the whole way back I won't have time to shower before meeting Damian. And the way my thighs feel, I'm definitely going back at a slower rate.

Great, I'm going to show up for my first day of school sticky and smelling like sweat.

"There's a shortcut," Mr. Beautiful offers. Pointing to the rocks at the edge of the beach, he explains, "That path will get you home in half the time."

I squint at the rocks, trying to find a path. All I see are big, beige rocks and short, shrubby bushes that look like they might like to scrape the crap out of my legs.

“It’s there,” he says with a laugh. “It starts out steep, but you’ll be on the flat after the first half kilometer.”

Finally spying the narrow path, I turn back and say, “Thank—”

But he’s already gone, running back the way he came.

I didn’t even get to ask his name.

“Thanks!” I shout after him.

Without turning or slowing he waves over his shoulder. I allow myself a few seconds of appreciation—watching him from behind is even more mesmerizing. Then, shaking myself out of that detour into fantasy, I turn and head up the path.

I’m back at the house in under twenty minutes, with just enough time to shower and dry my hair before I have to meet Damian.

Following Damian up the broad front steps of the Academy, I feel my jaw drop at the gorgeous building that is my new school. Clearly very old—ancient even—the whole stone front is lined with columns that stretch all the way to the roof. Above the columns is a triangle filled with carvings of men and women doing all different things—standing, sitting, lying down while eating grapes. It looks like a drawing I saw once of what the Parthenon might have looked like when it was new. Nothing like the single-story, boring to the point of hospital decor building that houses Pacific Park.

“This building dates to the relocation of the Academy in the sixth century,” Damian explains. He pushes open the massive golden front door and gestures for me to go in. “The only changes since that time have been technological modernizations. We have one of the most advanced computer labs in the world."

"Good to know some things on this island have reached the twenty-first century," I say, thinking back to the ancient computer at his house.

Then I step into the expansive front hall and all thought flees.

In front of me, directly across the stone tiled floor from the main door, is the biggest trophy case I have ever seen. And it is jam-packed with shining gold trophies.

"Wow," I whisper, unable to hide my awe.

"The Academy has an illustrious history," he says, walking up behind me when I zombie-walk to the glass case, spellbound by all the glitter.

"Are all these for sports?" I ask. Front and center is a big gold trophy that makes the Stanley Cup look like a wineglass. That must be for some major competition.

"Hardly," Damain says with a half-laugh. "The sports trophies are nearer to the end of the cabinet."

I follow the direction of his gesture with my eyes. I have to squint to see the section he's pointing to because it's halfway down the never-ending hall.

The hall is like twenty feet wide and just as tall, all shiny-smooth stone. Marble, probably. Clearly it runs the entire length of the building—all several hundred feet. Now I notice that there are windows in the wall behind the columns, letting in bright stripes of morning sunlight across the marble floor and reflecting off the glass-fronted cases. The whole space glows with the same soft amber color as the marble.

Every last inch of the interior wall is a trophy display.

"Then what—"

"Many of these are for academic competitions," he explains, answering my question before I finish. "But we also hold many historical artifacts on display. Artifacts too valuable to display in a museum. Our security is impenetrable."

"Artifacts?"

"This," he says, pointing to a no-larger-than-life-size apple that looks like it's been dipped in gold, "is the Apple of Discord, the cause of the Trojan War."

I lean in for a closer look. Other than being gold, it doesn't look any different than a regular apple. Then the letters of a Greek word carved on its side start to glow, like it knows someone's watching.

"Be careful." Damian pulls me back. "The Apple is tremendously powerful and dangerous. Do not get too close."

"Oh," I say casually, trying not to look impressed. "What else do you have?"

"There is one display I think you will especially enjoy." He strides off down the hall toward the sports section. When he stops in front of an almost empty case I nearly run into him.

All that's in the case is a little wreath of dried-up twigs. Not very impressive. Damian must think I'm easily amused.

Then I read the plaque.

Laurel presented to the first Olympic champion, Nikomedes, 919 BC.

Oh. My. God.

I blink up at Damian, disbelieving.

He smiles, a broad, self-satisfied smile that tells me he knows he impressed me and he isn't going to let me forget it. I don't care.

Reaching up, I finger the glass in front of the wreath, marveling at the thought that it had once crowned the very first Olympic champion ever. Kinda makes our medals seem like Happy Meal prizes.

"Come, Phoebe," Damian says, "we must discuss your schedule."

"B-but—"

He gently presses a hand to my back and leads me away. "There will be plenty of time for worshipping the athletic artifacts," he says. "You will be here for one year, at least."

Yes, yes, one year.

"Next time,"—he stops in front of a door and, unlocking it, ushers me inside—"I will show you the actual Sandals of Pheidippides."

It's a good thing Damian points me to the chair in front of his desk because I am on the verge of expiring from excitement. Suddenly, hurrying back to Athens to see the subway display—on my way back to civilization or not—seems like a really unnecessary expedition.

Who needs a replica when you can see the real deal?

CHAPTER 3

"YOU'RE THE *NOTHOS*."

Turning around in my desk, I stare at the girl behind me.

"The what?" I ask.

"*Nothos*," she says again. "The normal one."

"Normal?" I laugh. "Depends on your definition."

"As in not a descendant."

"Oh, then I guess so." It's true, after all.

She sticks out her hand. "I'm Nicole."

"Phoebe," I say, smiling as I shake her hand.

Nicole is the first person I've met at the Academy. Okay, so technically I'm only in my first class—World Literature of the Twentieth Century—and it hasn't even started yet, but still, a first is a first.

"Your stepsister is an evil harpy." Her voice is stone cold and I must look as frightened as I feel because she hurries to add, "In a purely metaphysical way."

"Oh." Whew. Not that I would be the tiniest bit surprised if that were true, given everything I've learned in the last eighteen hours. And beautiful but vicious pretty much describes Stella perfectly. "Tell me about it."

"Have you got a year?" she asks and I like her immediately.

Clearly, Stella is not high on her list of favorite people, either.

I am still laughing when the teacher, Ms. Tyrovolas—I can already see myself in detention for repeated mispronunciation, so I should probably just go with Ms. T—walks in. High school teachers at Pacific Park do not look like this: almost six feet tall, light brown hair curled and pinned up all around her head like a crown, and wearing something that looks like a cross between a sheet and an evening gown.

Staring is horribly rude, but I can't help it. I've never seen anyone who looked like that—not even in Los Angeles, where weirdos come out to play.

Without looking at me, Ms. Tyrovolas says, "I see you are unfamiliar with the costume of ancient Greece, Miss Castro."

I blink, not really knowing how to respond. She did catch me staring, after all, even if she had her back to me at the time.

The entire class turns to stare at me.

Trying to act cool, I swipe a hand over my head to make sure I haven't sprouted horns or anything. Haven't they ever had a new student in class before?

"Um, not really, Ms. Tra— um, Tivo— Tul—"

Nicole whispers, "Tyrovolas."

"Turvolis," I say, my voice catching. Why didn't I just go with Ms. T?

Ms. T turns around and everyone is instantly focused on their desks.

I try to smile, but I think it comes across more as a grimace.

"The tradition has been passed down since the founding of the Academy," she explains, "and I choose not to disregard our history."

At least I don't have to dress that way. My personal uniform of jeans and a T-shirt suits me just fine. On the rare occasion of a more formal event, Mom usually has to bribe me into dressy pants. A dress would cost her World Cup tickets.

Don't think she won't have to pay to get me into a bridesmaid's dress for the wedding.

"Tyrant is steadfast about tradition," Nicole whispers.

Which maybe explains why Ms. T is giving her a dirty look. With her short, bleached blonde hair—in an I'm-a-little-bit-punk and not at all I'm-a-cheerleader kind of way—half an arm of hot pink and white jelly bracelets, and silver glitter eyeshadow, Nicole is far from traditional.

"Thanks for the heads up," I say back. "So, are the teachers here . . . I mean, is Ms. T a—"

"Descendant?" Nicole asks. "Oh yeah. She's direct lineage from Athena. We're talking serious bookworm."

"I thought Athena was the goddess of war."

"You don't think Tyrovolas could kick some ass?" Nicole laughs. "I'm just teasing. War is only part of Athena's domain. She's also the goddess of wisdom, which makes her a big busybody with everything that goes on at the Academy."

Navigating this school is going to be a lot tougher than I ever imagined. I thought at least the teachers would be normal, but no luck there.

I need a new student handbook.

And the classwork? Let's just say I'll be struggling to maintain the B average I need to get into USC. Ms. T's syllabus looks like a work of world literature itself and we'll be reading more books in one year than I've read in my entire life. So much for Cesca's fantasy of me lounging on the beach—I'll be spending all my free time reading Kafka and Orwell and writing a twenty-five-page term paper.

She even teaches for the whole period—on the first day!—diving into the influences of Freud and Einstein on modern thought and the ramifications on everything from literature to war. By the time she dismisses us—the Academy doesn't have bells at the end of class—my brain is fried.

Only three more classes until lunch.

We walk out into the hall and there are students everywhere.

Unlike the hall inside the front entrance, the rest of the building looks pretty much like a school. The halls and floors are typical off-white and lined with lockers. Classrooms branch off on both sides, with big windows that look out over either the hills surrounding the school or the inner courtyard. All of the upper-grade classes meet on the second floor, while the lower grades take up the first. I guess that's so the younger kids can have recess out in the courtyard.

"Who do you have next?" Nicole asks.

I glance at the schedule Damian made for me. "Algebra II with Mr. C—"

"Cornball," she says and snatches the schedule out of my hand. "Me, too."

"—Cornelius," I finish.

"Look." She waves a finger at the schedule and the bottom half glows for a second. "Our afternoon schedule is the same."

Leaning in, I read the last three classes. *Physics II, Art History, and Philosophy.* "I'm supposed to be in Computer Applications and Biology," I argue. "I hate Art and I never had Physics I."

"No worries," Nicole says. "I'll get you through. Science is my thing and Mrs. Otis gives all As for art appreciation." She frowns at the schedule. "We'll just have to suffer through Dorcas together—no one gets out of here without Philosophy."

She shrugs and hands me back the schedule, as if she can't do anything more about it. Should I be upset? Should I go have Damian change my schedule back?

Or should I be thankful that someone seems happy to have me here and that maybe, just maybe, I've actually made a friend?

Folding the schedule, I stuff it in my pocket.

"Wow," I say. "How'd you do that?"

Nicole looks at me like I'd said the dumbest thing on the planet. "You really are *neo*, aren't you?"

"If that means out of my league, then yes."

"Don't sweat it, you've got me." Nicole takes my hand and pulls me over to a bare section of wall, out of the crowd's path. "I didn't start at the Academy until Level 9. It's pretty rough if you don't have help, and most kids here aren't into going out of their way to help a *nothos*—or, as some will call you, a *kako*. There are some basic rules you need to know."

This morning, Damian had seemed single-mindedly focused on gushing about the school's impressive history, leaving me to figure out the social stuff on my own. The only help he had offered me was having Stella as a guide. Not that I don't think she knows every last in and out, but spending all day trailing after her is not my idea of a good time. I had respectfully turned him down.

If Nicole had to go through this just a few years ago, then she is a lot more appealing as a mentor. Even if she is part descendant herself.

"What does *kako* mean, anyway?" I ask, remembering how Stella had called me that when we met. "It's not good, is it?"

Nicole shrugs. "It's a tactless way of saying you're not a descendant. *Nothos* is more politically correct."

I have a feeling that when she says "tactless" she really means "insulting."

"First of all," she says, moving on, "cliques at the Academy are a little different. There's almost no way to break in—not that you should want to—because they're pretty much determined by your association."

Association? I don't understand what she means and decide not to say anything, hoping I'll figure it out, but she must sense how clueless I am.

"Your family." She gives me a pointed look. "Your god."

Still not clear, I look around.

The second floor hall is full of students, and from the outside they all look fully normal. I see all the standard cliques. Populars here and nerds there. Jocks in a huddle and cheerleaders all around them. Freaks glaring at everyone from the corner and geeks trying to avoid getting knocked down. Stoners, burnouts, prudes, and skanks. Nothing unusual.

"Look at that group." Nicole points across the hall.

Clustered around a set of lockers, a group of girls with perfect hair, heavy makeup, and suggestive clothing cling to boys with metrosexual taste in fashion and gel-spiked hair. Miniskirts and tight T-shirts abound. Not so different from the populars at Pacific Park.

"Steer clear of them," Nicole warns. "The Zeus set. Power, privilege, and partying. They make Paris Hilton look like a Vestal Virgin."

The Zeus set? I guess I can see how being related to the ruler of all the gods would come with extreme popularity. Who would dare to cross them when you might wind up with a thunderbolt in the back?

One of the boys shifts, opening my view to the other side of the group. Stella stares back at me, willing one of those thunderbolts to hit me, I'm sure.

"Stella's one of them?" I ask, looking away before those gray eyes turn me to stone or something.

"Not exactly." Nicole flicks a sneering glance at the group. "She's one of Hera's."

"So then why—" I begin. Then I remember Hera's role on Olympus—Zeus's consort.

"There are alliances," Nicole explains. "Zeus-Hera is the strongest."

Figures. Not only is Stella a colossal evil, but she's got the popularity and the genes to back it up. I am more than thankful her powers are grounded right now. Otherwise Nicole would be carrying me to class in a baggie.

Looking around for something other than the evil stepsister to talk about, I ask, "What about them?"

Another group of students, all with sun-bleached hair, is gathered around a water fountain. They look like they washed up in the last wave. A lot of pooka shell necklaces and flip-flops. The guys are wearing brightly colored boardshorts and Hawaiian print shirts.

Some of the girls are in sundresses, some in camisoles and breezy skirts. One of the girls looks just like a picture I saw once of Cameron Diaz surfing.

"That," Nicole says, pointing at the surfer crowd, "is Poseidon's posse. Most of their brain cells have burned off from too much time in the sun."

At the center of the circle I notice a guy with white-blond hair that looks a little like Heath Ledger in *A Knight's Tale.*

"Forget it," Nicole warns when she sees me looking. "Deacon's dumb as a box of rocks." She tilts her head, as if considering him for a second. "Actually, that's an insult to rocks."

From the other end of the hall I hear a boy squeal, "I got it! I hacked into the Olympic mainframe!"

He's obviously a geek—complete with thick black-framed glasses and high-waisted pants. He's clutching a calculator-sized PDA in his hand, jumping up and down and revealing a total lack of coordination as he practically trips over his own feet and falls into the rest of his group.

"Geeks?" I ask.

"Hephaestus," she replies with a sigh. "I think he's embarrassed by them. I know I would be. Not one of them has a chance of scoring an Aphrodite like he did, but I bet one day they make Bill Gates look poor."

I always thought it was romantic how the deformed god of fire married the beautiful goddess of love. Kind of like a mythological *Beauty and the Beast*. Looking at his descendants, however, I'm thinking more along the lines of *Weird Science*—but these guys don't look coordinated enough to build the perfect woman.

Seeing all the cliques grouped according to ancestral god makes me wonder about Nicole. Seems like she doesn't hang out with anyone but herself—and now me. But she's part immortal, too.

"So, which god are you—"

She suddenly jerks me across the hall toward an open door, almost sending me sprawling on the floor.

"What the—"

"The Hades harem," she explains. "You do *not* want to mess with them."

And, peeking back out the doorway, boy can I see why.

The group just rounding the corner look like your average Goths—black hair, black clothes, black eyeliner—but with an edge. Pretty fitting for the god of the underworld's descendants.

Shoulder-to-shoulder, they stride down the hall, daring anyone to get in their way. The Zeus set stares them down, but most of the other students in the hall scamper out of their path. As they pass the doorway, a tall, thin girl with pale skin, shoulder-length black hair, and piercing pale blue eyes, stares at me with intimidating intensity. I know I must be a novelty and all, but she really doesn't need to look like she wants to melt me with her eyes.

"Who is that?" I ask, my voice barely a whisper.

"That," she says, grabbing my shoulder and dragging me into the classroom, "is Kassandra. Trouble on a cosmic scale."

I don't need her warning to know that.

"This is Cornball's class," she says, flopping into a desk in the last row. "Make it through this and it's all downhill until lunch."

"Great," I say, dragging my fascinated thoughts back from Kassandra and the Hades harem and following her to the back of the room.

I can do this. With Nicole's help I'll be in sync with the social patterns in no time, and all I have to do is get my Bs. No prob—

"I assume you all practiced the quadratic formula over the summer holiday," the big, beefy teacher at the front of the class says. "Take out a sheet of paper, solve for *x* and graph the solution."

He turns to the board and writes a list of ten equations, each one longer than a long distance phone number. Crap. Maybe USC will accept a solid C average.

Maybe I should have sat in the front row.

"How has your day been thus far, Phoebe?"

I look up at the sound of Damian's voice. What a question. It's a miracle I've made it to lunch, and the last thing I need is his interference in my half-hour of education-free time. My brain seriously needs to decompress.

"Fine," I say.

Really, though, my brain is on fire. I made it through Algebra on sheer luck—and a few answer prompts from Nicole. Cornball might have gotten his nickname from all the stupid jokes he makes during class, but when it comes to math he's as serious as an 8.0 on the Richter scale.

Modern Greek had been a little easier—being a first-year language class and all—but I was the only one in the class on the downhill side of puberty. You don't know how immature fourteen-year-olds can be until you're stuck in a room with a bunch of them for an hour.

The only thing that made World History, my last class before lunch, bearable was hunky Mr. Sakola. He looks like some fifties movie star, with a bright white smile, perfectly combed hair, and a really cute dimple in his left cheek. He's also as charming as Will Smith—with an equally beautiful wife, if the framed pic on his desk is any indication. The class, however, was another dumpload of information. I took enough notes to fell an entire forest.

So, by fine I mean exhaustingly rotten, but I don't say it.

"Good." He smiles like a principal—wide and proud, his sophisticated face cracking into sophisticated lines at the corners of his mouth and eyes. "Any problems or questions?"

"No . . ." I say, but even that's not true. "Actually, there is one thing."

He nods, encouraging me to clarify.

Though I have seriously considered not telling him this, I think it's in my best long-term interest to be as forthright as possible. After all, I don't want him out to make my life more miserable than it already is. So, I suck it up and say, "I, um, tweaked my schedule a little. . . ."

He nods again. "In what way?"

"Well—" I swallow, hoping he doesn't question my prerequisites. "I traded Computer Applications and Biology for Art History and Physics II."

More nodding. What's with all the nodding?

"As long as you keep up with your assignments, I don't foresee a problem. I just want to see you happy in your time here." Now his smile is more parental, small but still reaching his eyes to crinkle up the corners. He leans across the table to Nicole and whispers, "Miss Matios, the last student who tried to zap Philosophy out of their schedule spent a week as a pile of sand."

Then, without another word, he stands up and walks away, surveying the lunchroom like a General watching his troops.

"Man," Nicole says when Damian's out of earshot, "I'm glad I'm not you. I wouldn't want Petrolas for a dad."

"He's not my dad," I snap. I feel instantly guilty. It's not her fault I've been tossed into this little dysfunctional family. "Sorry. My real dad died a long time ago. Damian is just my stepdad."

She shrugs like I haven't just bitten her head off or she could care less that I did. I'm just relieved she doesn't make a big deal of the dead dad thing. I'm not always so touchy about it—therapist Mom head-shrank me through the whole grieving process—but I've been thinking about him more than usual since the whole stepdad thing started. Having a fake dad makes me miss my real one more. Great, another thing to look forward to for the next nine months.

At least Nicole doesn't seem to care if I'm a moody psycho. Something over my shoulder catches her attention. "Travatas!" she shouts across the dining hall, waving her arm in the air to catch someone's attention.

At the head of the lunch line is a cute boy—blond and wholesome in a Chad Michael Murray kind of way—with dark gold hair and wearing a MY CHEMICAL ROMANCE T-shirt. He looks up at Nicole's shout and smiles.

"Hey Nicole," he says, carrying his tray over to our table and taking the seat next to mine.

"Phoebe," she says, pointing her fork at cute boy, "this is Troy."

"Hi." I wave in greeting.

He smiles, showing straight white teeth and says, "Hi back."

"He's pretty much the only person in this school worth knowing." She starts to take a sip of her Dr Pepper, but then adds, "Besides me, of course."

Nicole is not short on confidence.

"Has Nicole been showing you around?" he asks, his mouth curling up at the corners.

"Yeah." I nod.

Nicole is way better as a guide than Stella would have been. I can just imagine my day as Stella's puppy dog, forced to trail after her and lick her boots when she got a scuff.

Even across the crowded dining hall, I can feel her glare.

She is at a table at the opposite side of the hall—far, far away from ours—sitting with the rest of the Zeus-and-Heras. She's sitting next to a boy with short, rusty blond hair who, from the confident way he is holding himself, is the leader of their pack. Tan, slick, and arrogant, he looks like her perfect match.

Troy must see me staring at her because he says, "I hear Stella's your stepsister." He takes and swallows a bite of vegetable lasagna. "Sorry."

What, did they have a school-wide briefing about me? It seems like everyone knows who I am, where I came from, and how I got here. Right now, about half the cafeteria is looking at me while trying not to look like they're looking. I'm like a celebrity, but not in a good way.

Don't they have better things to talk about?

"Am I the school's only gossip?" I ask.

"Pretty much," Nicole says.

I shrug. Great. "Then trust me," I say to Troy. "Stella is the least of my challenges."

"Yeah, I guess it would be hard to get dropped into this world." His eyes—a really pretty green with bright gold flecks in the center—are warm with sympathy. "Don't worry. . . . you'll get through."

He's sweet, which may be why I confess, "It might be easier if I had found out about this whole 'the gods are real' thing before the yacht docked on Serfopoula."

Troy's jaw drops. "They didn't tell you?"

"What," Nicole says, rolling her eyes, "like you're surprised? You know how Petrolas is about security."

"I know, but—" He shakes his head, like he can't believe it.

Join the club. "Let's just say this has been a summer of shocks."

"What *did* they tell you?" Nicole asks.

"Pretty much that the school was founded by Plato, moved here ages ago, and protected by the Greek gods. Oh, and that all the students are related to them."

She snorts, clearly not impressed with how little I know. "Leave it to Petrolas to give you the history without any real, useful info."

"Like what?" I ask, trying not to sound nervous.

I'm not sure I want to know how much more I need to know.

"Any use of powers that breaks school rules," Troy says, "like cheating or skipping class or altering a teacher's memory, is forbidden and earns serious detention time."

“No one wants a Petrolas detention,” Nicole says, sounding grim. “They make the Labors of Hercules look like kindergarten homework.”

“You should know,” Troy teases. “You’ve done more detention than anyone else in our year.”

“Are you volunteering to take my place next time, Travatas?”

Troy turns white. “N-no, I mean, I was only—”

Nicole throws a roll at him.

I laugh because this reminds me so much of the sparring matches between Nola and Cesca. For a second I feel like I’m back in L.A. with my best friends. Until Nicole says, “And whatever you do, don’t go into the last stall of the girls’ bathroom on the second floor.”

“Why,” I ask, afraid of the answer, “does it open a portal to a parallel universe, or something?”

“No,” Nicole says with a laugh. “It backs up all the time and makes the Physics room smell like a sewer.”

Troy hands me a roll and I toss it at Nicole.

“Don’t worry,” he says when we all get done laughing. “Nic and I will teach you the ropes. You’ll be a world-class social navigator before we’re done.”

“We’ll at least make sure you don’t run your ship up on the rocks,” she adds. “Lunch is the perfect chance to see all the little gorgons in action. Where should we start?”

The pair of them look around the dining hall, searching out examples for my education.

“How about with you?” I suggest. “What, um, gods are you related to?”

Nicole points at Troy. "Travatas is around fifty generations removed from Asklepios."

"Who's Askilopus?" I ask.

"Asklepios," Troy corrects. "The god of healing."

"That's neat," I say.

"Right." Troy rolls his eyes. "I'm just dying to follow in that millennium-long line of doctors and nurses."

Talk about pressure. I guess maybe that's not so great, after all.

Turning back to Nicole, who is looking around the room again, I ask, "What about you—"

"That's the Athena table," she announces. "They're all brainiacs, like Tyrovolas."

Troy leans closer and whispers, "Nerds."

Like I couldn't tell. As if the thick glasses and pocket protectors weren't clues enough, they're huddled around the table and bickering over trading cards. The cards flash and sparkle with every movement. I have a feeling these aren't your typical Pokémon.

"Those girls." Troy nudges me, pointing to a bunch of blondes standing near the door. "They're the cheerleaders."

Where does this guy think I'm from? Siberia? Southern California is the cheerleader capital of the world—well, second maybe to Texas—and I have no problem identifying them. The blue and white uniforms are a dead giveaway. Even in street clothes, the matching hair ribbons mark them as the cheer squad.

But, Troy is cute and I don't want to make any enemies on the first day—Stella is already enemy enough—so I just ask, "Whose are they?"

Troy frowns, confused, but Nicole understands.

"Aphrodite's." She does not hide the disgust in her voice, rolling her eyes as she adds, "You'd think she was the patron goddess of athletics instead of love, for all they throw her name around."

"Athletics," Troy explains, "fall under the patronage of Ares."

Looking up, I follow the direction of his gaze to a table in the center of the room. While I'm watching, the cheerleaders approach the table and fill some of the empty seats.

One, the blondest of them all, walks up behind a boy. His back is to me, so all I can see is his black curly hair. He stands up to embrace Blondie, settling his mouth over hers and smoothing his hand over her butt.

Holy crap!

Next to me, Troy says, "Looks like Griffin and Adara are on-again at the moment."

"Who?" I ask absently.

"Griffin Blake and Adara Spencer. They get back together every summer," Nicole says. "Never lasts more than a week into school."

Griffin Blake. The name rolls through my mind like gentle thunder. He is a god—okay, bad choice of words, but even with his face hidden behind the cheerleader he is the most beautiful specimen of boyhood I have ever seen.

After a brief fantasy about his luscious hair, I take in the rest of him, starting with his height—all six-foot-plus of him. (Wait, do they use feet and inches in Greece? Maybe I should say all two meters of him.) Tall and broad-shouldered, but with the lean, sleek athletic build of a runner. Which instantly appeals to me, of course.

There's something vaguely familiar about him.

His coal black hair curls over the white collar of the navy and sky blue striped rugby shirt he wears. Lifting his head from kissing Blondie, he turns to laugh at something someone at the table says.

It's him! The guy from the beach.

Those full and soft lips spread into the most beautiful, open smile I have ever seen. So much more than that half smile he had given me that morning. And I know, absolutely 100 percent know, that one day I want him to smile at me that way.

Then I see a girl at the table—one of the lesser blondes—pointing a finger in my gawking direction. Griffin's gaze turns on me, sees me openly staring at him, and erupts into laughter.

Winning that smile is going to be much harder than I thought.

"Absolutely not."

"What?" I turn back to Nicole to find her glaring at me.

"Trust me," she says with her customary bitterness. "You want nothing to do with Griffin Blake."

"Why not?"

"Because Nic and Gri—" Troy begins.

"Shut it." She gives him a warning look and then turns back to me, her bright blue eyes steady and serious. "Because no girl should leave the Academy with a shattered soul."

Without another word, she drops her gaze to her food and resumes eating. I look to Troy for answers, but his attention is fully on his plate, too.

Nicole's warning doesn't make any sense. Sure, he's with the cheerleaders and the jocks—normally a formula for making a jerk—but when we met on the beach this morning he was totally nice. He even got me home in time to clean up before school.

Nicole must be mistaken.

Griffin Blake is a really nice guy.

"Welcome to the Academy track and cross-country team tryouts," Coach Zakinthos says. "Some of you are familiar with the process, but for new students I will explain."

It may be my imagination, but I think he is talking only to me. Everyone else seems bored by his little welcome speech.

We're sitting on the soccer field at the center of a big stone stadium that's on the far side of the campus from Damian's house. It looks like a mini version of the Coliseum in Rome, complete with rows and rows of stone benches. We've already done group stretching and some stuff to get our blood flowing, like jumping jacks and push-ups—while Coach Z paces back and forth. His white and blue track pants whoosh with every step.

The apparel aside, he looks like he's never seen the athletic side of a sporting event. I guess being part-god is no guarantee of physical perfection. Approaching ancient, over fifty at least, he has a beer gut to rival diehard football fans. A light jog looks like a stretch, let alone actually making it on a run.

Maybe he coaches discus.

"Everyone will select up to five events and will compete in those events for a position on the team. The top three finishers in each will automatically earn a slot, but the final roster rests at the coaches' discretion. In distance running, there's just one race. Six boys and six girls qualify. Any questions so far?"

He looks right at me. There are at least sixty kids sitting on the field, but his question is only for me. I throw a sideways glance at Griffin, sitting near the back of the group with Adara between his legs and surrounded by the rest of the Ares clique. His piercing blue eyes are trained on me.

I start to smile, but as soon as he notices me looking, he scowls and looks away. Boys can be so strange.

When I don't answer, Coach Z glances at his clipboard. "There are twenty-five events to choose from. Throwers stay here with me. Jumpers go with Coach Andriakos. Hurdlers with Coach Karatzas. Sprinters meet Coach Vandoros at the starting line. And distance runners, Coach Leonidas is waiting for you at the entrance to the tunnel."

Around me, everyone gets up and heads off toward their coaches. I know I am going to the tunnel, but I hold back, waiting to see where Griffin goes.

Adara, her arms wrapped around his neck, gives him a quick kiss before bouncing off with the rest of the sprinters. He turns and sets off at a jog.

Toward the tunnel.

Omigod.

Heart thumping in my chest, I follow close behind. From the second I saw him on the beach I thought he looked like a distance runner, but now I know it's true.

That's one thing we have in common.

"Ah, Miss Castro," Coach Leonidas says as I walk through the tunnel, "you are a distance runner." He smiles and rubs his hands together. "Excellent. Tell me about your background."

Griffin is in front of me and he turns to hear my answer.

"Well," I say, trying to focus on running and not the gorgeous hunk watching me with the most beautiful blue eyes I've ever seen, "I ran cross-country and long-distance track for three years at my old high school."

"How'd you do?" Griffin asks.

I can't tell if he's teasing or asking, so I answer, "I won the Western Regional Championship twice."

"What about the third year?"

This time I can tell he's making fun—only to impress his obnoxious friends, of course. Why else would he be such a jerk when he was so nice to me this morning?

Well, while wanting him to smile at me someday might include a laugh or two, I don't actually want him laughing *at* me. It's a fine line. "Freshman year I came in second."

He looks like he's about to say something, but Coach Leonidas interrupts. "Wonderful," he says. "I'm sure you'll bring a lot to the team."

"Thanks, Coach Leo . . ."

Okay, so Coach Z said his name, but I can't remember how to pronounce it. Everything in this country is a tongue twister.

"Call me Lenny," he says. "Everyone does."

"Thanks," I say again, "Coach Lenny."

"Now that the pleasantries are out of the way," he says, "let's get to the running."

Everyone cheers—still full of the excitement of the first day of the season and not yet worn down by miles and miles and miles of running.

I cheer, too. After all the embarrassment and inferiority I've faced today, I'm ready to show them all what I'm really good at.

"We're going to start out with a nice, easy warm-up before we run the qualifying race." Coach Lenny looks happy, like he loves running and thinks it's great luck he gets to make a living doing it. "Follow me."

He turns and heads out of the tunnel, into the afternoon sun.

Now Coach Lenny looks like an athlete. There's no trace of belly, beer or otherwise, on his wiry frame—he's not hiding one, either, because his white tank and blue running shorts leave little to the imagination. He sets the pace—the twenty kids who'd assembled in the tunnel fall in behind him—a gentle run that's not about to get anyone sweaty. I focus on the footfalls of his sneakers, counting out the rhythm in my mind and letting it sink into me.

The steady rhythm matches my heart rate.

I am vaguely aware that our pace is increasing. As we build up speed I stay focused on Coach Lenny's sneakers, never letting him get more than a few feet ahead of me.

I get lost in the run.

Barely noticing my surroundings, I'm surprised when he looks over his shoulder and announces, "We'll make two more laps around the stadium before heading to the course."

I'm in the middle of the lead group, content for the warm-up to hold back my pace. Don't want to wear myself out before the qualifier.

I love everything about running: the steady rhythm of my sneakers hitting the ground, the adrenaline and endorphins pulsing through my bloodstream, the cotton of my PAIN IS WEAKNESS LEAVING

THE BODY tee rubbing against my skin with every step. If I could do it without winding up in a tree or a ditch, I'd close my eyes and just . . . feel.

Running is when I know I'm alive.

Everything else is downtime.

Step, step, step, breathe. Step, step, step, breathe.

That pattern is my comfort.

Nothing else that happened today matters anymore. The craziness of my life melts away. In my mind, I'm back home—running on the beach with Dad shouting encouragements and urging me to push myself. No gods, evil stepsisters, or mind-muddling boys allowed. All I know is I'm running and I feel perfect.

"Hold up here," Coach Lenny announces, stopping us at a clearing with a smooth dirt path that leads into a pine forest. "Everyone walk it out, bring your heart rate back down. Get a drink of water."

He points to a drinking fountain near the head of the trail. I wait until everyone else has taken a drink before getting my own.

Someone taps on my shoulder, just as I suck down a big gulp.

Coughing, I turn to find Troy standing behind me, a big grin on his face.

"Hey," I say, wiping at the water dripping down my chin. "What are you doing here?"

"Thought you might need a good luck charm."

He holds out his hand, keeping it fisted so I can't see whatever's inside. I hold out mine beneath his. With a twist of his wrist, he opens his fist and I feel something fall onto my palm.

"A feather?"

"Yeah," he says, blushing a little. Pink looks good on his cheeks. "To help you fly faster."

"Thanks," I say, blushing myself. "That's sweet."

"You running today, Travatas?" Coach Lenny asks.

"No way." Troy backs away. "Just saying hello."

"If you stay, you run."

Troy turns to me, looking a little panicked. "I've gotta run. I mean go." He glances nervously at Coach Lenny. "I'll see you tomorrow."

He's gone before I can say, "See ya."

I don't have time to laugh at his hasty escape, Coach Lenny blows his whistle and calls us all to the starting line.

"I'm going to lead the course," he says. "And I'll be waiting back here when you finish the circuit. Follow the path marked with white flags."

Holding up his stopwatch, he turns to the course, blows his whistle, and starts the race. My heart rate kicks up at the shrill whistle, knowing this is the moment I have to prove myself.

Monitoring my pace, I stay in the middle of the pack. I've always been a strong finisher and it's better if I conserve some energy for the last kilometer than burn it all off at the start. A couple kids bolted out of the gate and I know they will be running out of steam halfway through.

I maintain my pace, just like Dad taught me.

Step, step, step, breathe. Step, step, step—

"Why bother trying out?"

Griffin's question—from right next to me—startles me and I trip over my own feet, but manage to stay upright and moving forward. It takes several steps before I get my rhythm back.

"What do you mean?"

I risk a glance.

His blue eyes are focused on the course and his mouth is twisted in a smirk. "You'll never qualify," he says. "You're a *nothos.* You can't keep up."

Who is he to tell me what I can and can't do? He doesn't know me. Cute boy or not, I can beat his tail.

"I'm keeping up with you," I snap.

"Only because I'm letting you."

His expression doesn't change and he doesn't look away from the course, but I can tell he's laughing at me. I really can't stand it when people laugh at me.

I feel a little surge of extra energy—adrenaline—and pick up my pace.

"When the race is over," I say, letting his taunts get the better of me, "you can let me know how it feels to be beat by a *nothos.*"

That hits home. His anger doesn't show on his face, but his hands ball into fists and his movement becomes a little tighter.

"That," he says through clearly clenched teeth, "will never happen."

What happened to the super sweet guy I met on the beach? This is more like the guy Nicole warned me about. "Were you possessed by the Furies after we met this morning? Or did I just catch you off guard before you'd had your jerk juice?"

"This morning," he snaps, "I didn't know who you were."

"Oh," I say, "you're only nice to strangers. Now that we're acquainted you have to be rude. Got it."

"If I were being rude," he said, his voice cold and hard, "you would know it. I'm only amusing myself to pass the time. In about half a kilometer you'll be in my dust."

Well, I didn't get to be Western Regional Champion—twice—without learning how to ignore head games. Cross-country is full of trash talk, but it's only effective if you let it get to you.

"Whatever." I shrug, "We'll see at the finish line."

Looking ahead, I realize we have dropped back a little from the main group. I can't let him get me off my race. I count to three before kicking up my pace another notch. Already I can feel myself closing the gap.

"Never," Griffin says as he speeds up, "mess with a descendant of Ares, *nothos*."

Then, before I can reply, a flash of light glows at my feet and the next thing I know I'm tumbling headfirst into the packed dirt path.

Griffin and the other runners disappear around a bend in the course and all I'm left with is a thin cloud of dust. Jumping to my feet, I look down to find my shoelaces untied, or, more accurately, untied and retied together.

Stepping out of my shoes rather than bother untying the supernatural knot—which is probably impossible to undo, anyway—I turn and start the long trudge back to the starting line.

CHAPTER 4

WHEN COACH LENNY crosses the finish line, I am sitting in the dirt, trying to unknot my sneakers without success. After trying to unravel the knot for nearly half an hour, it hasn't budged a millimeter. Either I'm going to have to cut the laces or buy new Nikes.

"What happened?" he asks, slowing to a stop at my shoeless feet.

I shrug. "I tripped."

"Tripped?" he asks between panting breaths. He starts pacing around me in little circles. "So you just give up?"

"What do you want me to do?" I shout, flinging my hopelessly joined sneakers into the woods. "I'm just a plain old, non-god-related person. I can't keep up."

Even if I could, no one would let me. Except for my mom—and maybe Damian—nobody wants me on this stupid island. I wish I could go home. Only I don't have a home to go home to. At this point, a year with Yia Yia Minta—with her stinky goat cheese, chain smoking, and spitting on everything for good luck—would be a blessing.

Coach Lenny squats in front of me. He stares into my eyes, like he's trying to see all the way into my brain. Heck, he's part-god. Maybe he can.

The sounds of footsteps and heavy breathing coming from the course indicate the first group of racers. Griffin, of course, is in the lead. I wonder if he cheated against everybody else, too.

Coach Lenny looks from me to Griffin and back again. His lips firm into a tight line. I can see the muscles in his jaw clenching.

"Did he use his powers against you?" Coach Lenny pronounces every word very carefully. He sounds really angry.

Griffin, walking around the starting area with his hands on his waist, looks at me like a puppy caught peeing on the rug. Nicole and Troy said the whole powers thing is strictly controlled and that using them against someone else is a big no-no. Like when Stella zapped my backpack.

I bet sabotaging my race is worth more than a week of grounded powers.

His fate is in my hands.

I smile at Griffin, majorly satisfied to see his ears turn red. I don't know if he's embarrassed for being such a jerk or afraid that I'm going to rat on him, but I like both options equally.

Either I turn him in and get revenge for his jerkiness this afternoon, or I cover for him and then he owes me one. Big time.

"Oh no," I say with a wide, innocent grin, batting my eyelashes for effect, "Griffin would never do something so underhanded, would he?"

I'm not fully sure why I don't squeal. Maybe I like the idea of being one up on him. Or maybe I think the whole thing isn't worth the trouble. Or maybe—and this is a terrifying possibility after what he's done to me—I still want him to like me.

Or at least the him that I met that morning on the beach.

The him he's showing this afternoon can go take a leap.

Griffin exhales loud enough for me to hear, like he's beyond relieved that I didn't rat on him.

A few more runners cross the finish line. Griffin congratulates them as they arrive, and then they pat him on the back for coming in first. They might dismiss his red cheeks and ears as a result of running, but I know he's embarrassed. He knows he won unfairly.

Coach Lenny eyes me suspiciously. I'm a horrible liar and he can probably tell I am covering for Griffin. But he apparently decides to let this one slide and walks away.

Now it sinks in that I am going to have to walk all the way back to Damian's house—across the whole campus and a very rocky hill-side—in my socks.

I glare at Griffin, bent over the water fountain and showing off his cute butt—I mean his rotten backside. Well, I am *not* going into the woods sock-footed after a pair of shoes when it's his fault I threw them in there.

Jumping to my feet, I stomp across the starting area as best as I can without shoes and tap him on the shoulder.

"Get my shoes back," I demand.

He jerks up and spins around, like he's shocked that I have the nerve to talk to him. "Excuse me?" he asks, like I'm the one being rude.

Only I can't really remember what I was asking him because his lips are all glossy and wet from the drinking fountain.

"I, um . . ." I swallow hard, hoping that will clear my brain. "Shoes. They're . . . in the woods."

I wave my hand back over my shoulder in the general direction that my shoes had gone. Then, while my eyes are locked on his lips, his tongue darts out to catch an extra drop of water at the corner of his mouth. I sort of shudder all over and I think it's with only the biggest display of willpower that I don't whimper.

His mouth kicks up at one side in that cocky grin.

Like he knows just what kind of thoughts I'm having.

That shakes me out of it.

I drag my eyes away from his lips and focus on his eyes—his bright blue, hypnotic . . .

"My shoes," I say as forcefully as possible. "I tossed them in the woods. Get them back."

"Why would you throw your—"

"Because I couldn't get them unknotted, thank you very much."

"Oh," he mouths, scowling. As if he hadn't realized I couldn't untie his supernatural knot.

Then, before I can blink, he holds out his hand to the woods and then my shoes are there—laces unknotted and tied into neat little bows. He holds them out to me and, as soon as I take them, turns and walks away.

I stare after him, confused.

I feel like I've missed something again, like I should thank him for undoing the rotten thing he did in the first place. Like he's pushing me away and pulling me in at the same time.

And I thought girls were supposed to be the complicated ones.

Forcing myself to forget Griffin and his contradictions, I slip back into my shoes and start for Damian's house. No point hanging around to hear I didn't make the team. Great! There goes USC. There goes the one thing I could count on to keep me going on this stupid island. There goes my life for the next year—and beyond.

"Wait a minute, Castro," Coach Lenny calls out. "We have a meeting in the locker room to announce the team roster."

Yeah, right. Does he think I enjoy humiliation? I didn't even finish the race—not that it was my fault or anything, but quitting is quitting. Oh well. Since I have to stop by school anyway to pick up my homework, I might as well sit in on the announcement. With Griffin coming in first, I'm sure there's no way he's not on the team, but maybe I'll get the satisfaction of seeing Adara get cut.

The locker room is deafening loud with everyone talking at once. The coaches are locked away in Coach Z's office, making their decisions and everything.

Even surrounded by sixty kids I feel completely alone.

No one is talking to me, but plenty are talking *about* me. And staring at me. And pointing at me. And laughing at me.

Rather than sit there and take it, I go get a drink from the water fountain. A nice, long drink. I don't think I've ever drunk so much at once—except for the time I ran the Death Valley Marathon. Being waterlogged is definitely more appealing than sitting around being stared at like a talking dog.

When I can't drink any more, I glance around the hallway while wiping at my mouth. A little ways down I see a display case and wonder what this one holds. More Olympic medals? More artifacts from the first marathon?

No, just a big collage of pictures of last year's track team.

A bunch of guys in blue running shorts dumping a cooler full of ice on Coach Lenny's head. A group of girls posing around Coach Z. Adara and Griffin kissing on the starting line.

Gag me.

I've had enough. I'm not going to stand around and wait to hear how I suck and I should never run again and—

"She didn't even finish the race," a deep male voice says.

Looking around I don't see anyone in the hall.

"Because Blake used his powers on her," a voice that sounds like Coach Lenny says.

The voices are coming from a slightly ajar door. It's wrong and sneaky and all those things, but I tiptoe up to the door and listen. They are talking about me, after all. I think I have a right to hear.

"If he did," the first voice—I think it is Coach Z—says, "then we will have to ground his powers."

"I can't prove it," Coach Lenny responds, sounding exasperated. "She wouldn't admit what he had done. She's protecting him."

I knew he hadn't believed me.

"That doesn't change the fact that she didn't complete the race. How do we know what she can do on a course—"

"She kept up with me during warm-up, damn it!"

Wow, Coach Lenny sounds really upset. Maybe he doesn't like the idea that a normal girl could run as fast as him. Man, these descendants sure are a bunch of egotistical freaks.

"I was going to keep it at a slower pace," Coach Lenny explains, "so I didn't wear her out. But she kept up. So I pushed harder. And she kept up. By the end I was almost running full out and still she kept up. She was barely winded when we stopped. The girl has phenomenal talent, powers or not."

Wait a minute. He actually sounds impressed.

"Really?"

They both sound impressed.

"Petrolas said she might surprise us, but I'm not sure, Lenny," Coach Z says. "We still don't know what she will do under the pressure of competition."

I almost reveal my presence by shouting, *I live for competition!* But I don't think getting in the middle of this conversation is going to help my cause.

"Z, if you're not convinced then give her a trial slot on the team. Let her show us what she can really do in a race when no one zaps her laces together."

There is a long, painful silence. I can picture Coach Z sitting there thinking, rubbing his big potbelly while he decides whether or not I'm worth a shot.

I am holding my breath. If he doesn't answer soon I'll probably pass out, and then they'll find me in a heap outside their door.

"All right," he finally says and I suck in oxygen. "She can train with the team and she'll run in our first meet. If she doesn't place in the top three then she's out. That fair?"

Fair? Insanely! Because even though everyone else may have godly powers, I haven't placed lower than second in . . . well, ever.

"Great," Coach Lenny says, sounding very happy. "Let's go announce the team."

I turn and take off at a dead run for the locker room. I am just taking my place in the back corner of the room when the coaches walk in. It is a major struggle not to break into a massive grin. Adara glares at me from across the room, but I can't even muster a scowl.

"Everyone, may I have your attention, please." Coach Z thumps his clipboard against his leg until everybody quiets down and looks at him. "The team roster will be as follows . . ."

As he starts to read off names by event, I glance at Coach Lenny. He is looking at me with a proud smile on his face. I give him a beaming smile. I can't help it, even if it gives away my eavesdropping.

He smiles back. Then he cups a hand over his ear like someone listening at a door and winks at me.

I laugh out loud. Man, you can't get away with anything at this school.

"How was your first day?" Mom asks as I fly into the house and let my backpack drop on the floor with a thud.

She is sitting at the dining table with magazines spread out in front of her. They are all wedding magazines. She has months to plan, so I don't know why she's obsessing.

"Long," I answer before heading to the kitchen for my traditional after workout snack: Gatorade and a PowerBar.

Only we don't have either.

"Oh, I forgot to tell you," Mom says. "Hesper goes to the market on Serifos once a week. She'll get what you need on Friday."

Closing my eyes, I wonder what she'll forget to tell me next? First, the whole immortal thing. Now, the once-a-week grocery shopping thing. Maybe next I'll find out Alexander the Great is coming back to life and bringing his army to dinner.

“Whatever.”

I slam the refrigerator door shut and head back to the living room to grab my backpack. What I need right now is a refuge from life. I really wish there was a lock on my bedroom door.

“What were your classes like?” she asks. “Do you like your teachers?”

“They’re okay.”

“What about the students? Did you make any friends?”

“A couple.”

“What god do they belong to?” Her voice takes on that professional analyst tone. “Damian tried to describe the social dynamics of the school, but I’d like to hear your—”

“Just drop it, okay? I’ve got a ton of work to do.” I want to stomp off to my room, but my thirst gets the better of me. I drop my backpack and go get a glass of water—from the tap. Is bottled water too much to ask for?

“Honey, I know this is a lot to face all at once.”

“I’m fine. So there’s no Gatorade. I’ll dehydrate like a normal person, all right.”

She looks a little hurt, but that was pretty much what I was going for. Everything about this situation is great for her and crappy for me.

“Do you think—” she starts to say, but then stops.

I fling my backpack over my shoulder and head for my room. I can sense Mom trailing behind me, but I’m happy to ignore her. Unzipping my bag, I start setting the massive textbooks out on my bed. I think I have more homework tonight than I had in my entire three years at Pacific Park.

“Damian told me the cross-country tryouts were today,” Mom says from the doorway. “How’d they go?”

I shrug. “I made the team.”

“That’s wonderful. I never doubted you would.” She falls silent.

“Look, Mom.” I carry my Algebra II textbook to my desk and drop it on the smooth wood surface. “I have a ton of homework to do, so . . .”

“Oh.” She looks around and sees all my books on the bed. “Of course, I’ll just leave you alone to get to work. I’ll let you know when dinner’s ready.”

“Fine,” I say. And then, because I feel a little guilty for being so mean, I add, “Thanks.”

One hour and thirty quadratic equations later, my eyes are blurry from staring at so many numbers. I think I can solve for *x* in my sleep now. The house is oddly silent—the Stella monster must be out somewhere and I haven’t heard Damian come home. I haven’t even heard Mom moving around.

Emerging from my room for a glass of water, I see Mom still hunched over the magazines on the dining table.

“Hi, Phoebola.” She smiles as I approach.

“Hi.” I smile back.

Somehow, this feels more like the old us. Maybe because no one else is home, but I feel like we’re back in L.A. and giggling over fashion magazines again.

Spurred by sentimentality, I slide into the chair next to her. “Whatcha looking at?”

She groans. “Bridesmaid dresses. There are so many styles and colors to choose from I don’t even know where to start.”

"Well," I say, studying the pictures laid out in front of her of skinny models in brightly colored shiny gowns, "maybe you should pick your wedding colors first. Then you can just pick a style you like."

"What an inspired idea." She pulls out some papers with scraps of color stapled to them. "Here are some of my color choices. What do you think?"

She looks at me all serious. I know that in the great big scheme of things choosing wedding colors is not an awe-inspiring responsibility, but the fact that Mom is seriously asking my opinion makes me feel really important.

I think she has almost every color in the world on these sheets, but they are grouped into a few coordinating palettes. One has a horrid pea green that wouldn't look good on anyone—not even Adara. I shove that one aside. Some have different shades of orange and yellow that seem more Halloween-y than wedding-y. I put those aside with the pea green. That leaves two choices: one with three shades of pink that my mom would never be caught within spitting distance of and one with three shades of blue and a teal green.

"This one," I say, pointing to the blue and green palette. "Everyone looks good in light blue. And it goes with the whole Mediterranean setting."

Mom studies the colors, like she's picturing the whole wedding and adding touches of blue and teal everywhere.

"I like it," Mom says, smiling and warming up to the choice. "And blue and white are the colors of Greece. It seems only fitting since I will soon become a Greek citizen."

"What!" My jaw drops and I stare at her. "You're becoming a Greek?"

“Of course,” she says with that happy-mushy smile on her face. “Damian cannot leave the Academy. His job and his life are here. And here he is protected. In America, he would always be vulnerable to discovery.”

“But you can’t just un-become American,” I insist.

Okay, so my problem isn’t really that she wants to renounce her American citizenship. If she becomes a citizen of Greece then that makes this whole thing so much more real. Like she can’t ever turn back. Like I can’t turn back.

“What about me?” I ask.

“Damian and I love each other. We are going to make a life together and that can only happen here.” She takes the discarded color schemes and drops them in the wastebasket in the kitchen. “That doesn’t mean that you’re not a major part of that life, even when you choose to return to the States. You are my daughter. My love. My everything. That will never change. But don’t you think I deserve a little happiness after all these years?”

We *were* happy. In California.

Mom had her practice and Aunt Megan and Yia Yia Minta.

I had Nola and Cesca and a track team full of friends.

Everything was great. So why did we have to move all the way around the world just for a guy?

“Besides,” she says, her voice all wistful. “I like Greece. It makes me feel closer to your father to be in his homeland.”

“Homeland?” I ask, shocked. “Dad was from Detroit. Motown is his homeland.”

“His family is Greek. In his heart he was always Greek.”

“That’s creepy.” I stand up and start pacing. “You marry this new guy and move to Greece to be closer to your dead husband?"

She gasps as I say it. I know that was pretty harsh, but it's the truth.

"Phoebe," she begins, and I know she's serious because she uses my real name, "what your father and I had was very special. Nothing—not his death, not my remarriage—will ever change that. Damian understands."

Well, I don't understand. Mom may think it's fine to snag a new husband, but I don't need a new father. And being in Greece will never make me feel closer to the one I had.

Sure, I've been thinking more about Dad since we got to Serfopoula than I have in ages, but that's because of the stepdad thing. Mom is probably going through the new husband thing. It's displaced guilt or something because she feels bad for remarrying. That's her baggage.

Dad was perfect and now he's gone. I can't get him back and don't want to replace him.

"Fine." I stalk into the kitchen, wiping at the tears I don't want Mom to see, and refill my glass of water. "You stay here and become Greek. I'll send you a postcard from USC when I graduate."

With a satisfying slam, I shut myself in my bedroom and fling myself on the bed. I can picture Mom watching me storm away, shrugging at my infantile behavior, and going back to planning her wedding.

It's like I don't even matter anymore.

Rolling to the edge of the bed, I reach over to the desk to grab my Physics II book. If it's like everything else at this school my eight homework problems are going to turn into a major scientific treatise.

When Mom knocks on my door to call me to dinner I ignore her. The last thing I want is to face another meal of goo-goo eyes and green sea slugs—even though Stella's powers are grounded, I don't put it past her to bring *real* ones this time. Besides, I still have half a book to read for Ms. T.

My door swings open. "Phoebe, dinner is—"

"Mom!" I shout, jumping off my bed. "You can't just barge into my room. Don't I get any privacy?"

"I'm sorry. When you didn't answer I—"

"Look, I don't want dinner. I'm not hungry." Actually, I'm starving, but I would rather go hungry until lunch tomorrow than have a *family* dinner. "I have a lot of work to do, so just leave me alone."

The hurt in her green eyes makes my heart ache. Not enough to take back what I said, though.

I'm surprised she's not shouting right back at me.

"All right," she says softly. "I understand your need for distance. I'll ask Hesper to leave a plate of leftovers in the fridge."

I shrug, like I'm not interested. Like I'm not already plotting to sneak out and consume that plate after everyone's in bed. "Whatever."

Her sad smile says she already knows what I'll do.

Without another word, she turns and walks away.

Animal Farm in hand, I collapse on the bed.

All animals are equal, but some animals are more equal than others.

Sounds like my life.

Maybe this book won't be so bad, after all.

Two hours and forty-seven pages later I'm still twenty pages from being done with my reading assignment.

I can't face another page of *Animal Farm* without a break, so I head to Damian's office to check e-mail. He's there, bent over a stack of papers. It's a really big stack and I wonder if he has to get through the whole thing tonight.

He sure seems to be busy all the time.

I'm not sure if I should interrupt, so I hover in the doorway. He looks up and smiles.

"Good evening, Phoebe." He pushes his papers aside and smiles at me. "How is the homework coming?"

"All done," I say cheerfully.

Okay, so I still need to read another twenty pages of *Animal Farm* and choose a painting from the Art History book to study for the semester, but everything else is finished.

"Please," he says, gesturing to the computer, "feel free to check your e-mail. But be sure and leave enough time to finish your reading."

How did he know? Either I'm that transparent or he can read minds.

"I don't read minds so much as I read emotion," he says. "I sensed your guilt over lying to me."

"I wasn't ly—"

"You were stretching the truth." He gave me a disapproving principal look.

"Fine," I relent. "I'm *almost* done."

He points to the chair in front of his desk. "Please, take a seat."

Nervous about his "discussion" tone of voice, I sink into the chair with a sense of despair. I'm about to be lectured, I just know it.

"Don't worry," he says, again reading my mind—or emotions, or whatever. "I know this is a difficult transition for you. There are many changes occurring simultaneously. Whatever your opinion of me and my relationship with your mother, I would like you to trust me. No matter what problem you are having you can discuss it with me and I will advise you as best I can. In the strictest confidence."

I nod, knowing this is a really kind offer. There is still some part of me that won't just open up and accept his help. Not out loud anyway. But it's good to know it's there. If I need it.

"You should know," he adds, pulling his pile of papers back over and starting to look through them again. "Ms. Tyrovolas frequently gives a detailed quiz over reading assignments."

"Oh." Cool. Insider information. I'm beginning to see how having Damian as an ally could be really useful. "I'll just check my e-mail real quick, then."

He nods and keeps reading his papers.

Anxious to see if Cesca and Nola e-mailed me and get back to finishing the *Animal Farm* pages, I jump into the chair in front of the computer and log on to my account.

I have two messages.

To: lostphoebe@theacademy.gr

From: coachlenny@theacademy.gr

Subject: Training Meeting

Phoebe,

As you overheard, your place on the team is conditional on your placing in the first meet. That is in three weeks. Come by my office after school so we can talk about your training schedule.

Coach Lenny

I send him a response saying I'll be there as soon as I get out of Philosophy. Then I save his message in my Running folder and move on to the second message. It's not from California.

To: lostphoebe@theacademy.gr

From: gblake@theacademy.gr

Subject: No Subject

Making the team was the easy part.

G

Teeth grinding, I click the delete button. That message disappears. . . . but another pops up in its place. I hit delete again. Another message pops up. Delete. Pop-up. Delete. Pop-up, pop-up, pop-up. Delete, delete, del—

To: lostphoebe@theacademy.gr

From: gblake@theacademy.gr

Subject: No Subject

You can't get rid of me with the delete key.

Remember who has powers.

G

ℭ

"Son of a—"

"Something wrong?" Damian looks up from his papers.

"Um, no," I mumble.

To: gblake@theacademy.gr

From: lostphoebe@theacademy.gr

Subject: Balance of Power

Remember who can tell Coach Lenny about zapped shoe-laces.

P

I send the message and Griffin's annoying pop-ups disappear. Very satisfied, I am about to close out of e-mail when the instant messenger opens.

TrojanTiger: Phoebe? you there?

Who is that? Maybe it's Griffin trying to get at me another way—that guy spends way too much time devising ways to torment me. And all I've done is dare to go to his school. Can't he tell I don't want to be here any more than he wants me here?

Besides, isn't a Trojan-something a really bad virus? Maybe he's trying to trash my computer. I almost think about letting him, because he'd really be destroying Damian's computer and that would get him in a lot of trouble.

But I decide it's not worth it. I need to get back to my reading. My cursor is over the close button when another message comes through.

TrojanTiger: it's me Troy.

LostPhoebe: Troy! I thought you were someone else.

TrojanTiger: disappointed?

LostPhoebe: no!!!

LostPhoebe: relieved

TrojanTiger: <vbg> how were tryouts?

LostPhoebe: made the team

TrojanTiger: knew you would

LostPhoebe: that makes one of us

TrojanTiger: ha ha

The cursor blinks at me. I don't know what else to say. I mean, Troy is being super nice to me, but why? And do I want a guy to be super nice to me? Sure, he's cute and sweet and everything I *should* want in a guy, but do I? When do girls *ever* like the guy they should?

Besides, it doesn't look like he knows what else to say, either.

Blink, blink, blink.

TrojanTiger: still there?

LostPhoebe: yeah

LostPhoebe: you?

TrojanTiger: yeah

LostPhoebe: okay

Blink, blink, blink.

TrojanTiger: well

TrojanTiger: just wanted to check in

LostPhoebe: thanks

TrojanTiger: better go finish my homework

LostPhoebe: me too

LostPhoebe: more reading for lit

TrojanTiger: finish!

TrojanTiger: tyrant quizzes

I glance at Damian. He's focused on his stack of papers and doesn't notice me watching. I'll give him one point on the plus side for cluing me in about the quiz.

LostPhoebe: heard about that

LostPhoebe: almost done

TrojanTiger: okay see you tomorrow?

LostPhoebe: of course!

TrojanTiger: save me a seat at lunch

TrojanTiger: unless you sit with Ares now

LostPhoebe: as if!

LostPhoebe: they wouldn't have me even if I wanted to

LostPhoebe: and I so don't want to!

TrojanTiger: good <vbg>

LostPhoebe: night

TrojanTiger: night

The message window closed.

I sigh. *Animal Farm* is calling.

Sliding the keyboard tray back under the desk, I stand and head for the door.

Damian stops me before I get there. "Since you rely so heavily on electronic communications to keep in touch with your friends," he says. "Your mother and I have decided you need a laptop computer."

I spin back to face him. "Really?"

"And an Internet connection in your room." He hasn't looked up from his papers, but I can see him smiling just a little at my enthusiastic reaction.

"That's great!"

"Hesper will pick up the computer when she travels to Serifos on Friday. The connection will be installed tomorrow."

Friday? That's only two days away. Two days until complete freedom of Internet access in the privacy of my room.

"Wow, Damian, that's—" Amazing? Wonderful? Terrific? Nothing seems to say exactly what I mean, so I just say, "Thanks."

"You're welcome."

Turning, I start to bounce out of the room.

"Just don't spend all your time conversing with Mr. Travatas. Your studies come first."

Man, I can't keep any secrets.

"Hey, Damian?" I ask over my shoulder. "Can you read emotions through walls?"

"No," he says with laughter in his voice.

"Good." I move through the doorway, to the other side of the wall. "Because I'd probably get in trouble for what I'm feeling right now."

To my total shock, Damian laughs out loud.

"I don't need to read emotions to know what you're feeling at the moment," he says. "But I promise not to use it against you."

With a smile, I hurry back to my room.

For the first time since we landed on this island I feel like more than two things in a row are going right. It might not last, but I'll take it while I can.

CHAPTER 5

"YOU MUST TRAIN HARDER than ever before." Coach Lenny looks at me across his desk. "Not only must you surpass our own runners, but the other teams we will be competing against are very good."

"All right," I say. "I'll do whatever it takes."

"Thankfully," he says as he flips open his calendar, "you won't be competing against Blake. But you will be running the same course."

I fall silent. Even though Coach Lenny knows Griffin zapped me, I'm still not a rat. Besides, a girl has to stand by her lies, right?

"Don't worry about him, though," Coach Lenny says. There is a wicked gleam in his eyes and he smiles. "Coach Z and I have agreed to ground his powers for the day of the race."

"Okay," I say mildly. But inside I'm jumping for joy.

Griffin is going to be so pissed off!

"Actually, we have decided to ground everyone's powers." He winks at me. "The team is always prohibited from using their powers in a race, but this time we're making sure."

Wow. If everyone only hates me now, they're going to really despise me by the time I get out of here.

Coach Lenny starts scribbling on the card, down to business. "Even with their powers grounded, your teammates will still have exceptional strength and stamina. I want to make sure you blow them away." He hands me the card. "Do these exercises each night before you go to bed."

I read the exercises.

25 sit-ups

15 push-ups

50 jumping jacks

repeat 4X

"Okay," I say. "No problem. What else?"

He starts writing on another card.

"Hydrate. Drink at least sixty-four ounces of water a day. And consume plenty of protein and complex carbohydrates." He slides the second card across the desk. "You're going to need the energy."

The second card says, *6:00am M-F & 8:00am Sat-Sun.*

I look at him, confused.

"We will meet every day before school and every morning on the weekends for a training session. In addition to the daily practices after school and on Saturday afternoons. By the time I'm through with you, you'll be in the best shape of your life. You'll be ready to win the Athens marathon."

"Great." I slip the cards into my backpack. "I'm ready to work."

He smiles at me. "Get changed for practice. I'll meet you on the course."

I head off to the locker room, anxious for the freedom of running. After the day I've had I could run a hundred miles. Hey, it's cheaper than therapy.

Ms. T's quiz had been more like a final exam. If I hadn't read every word of the assignment I would have flunked big time. I make a mental note to thank Damian and Troy for the inside scoop.

"Look what the sympathy vote dragged in," a syrupy voice says when I walk into the locker room. A flurry of giggles erupt around Adara.

Lifting my chin a notch, I stalk to my locker and spin the combination. In these situations it's always better just to ignore the vicious cheerleader taunts. Witty retorts only wind up pissing them off more.

"What's the matter, *kako*?" She walks up beside me and plants one Reebok-shod foot on the bench. "Afraid to tangle with a goddess? Afraid you'll lose?"

I clench my jaw, but still say nothing. Jerking my sweatpants out of the locker, I fling them onto the bench—next to her foot—and begin unbuttoning my jeans.

Out of the corner of my eye I see her lean down, blonde hair swinging over her shoulders, and snatch up my sweats.

"Give those back," I demand.

She stands up on the bench and holds them over her head. "Come and get 'em."

With a growl I leap up on the bench with both feet. Leaning back, she holds the pants just out of my reach.

"Give them back," I warn. "Or I'll—"

"You'll what?" Her lower lip pouts out and she flutters her eyelashes. "You'll call your daddy to take them from me?"

ꟷ

I gasp. At first I think she must not know my dad is dead—maybe gossip at the Academy is not up to Pacific Park standards.

Then she adds, "Oh, that's right. Your dad's dead."

I don't know how she knows, but she does. And she doesn't care.

Adara drops my pants to the cement floor, where they land in a puddle of shower water. That's the last straw.

My vision goes fuzzy, like someone is shining a really bright light in my face.

With every ounce of power I can dredge up—fueled by desperate fury and the Twinkie Nicole split with me between fifth and sixth periods—I lash out violently with both hands, slamming my palms against her chest. Adara flies off the bench, sailing through the air until the cinder-block wall stops her.

She drops to the floor in a silent heap.

I watch, unemotional, as she struggles to regain her breath. Guess the wall knocked the air out of her. I'm so sad. Then, as she scrambles to her feet and dusts off her track shorts, I casually pluck my pants out of the puddle and pull them on.

My hands are shaking with adrenaline. For a minute there I felt invincible, like I could do anything. I guess I didn't know my own strength. My weight training is usually low weights and high reps so I don't build bulky muscles. Maybe I'd better drop down to lower weights.

Her cheerleader groupie friends rush to her aid, but she just shrugs them off. "You'll wish you hadn't done that."

"You know, Adara," I say, sauntering toward the door, "I don't think I will."

“I’ll make your life miserable.”

“Take a number,” I throw over my shoulder as I hurry into a jog, heading for the track. I am so ready for the exhaustion two hours of running brings.

“Can we call a truce?” Stella walks into my room and sits on my bed like she owns it.

Ew, now I have to wash my sheets.

I eye her skeptically. “What’s the catch?”

“No catch,” she assures me. “I just think we should try getting along like sisters. After all, it’s going to be a long year if we fight the whole time.”

I agree. But I don’t believe her.

Stella doesn’t have a let’s-get-along bone in her body. And her eyes still have a little rim of ice around the edges.

“I’m not buying,” I say before returning my attention to conjugating Greek verbs—and they’re kicking my tail. Can’t they use the regular alphabet? “Just pull whatever prank you want to pull so I can get back to my homework.”

“So untrusting, Phoebe.” She stands and starts to leave. “I speak fluent Greek, you know. I was going to offer my help. . . .”

I want to ignore her, really I do. But just then I’m trying to figure out the aorist tense of *to be*, which is just one of the like forty tenses I have to conjugate.

“Wait!” I blurt.

“Yes?” I can tell from her tone of voice that she knows I’m desperate. She pauses in the doorway, but doesn't turn back around. Like she's waiting for me to beg. That's never going to happen, but I am open to negotiations.

"What do you want?" I ask. "Honestly."

Her shoulders lift beneath the pink polo shirt she's wearing. "Nothing significant."

"Stella—"

"Three things." She whips around and shuts the door sharply behind her. "In exchange for Greek tutoring I want three things from you."

I narrow my eyes at her scheming demand. "I'm listening."

"First, you never speak to me at school."

Like that's a hard one to uphold. I'm always having to stop myself from finding Stella to tell her every detail of my day—not!

She's waiting for me to answer, so I nod.

"Second, I want you to tell Daddy you want a subscription to *Vogue* and *Cosmo*."

"But I don't read—"

"It's not for you, *kako*." She rolls her eyes at my ignorance. "He won't let me read them because he thinks they're 'useless social trash' that give women 'a distorted view of physical perfection' or something like that."

"What makes you think he'll let me—"

"He wants to win your affection," she interrupts—again. "He'll give you anything you want."

"Fine," I say. "*Vogue* and *Cosmo*." Though I have to say I pretty much agree with Damian. I'd rather get a useful magazine, like *Her Sports*.

“And third—” She drops her voice to a near whisper, so low I have to step closer to hear her. “I want you to break up Griffin and Adara.”

My jaw drops open.

Of all the things I might have imagined she was going to ask for, that was nowhere near the list. That wasn’t even in the same universe as the list.

What about that boy I saw her sitting with at lunch? I got the definite impression there was something going on between them. In any case, I’m not about to get in the middle of that social mess.

“No way,” I say, thinking the pair already hates me enough. Even a perfect 4.0 isn’t worth getting in the middle of that relationship. “Besides, everyone says they always break up after the first week of school.”

“Not this year,” Stella says with a sadness in her voice I didn’t think she was capable of. She must be faking.

“Why do you care if they’re together?”

She looks away for a second and when she looks at me again her eyes are lined with tears. They look real, but with Stella who can tell? “I want Griffin for myself. This is my last year, my last chance.”

“Then why don’t you just ask him—”

“Because Adara is my friend,” she snaps. “I don’t want to ruin that, I just want to—”

“Steal her boyfriend?” Sure sounds like a friend to me.

“Do we have a deal or not?”

“Sorry,” I find myself saying. “I’m not getting involved.”

“Oh, I think you will,” she says, her jaw firm.

Walking to the door to usher her out, I start to explain, “No—”

“You will if you want to get back to America next year.”

My hand freezes inches from the doorknob.

“I know you’re counting the days until you can leave, until you can go away to college.” She walks up behind me and whispers in my ear. “Dad thinks that’s a bad idea. He thinks you should stay on through Level 13 and attend university in Britain.”

“Absolutely not—”

“I heard him talking with your mom about it.” Her smile is wicked. “She agreed.”

“She would never—”

“She would and she did.”

“Stop interrupting me!” I shout, but I’m more mad about the whole college thing.

Her face changes and suddenly she looks like the dutiful student body president, which she is. “I think you’re right, Dad,” she says in the singsong voice of a butt-kissing tattletale. “Phoebe confided in me that she has been struggling with her classes. She’s afraid that the rigors of collegiate academics will be too much for her.”

“You wouldn’t dare,” I warn.

“Oh, I would.” She fake-smiles. “Of course, I could just as easily be swayed to testify to the opposite.”

Suspicious, I ask, “How could I be sure you’d help me?”

She shrugs. “I’m going to Oxford. The last thing I want is to spend more time trapped on an island with you. I’d rather have an ocean between us.”

At least she is being honest.

I weigh my options. I can tell Stella to go take a flying leap, leaving me struggling through Modern Greek and maybe stuck on this island for an entire extra year. Or I can accept her terms, get an A in the class, jet off to USC after this one wretched year, and probably get cursed into oblivion by Adara.

Of course, with the second option there is a potential added bonus. In wrenching Griffin away from Adara, I could conceivably end up keeping him for myself—which means I would get to see Stella lose out on something she really wants. A rare occurrence, I think.

Win-win.

"All right," I finally say. "You help me, I'll help you."

She actually smiles, a genuine, nonthreatening smile.

That won't last.

"But I can't make any guarantees," I add. "How am I supposed to break up the golden couple? What if I can't split them up?"

"You'll find a way." She turns to walk away. "I hear cross-country teammates grow very close. Steal him, dump him, and I'll clean up the pieces."

She opens the door and starts to leave.

"Hey," I cry. "What about my homework?"

She looks back over her shoulder. Her smile is sinister. "As soon as you meet your end of the bargain, I'll fulfill mine."

Then she walks out of the room, slamming the door.

I send my Modern Greek textbook flying after her.

"Phoebe?" a muffled voice calls to me. Then louder, clearer, "Phoebe?"

“Mmnff,” I grumble and settle back into my dreamland.

“Phoebe!”

I shoot up in my chair. “Wha—what’s going on?”

“Phoebe, honey,” Mom says, laying a hand on my shoulder, “you fell asleep over your homework.”

A quick glance at my desk reveals some sleep-crumpled papers and, thankfully, no drool puddle. Peeling a sheet of notebook paper off my cheek, I check and see that I had finished my Art History questionnaire before dozing off.

“Thanks,” I say, smoothing out the paper and slipping it into my binder. “I guess practice wore me out.”

“Did you want to check e-mail before Damian and I go to bed?”

Ew. I shudder at the thought of Mom and Damian going to bed together. I mean, I know this isn’t our first night here, but I don’t need the reminder of where my mother sleeps.

“Sure,” I say before she can elaborate. “I’ll go do that right now.”

She stops me before I hurry out of the room. “Is everything all right, Phoebola?”

“Sure,” I say again. “Why wouldn’t it be?”

“You seem a little . . .” She gives me a sad look. “. . . withdrawn.”

“There’s a lot going on,” I explain.

“Are you having trouble with your classes?”

“No,” I assure her. “I mean, sure it’s loads more work than we ever had at Pacific Park, but I’m making it through.”

“Then it’s your classmates.” She frowns like she’s thinking hard about something. “I thought you said you’d made new friends?”

“Yeah.” And a few enemies. Not that I’d tell her that—it would be like tattling to the principal. “Nicole and Troy are great.”

"What about your track teammates?"

I can't help rolling my eyes. "I don't have to like them to run with them."

"Want to talk about it?"

I'm tempted. I mean, I haven't spoken to anyone but descendants since we got here. And she's the only non-descendant I'm allowed to talk to about everything that's going on. Besides, before the stepdad entered the picture we were like best friends. We talked about everything. I could talk to her about things I couldn't even talk about with Nola and Cesca. I cried on her shoulder when jerky Justin dumped me and she didn't even try to shrink me.

But I can't forget what Stella said about Mom agreeing that I should stay here—or the fact that it's Mom's fault I'm in this mess in the first place.

"No, I'm exhausted," I say. "I'm just going to check e-mail and go to bed."

"You would feel better if you got things off your chest."

"Really," I insist. "I'm fine."

I can tell she isn't satisfied. Maybe if she were just in parent mode I would talk to her, work through things rationally. But I'm in no mood to unload my issues—especially not on Super-Therapist Mom.

"You know, I've been thinking." She smiles big, in a way that means she thinks she has a fabulous idea. "Why don't we have a mother-daughter day? We could go to the village and browse the little shops and have sundaes at the ice cream parlor."

"I don't know, Mom. I've go so much going on—"

"You can't run and do schoolwork *all* the time." She brushes a loose lock of hair off my face. "How about Saturday? It might be tough, but I'll clear my hectic schedule."

For a second, it's like the old Mom and Phoebe are back. She's joking with me and I'm rolling my eyes at her corny humor. Maybe it would be good to spend some time together. Besides, I haven't seen the village yet, except for from the dock. Who knows, it could actually have a cool shop or two. I could get souvenirs for Nola and Cesca.

"Sure," I say. "Saturday."

With a quick wave, I leave her alone in my room and retreat to Damian's study and my electronic connection to the civilized world.

I click open my e-mail. The little smiley faces next to Cesca and Nola's e-mail addys are bright yellow. They're online!

Two mouse clicks later I have my IM open.

LostPhoebe: hi!!!

GranolaGrrl: Phoebe!

PrincessCesca: finally! been waiting online all day

GranolaGrrl: no we haven't

LostPhoebe: glad ur here

LostPhoebe: did you get my e-mail?

PrincessCesca: of course

GranolaGrrl: things can't be bad as you think

GranolaGrrl: nothing ever is

PrincessCesca: have you been to the beach yet?

LostPhoebe: just for a quick run

GranolaGrrl: I bet they're polluted anyway

GranolaGrrl: all those years of combustion powerboats cruising the Mediterranean

PrincessCesca: ignore enviro-freak

PrincessCesca: dish on the guy scene

GranolaGrrl: <insulted>

LostPhoebe: well there are a couple of really cute guys

GranolaGrrl: I resent being labeled an enviro-freak

PrincessCesca: which one is taking you to homecoming?

GranolaGrrl: I prefer to be called environmentally active

LostPhoebe: I don't think they have a homecoming

LostPhoebe: besides, one of them already hates me

GranolaGrrl: hate is the mirror of love

PrincessCesca: what about the other guy?

I pause, thinking about Troy. He's cute. And nice. And a good friend. And nice. And thoughtful. And nice.

Sigh. Nice is not necessarily boyfriend material.

Not even crush material.

At least not for me.

LostPhoebe: Troy is just a friend

GranolaGrrl: boy friends make the best boyfriends

PrincessCesca: <rolls eyes> what about the other?

LostPhoebe: the one that hates me?

GranolaGrrl: he doesn't hate you

PrincessCesca: yes, him

What can I say about Griffin Blake?

That he zapped my shoelaces together? Oops, can't reveal the whole secret-island-of-the-Greek-gods thing.

That he makes Orlando look like a Troll? Nope, that would give away too much of my unwanted interest in him—why do I always crush on jerks?

That I've been commissioned by my evil stepsister to break up him and his girlfriend? Stella is the last thing I want to chat about. Besides, that leads me down the path of thoughts about my *real* reason for accepting her deal—something to do with how my heart pounds like a bongo every time I see him—and those are thoughts best left unexplored.

Somehow, none of these seem appropriate.

LostPhoebe: nothing to tell

LostPhoebe: promise

PrincessCesca: you only promise when ur keeping a secret

GranolaGrrl: we should respect her privacy

PrincessCesca: for crying out loud

PrincessCesca: don't you want to know about the guy our best friend is crushing on?

GranolaGrrl: of course, but that doesn't mean we have to pry

LostPhoebe: I'm not crushing on him

PrincessCesca: yes it does

PrincessCesca: that's exactly what it means

GranolaGrrl: she has a right to her privacy

PrincessCesca: she has to tell us, we're her best friends

LostPhoebe: stop!!!

The rapid-fire IMs stop. I stare at the blinking cursor, thinking how much I miss hearing them argue in person. It's just not the same on the computer. The scrolling IM chat is making me dizzy.

GranolaGrrl: are you all right?

LostPhoebe: why does everyone keep asking me that?

PrincessCesca: well are you?

LostPhoebe: I'm fine

LostPhoebe: it's late and I'm tired

GranolaGrrl: you should get your rest

PrincessCesca: what time is it there?

I check the clock on the computer. It's after eleven. Crap, I have to meet Coach Lenny at six.

LostPhoebe: almost 11:15 and I have to get up early

GranolaGrrl: we'll let you get some sleep

PrincessCesca: but don't think we're letting this crush thing go

LostPhoebe: thanks

LostPhoebe: I miss you guys

GranolaGrrl: we miss you, too

PrincessCesca: Pacific Park is the pits without you

PrincessCesca: Justin acts like king of the school

PrincessCesca: he's an a$$

LostPhoebe: not sorry to miss that! ☺

GranolaGrrl: 'night

PrincessCesca: good night

LostPhoebe: bye

I sign off, sad to be so far away from my friends when I need them the most.

I am lying in my bed, almost ready to drift into blissful sleep when I remember Coach Lenny's exercises. He'll kill me if I don't do them. Jumping out of bed, I dig the note card out of my backpack and start counting sit-ups.

"One, two, three . . ."

Who knew it could take an hour to do one hundred sit-ups, sixty push-ups, and two hundred jumping jacks. By the time I collapse back in bed I'm exhausted. I fall asleep the second my head hits the pillow.

When my alarm goes off I feel like I've slept all of five minutes.

It's going to be a rough day.

"You look like Hades," Troy says as he sets his lunch tray next to mine.

Through some great miracle of adrenaline or alpha waves, I am still awake despite a pop quiz in Algebra and a documentary on the Ancient Egyptian practice of mummification. But it's a near thing.

"Thanks," I mumble, struggling to keep my head from dropping onto my plate of hummus-smothered meat loaf. And I thought there was no way to make meat loaf worse.

Food is the last thing on my mind, though. We are doing pendulums in Physics today and I just know the swinging and circling is going to trigger my motion sickness. I'm trying not to consume anything I don't want to see again.

“I had a late night,” I explain. “And early morning practice.”

“I thought practices were after school?” he asks.

“They are,” I say. “But I have to practice extra.”

“Why?” Nicole prods her meat loaf like she’s afraid it might get up and walk off the plate. “You made the team.”

“Only if I finish top three in the first meet.”

Nicole lets out a low whistle. I’ve always wanted to be able to do that. I can’t whistle at all, despite years of secret training and even a hands-on lesson from Justin that I’d rather forget.

“I have faith in you,” Troy says. “I’ll help any way I can.”

I smile at him. He’s so sweet and looks really cute with that goofy grin on his face. And that golden blond hair spiking off in every direction doesn’t hurt his star quality good looks. And he seems to like me. Maybe Troy could be more than a friend, after all.

“Thanks.” I blush even though I know he can’t read my thoughts.

His grin deepens.

Oh yeah, he’s part god. . . . maybe he can. Which leads me to wondering . . .

“I have a question,” I say to both of them.

“Shoot,” Nicole says.

I think about it for a few seconds, trying to get the words right. Trying to figure out how to ask what I really want to know.

“Are your powers unlimited?” I finally ask. “I mean, can you do pretty much anything you want?”

“Yes and no,” Nicole says.

“Great.” I venture a tiny bite of blue Jell-O. “That clears it up.”

Troy swallows a giant forkful of meat loaf before saying, “It’s not a simple question. In one sense, there are no limitations on what we can do. But—and this is a big but—just because we have the potential to do something doesn't mean we have the ability."

"I'm working on no sleep," I plead. "Can you please elaborate?"

"Our powers don't come easy," Nicole explains. "When we're born we can't really tap into them. They're there, but it takes years—a lifetime, really—of training to learn how to use them."

"There are exceptions, of course." Troy sets down his fork to chug a pint of milk. "The closer you are to the god on your family tree, the stronger your powers are from the start. Most of us are pretty far down the branch."

"How do you train?" I ask. It's not like I've seen classes out in the courtyard working on moving things with their minds.

"That's complicated." Nicole pushes her untouched meat loaf to the side. "Part of it is learning how to focus your energies—how to channel the powers into what you are trying to do. But a big part of it has to do with self-knowledge. You have to know yourself, understand yourself so you can sense the extent of your powers. The better you know yourself the more focused your powers get."

"Wow," I say. "That sounds so . . ."

"Vague?" Nicole suggests. "It is."

"I was going to say dangerous. What if someone suddenly reaches a new level of self-knowledge and, like, accidentally blows someone to pieces."

"Oh, don't worry," Troy says cheerfully, "there are controls."

"Controls?"

"Yeah," Nicole adds. "Since we're not fully gods, the Mt. Olympus twelve placed a protective order over our powers."

"What does that mean?"

“It means we can’t kill anyone—either accidentally or on purpose—using our powers.” Nicole stares at the table, like she’s lost in thought. Her voice sounds far away. “Only the gods can act irreversibly.”

Silence falls on our table. Nicole sits lost in thought. I feel like I’m missing something important. Gesturing with my eyebrows, I try to silently ask Troy what’s going on. He just shakes his head and goes back to shoveling down his tray of food.

I definitely get the hint that Nicole has a lot of buried secrets. This is just how they both reacted when we were talking about Griffin the other day. I totally don’t expect them to dish on all the buried past in the first week of our friendship, but I wonder if those two secrets are related?

Still, it’s clear that this is a subject best avoided for the moment.

“I’ve been wondering about the gods,” I say, trying to fill the awkward silence. “Do they come cheer at football games? Or speak at graduation or anything?”

Troy snorts, quickly wipes a napkin across his mouth, and says, “Not likely. They’ve been under the radar ever since man stopped worshipping them.”

“Why?”

“No one knows for sure,” he says.

“They’re pouting,” Nicole says, back to her old snarky self just as quickly as she left.

“They are not pouting,” he argues. “They’re gods. They don’t need to pout.”

“I don’t care if they need to.” Nicole grabs an apple slice off Troy’s tray. “They are.”

ℴ∞ℴ∞ℴ∞ℴ∞

"That's ridiculous," Troy says, offering me an apple slice and then setting the bowl in the middle of the table.

"Makes sense to me," I say. "For what I know, anyway. If someone suddenly loses stuff they thought they deserved then they might pout." Not that I know this from personal experience or anything.

"They aren't," Troy insists, though I sense he knows he's losing the argument.

Nicole leans forward over the table, staring Troy square in the eyes, and asks, "Who do you think is in a better position to know?"

He scowls, like he's confused. "Why would you know—"

"Have *you* ever been to Mount Olympus?"

He starts to shake his head. Then, all of a sudden, his eyes get real wide and his mouth drops open. "Oh gods," he says. "I totally forgot."

"Yeah, well," Nicole says, returning to her seat, "I haven't."

"Forgot what?" I ask.

"Nothing." Nicole waves off my question. "It's not important."

Yeah, and running is just my hobby. I don't need Mom's therapy degree to know that whatever they're talking about—Nicole visiting Mount Olympus?—is a majorly big deal. I also don't need to read minds to know that this is an I'm-not-going-to-find-out-about-it-anytime-soon kind of secret.

"Are you going to the bonfire tonight?" Troy asks out of nowhere.

"Bonfire?"

"Every year," Nicole looks up, sounding unimpressed by the whole thing. "On the first Friday of school, all the groups come together for a big, raging bonfire on the beach. It's the only time all the gods get along."

From what I've seen, the god cliques don't mix. "Why do they get along at the bonfire?"

"It's a night to honor Prometheus," Troy explains.

"The guy who stole fire and gave it to people?" I ask. See, I did pay attention in English class.

"Yeah," Troy continues. "When he did that it created a kind of bridge between man and the gods. Without that link," he says, smiling, "none of us would be here."

"So we honor him by throwing a huge party, lighting up the beach, and pretending like we don't hate each other the rest of the time."

"Ignore Nic," Troy admonishes. "It's the best party of the year."

"Sounds like fun." I could use a few hours of homework- and training-free fun. And at least I get to sleep late tomorrow since I don't meet Coach Lenny until eight on Saturdays.

"It starts at nine." Troy looks down at his hands. "How about I come by—"

Another low whistle from Nicole interrupts whatever Troy is saying—and I'm a little annoyed because I think he's on the verge of asking to be my *date* to the bonfire.

"Those two are taking PDA to a whole new level." Nicole grunts in disgust and returns her attention to her food.

A few feet away, Griffin and Adara are sucking face like they're attached at the mouth. Wow, they could at least keep their oral fixations behind closed doors.

I'm about to make some dismissive comment and return my attention to Troy when a paper airplane comes flying into my meat loaf. Looking around, I see Stella watching from three tables away, gesturing at the airplane and indicating I should open it.

Frowning, I pluck the airplane's point out of the mush and unfold the paper.

Don't forget our deal.

Now's the perfect chance to start.

The deal. Right, I'm supposed to magically come between the golden couple. I must have been seriously sleep deprived when I agreed to this. There's no way I'm going to—

The paper in my hand glows for a second and more words appear.

I get my powers back in three days, kako.

Want to eat earthworms next time?

"What does *kako* mean again?" I ask.

"I told you," Nicole says. "It means you're not a—"

"No," I interrupt. "What does it *really* mean?"

Troy looks up from his meat loaf and gives me a sympathetic smile. "It means you have bad blood."

I start to crumple the note into a ball, ready to fling it back in Stella's face. Nothing more than she deserves. But something holds me back.

The paper glows again.

And don't tell anyone you're doing this for me or you'll never get off this island!

As soon as I finish reading the last word, the note glows again and I'm there holding a blank sheet of paper.

If she doesn't have her powers, how did she zap the note?

I look up and another highlight-heavy harpy is huddled close to Stella, her finger pointing at me. Guess it pays to have supernatural friends. Before Stella's friend can zap me into a bat or something, I stand up abruptly, knocking my tray and sloshing orange Fanta all over my meat loaf.

That could only be an improvement.

"I'll be right back," I say, throwing Stella a good scowl so she knows how unhappy I am about being forced into action.

I have my own reasons for doing this, but if doing this her way keeps her from suspecting my motives then I'll go along. No point in antagonizing her when I just got her off my back.

"Something wrong?" Troy asks.

"No," I assure him. "Just something I have to take care of."

My stomach rolls as I approach them—I'm not sure if it's because I'm nervous or repulsed about what I have to do. I glance quickly over my shoulder. Stella nods encouragingly. Nicole and Troy stare at me like I've lost my mind.

But sometimes a girl has to make the tough choices.

Deep down inside I know this is more than just a deal with Stella. In spite of all the warning signs that keep flashing GRIFFIN BLAKE IS A BAD IDEA, there is something about him that I can't resist. Something I saw that first morning on the beach before he knew who I was. Something that even his sabotaging my tryout didn't completely erase. The runner in me wants to believe that someone who loves the sport as much as he obviously does—who loves it as much as I do—has to have a pure heart in there somewhere. I can't let go of that hope, so I have to go after it.

Sucking up all my courage, I reach out and tap Griffin on the shoulder. At this point I really have no idea what I intend to say, but just hope that something intelligible will come out of my mouth when the time comes.

Without releasing Adara from his embrace, Griffin turns to look over his shoulder.

Behind him I can see Adara glaring at me with deadly daggers in her vapid gray eyes. I think I'm probably lucky there aren't real daggers slicing through me right now. Pissing her off is definitely a bonus.

The look Griffin gives me isn't much more inviting.

"Well, *nothos*," he snarls, "what do you want?"

CHAPTER 6

GRIFFIN'S FLAME-BLUE EYES glare a hole in me.

My knees go a little weak at being so close to him. No matter how many times I tell myself this one is a L-O-S-E-R, my heart still beats faster whenever I think of him. I can feel the adrenaline coursing through my body—prepared to flee if the embarrassment meter reaches the warning zone.

"Um, I, uh . . ." Great start, Phoebe. Why don't you just sink into a puddle at his feet? Then he can rinse off his shoes in your pathetic—

I lurch as I feel a sharp pinch in my butt. Spinning around, I see Stella and her friend laughing uproariously.

Grrr.

"Did you want something?" Adara asks, her voice dripping with disdain. "Or did you just want to stand close enough for us to see the pathetic look in your eyes?"

That does it! Suddenly, I know I am going to relish stealing Griffin away from her.

"Actually," I focus my attention and my gaze on Griffin, batting my eyelashes at him like a flirting fan-girl. I tell myself Adara isn't even there. "I wanted to ask for your help."

Bat, bat, bat.

Biting my lip, I try for my most seductive girl pose.

Griffin snorts. "With what?"

"With the cross-country course," I say as I step closer and increase my batting speed to mach two. "You must know all the bumps and . . ." I place my hands on my hips, tugging my T-shirt tighter across my chest in the process. ". . . curves."

The corner of his kiss-begging mouth lifts up in a smirk. "Why would I want to help you?"

He talks tough, but his eyes never leave mine—like he's really trying to figure out why I'm asking for his help.

Time to play my blackmail card. Stepping forward, I place my hands on his shoulder and lift up on tiptoe to whisper in his ear, "Because you don't want me to tell Coach Lenny about the shoelaces."

I can hear his jaw grind in frustration.

Lowering back to my heels, I add, "But if you're all talk about running, then I guess you can't help me after all."

With nerves of steel, I turn away. My heart is racing and I can't feel my hands or my feet. But somehow, I start walking and keep moving forward. I take three steps before he calls out.

"Meet me at the starting line at noon on Sunday." His voice is cocky—without turning around I can tell he's acting like this is some big joke. "I'll show you how to run the course."

"See you there," I say casually and then keep walking.

Stella, who has been watching the entire show, smiles and nods at me. I guess she approves of my first effort. Hopefully, that means I won't have to worry about her zapping my food into something from the low rungs of the animal kingdom anytime soon.

But if she knew how much I am looking forward to the meeting with Griffin, she wouldn't be smiling at all.

Back at my lunch table, Troy is intently focused on his tapioca pudding. Nicole is staring at me like I've lost my mind.

"Have you lost your mind?" she demands.

I shrug, too elated and terrified by the whole situation to even answer. My mind races, imagining what I'll say to Griffin on Sunday, how I'll act, what I'll wear. This isn't about Stella—this is about me.

"Earth to Phoebe." Nicole snaps her fingers in front of my face.

"What?" I shake myself out of the daydream.

"What were you thinking?" Her eyebrows jump up in disbelief. "Griffin Blake is a centaur's rear."

"I just . . ." I struggle to find something to say that won't be a total lie. Or the total truth. ". . . thought he could help me out."

Nicole flings her fork down on her plate. "You're crazy."

Maybe . . . but I can't keep the smile off my face.

Troy, who hasn't said a word since I got back to the table, stands up and grabs his tray. "Maybe Blake can take you to the bonfire."

Before I can answer he turns and walks away.

He sounded really upset.

I watch him walk over to the conveyor belt, toss down his tray, and leave the room. Without once looking back at our table.

"What was that about?" I ask.

Nicole stares at me. "Are you that dense?"

"What?" I look at her, confused.

She shakes her head. "No wonder you made a fool of yourself over that ass. You're clueless when it comes to boys."

She spears a bite of meat loaf with her fork. I think she is actually going to eat some of the questionable stuff, but instead she flicks it up in the air. The meat blob sticks to the ceiling for a few seconds before plopping back down on our table.

"Did you really not know what was about to happen?" she demands.

I can tell she expects me to know what she's talking about—other than she thinks I should stay far away from Griffin, but I already *know* that and it doesn't make a difference. "I don't know—"

"Troy was going to ask you to the bonfire."

I can almost hear the unspoken *stupid* at the end of her statement. Yes, I knew Troy was going to ask me. And I was even going to agree.

"We can all go together," I offer. "As friends."

"You could do worse than liking Troy, you know." She glances back to the golden couple, who are continuing their bid for the PDA record. "Wait—you already have."

I sigh, because she's right. After everything I went through with Justin, I know how much it hurts when bad crushes happen to good people. But no matter how many times I tell myself he's pure bad news I just can't get my mind off Griffin. I am living proof that crushes are blind, deaf, and dumb.

"I know," I say. "But I can't—"

I shake my head.

I'm afraid of blowing my friendship with her—and with Troy—all because I can't control my stupid crush on Griffin. There, I've said it. I have a crush on Griffin Blake.

Okay, I didn't really say it—I thought it.

Admitting there's a problem is the first step to recovery, right?

“I understand,” Nicole says, her voice full of sympathy. “You can’t always choose who you fall for.”

“Exactly.”

“Don’t worry.” She sounds upbeat and I’m relieved that she’s not casting me away just because my heart has bad taste. “Eventually he’ll break your heart and maybe Troy and I will be there to glue the pieces back together.”

That’s a cheerful thought.

“I hope you won’t have to.” I smile. Nicole is a true friend—which makes me think of Cesca and Nola. They would love Nicole. Cesca would love her willingness to say what she’s really thinking and Nola would appreciate how she is an individual and doesn’t care what others think of her. We would make a great foursome. Maybe one day we can all hang out together.

“So, I can’t talk you out of this?”

I shake my head. Time for full disclosure. “There’s more to this than a, um, crush.”

She lifts her eyebrows.

“I made a bargain with Stella.”

She doesn’t say anything, just keeps looking at me expectantly.

“She’s offered to tutor me in Modern Greek and to help convince her dad not to keep me here for another year.”

“In exchange for what, your firstborn child?”

“In exchange for splitting up Griffin and Adara.”

Another low whistle. “You made a deal with Hades, you know.”

“Yeah,” I say, defeated. “I know.”

“Cheer up,” she says as she stacks our trays of untouched—except for the blob she flung at the ceiling—meat loaf, "I'm going to help you in this idiotic quest for Blake."

"Really?" I ask, suspicious of her sudden turnaround. "Why?"

"Because I think this bargain is just your excuse." She grins wickedly. "You want him, and the sooner you catch him the sooner he'll break your heart. And the sooner you can recover. I'd hate for you to spend the entire year pining over him." She picks up our trays. "He's so not worth it. And if you break his heart instead, so much the better."

I have a feeling that Nicole has her own motives, but I just ask, "When do we start?"

"Tonight," she says decisively. "We'll launch Operation Anteros at the bonfire."

"Anteros?"

"The god of avenging unrequited love." Nicole flashes me a devious smile. "Blake doesn't stand a chance."

I float all the way to Physics, daydreaming about the romantic bonfire and how Nicole is going to help me catch Griffin Blake so I can get him out of my system. Something in the back corner of my mind screams that I don't want to get over him, but I ignore it.

Evening is cool on the beach, but the sun-warmed sand and the roaring bonfire more than keep me warm. The water of the Aegean stretches out before me as far as I can see, until it disappears into the setting sun. An inky blue sea with crimson reflecting on every ripple. I can imagine those thousand ships setting sail, gliding silently over the waves to rescue Helen from Troy—whether she wanted to be rescued or not.

"The island is pretty romantic at night," Troy says from behind me.

I turn, surprised to see him after he stormed off at lunch—not that I blame him considering the fool I made of myself over Griffin. Only a great miracle of willpower kept me from losing my own lunch.

"Yeah," I say brilliantly. "It's beautiful."

Boy is it.

Nicole and I had gotten to the beach just before sunset, so I am watching the sun turn the Aegean into a sea of flames. Everything glows in a million shades of orange. Even the village buildings—walls of the same white plaster as Damian's house—perched on the cliffs above the water reflect the warm light, turning them a pinkish shade of peach. It's breathtaking.

For a few seconds I am even thankful to be on this stupid island, just so I could watch this sunset.

"They say that Leda, a handmaiden of Helios who was in love with the sun god, built this island by hand," he explains. "She carried soil from Serifos one fistful at a time."

"Why?" I ask, wondering what would possess someone to undertake such an overwhelming task.

"Each night, when Helios drove his chariot below the horizon, she wept for the loss of him." Troy's voice is soft and hypnotizing. "She built this island so she could watch him until the last ray of his light disappeared from view."

"Wow." That's devotion. And one of the most romantic things

I've ever heard. I turn away from the waning sunset to look up at Troy. "So the island was built for watching the sun set?"

He shrugs. "It's just a fairy tale. A bedtime story men made up to tell around the fire at night."

From the far-off look in his eyes—which are *not* looking at me—I can tell he's still hurt.

"Until a few days ago," I return, "I thought you were a fairy tale."

"There's a difference. Myths and fairy tales aren't the same thing."

"Then explain it to me."

Still gazing at the water, he says, "A myth is a tradition, a legend created to explain the unexplainable. The gods are unexplainable, hence they are myth."

"And fairy tales?"

I watch his face closely, looking for a reaction. Finally, after several long seconds, he turns to look down at me. He meets my gaze head on, concentrating like he's trying to figure me out. Good luck with that. Eventually his features relax and he smiles a little.

"A fairy tale," he says, "is a story we wish were true."

I smile in relief. Whatever Troy and I are destined to become, I know we're friends. And I'm glad my stupid deal with Stella hasn't come between that.

Which reminds me . . . "There's something I need to tell you."

His eyebrows lift.

I stand up so I can tell him eye-to-eye.

"It's about me and the evil stepsister."

"I'm listening," he says.

It's better he knows what's going on so next time I make a fool of myself with Griffin he doesn't jump to any crazy conclusions. The reality of the situation is bad enough.

"What happened in the lunch room today wasn't about me wanting Griffin." At least, not *just* about me wanting Griffin. "Stella and I made a deal."

He looks skeptical. "About what?"

"If I break up Griffin and Adara she'll tutor me in Modern Greek—"

"I could help you with Modern Greek."

Why hadn't I thought of that? "That's not the only thing. If I do this she'll help convince her dad that I don't need to stay on for Level 13."

"And if you don't?" He crosses his arms over his chest.

"She'll convince him that I do."

He scowls. "Why that conniving, blackmailing—"

"I know . . . but I agreed."

"So," he says slowly, "you want to get off this island so bad you're willing to make a deal with the gorgon?"

"Yes." He sounds so sad that I feel kinda guilty. But undeterred. "I just wanted you to know, so you would understand, because I don't want to lose your friendship."

I place a little extra emphasis on the word friendship, trying to make him see that that's how I think of him. As a friend.

From the look in his eyes, he knows exactly what I'm saying.

"All right." He smiles, like he's trying to show that he's fine with that. "If that's what you really want I'll do whatever I can to help."

I tug my zip-front sweatshirt tighter around my waist. The sun is gone now, and the beach is downright chilly. Maybe all that cool air blowing off the water.

“Thank—”

“Well, well, well,” a whiny voice I’m starting to get sick of says, “look who showed up at the bonfire uninvited.”

Flanked by two other cheerleaders, Adara is wearing a white crocheted bikini top and a pair of white cutoff jeans shorts. I’m shivering in my jeans and sweatshirt—she must be freezing.

The thought makes me smile.

“Hi, Adara,” I say with sugary sweetness. “I love your swimsuit.”

She scowls, but can’t resist the compliment. “Thanks—”

“Of course, I loved it when everyone in L.A. was wearing them last summer.” I turn to Troy and whisper dramatically, loud enough for everyone to hear, “It’s *so* last season.”

Adara’s mouth drops open. “Listen, *kako*. Tonight is for descendants only—no godly blood, no bonfire. Leave now before you embarrass yourself.”

“Leave off, Adara,” Troy says. “She’s with me.”

“Really?” she coos. “She was panting over my boyfriend at lunch today. Are your attachments always so fleeting, *kako*?”

Troy lunges forward, but I grab his shoulders and hold him back. He gives me a look that says he’s clearly willing to throw down with Adara for me. I shake my head.

“She’s not worth it,” I say. “You have to pity someone who doesn’t understand the concept of friendship.”

Adara sidesteps Troy, stepping right up into my face.

“Stella may be softening toward you, but I know better.” We are nose to nose when she sneers, “You are a disgrace to the Academy and your very presence sullies a reputation over two thousand years in the making.”

I know this shouldn't bother me. I mean, she's a jealous, vindictive cow. Still, I have a feeling that she's not the only student at the Academy who feels that way. Since I can't really argue that point—I mean, I can't like suddenly make myself the descendant of a god—I resort to hitting Adara where it hurts.

In her superficial face.

"Wow, I have never seen pores that big," I say with a gasp of awe, tilting my head for a closer look. "Those blackheads look like Dalmatian spots."

While she struggles to think of some witty comeback—I'm not waiting around all night for *that*—I take Troy by the hand and lead him down the beach toward the blanket Nicole has spread out.

He stumbles a little as I tug him, but catches up quickly.

"She's going to hate you." He sounds genuinely concerned.

I roll my eyes. "She already does."

From behind, she shouts, "At least I'm not wearing shoes from the last decade."

I glance at my footwear.

My Chuck Taylors are brand-new. In fact, they're so new they need a little wearing in and maybe a few scuffs. Besides, black All Stars are always the height of fashion.

And the originals date back to the fifties. Adara could use some work on her fashion history.

"You're right," I shout back over my shoulder, darting a glance at her standing petulantly with her hands on her hips. "Those beaded flip-flops you're wearing are only two seasons old."

"Aaargh!!!" Her scream echoes across the beach.

Everyone turns to stare at her as she stomps her foot on the sand. Does she think that's making a statement?

"You'd better get off this island as soon as possible," Troy says, laughing. "The longer you stay the greater the chance that Adara blasts you to Hades."

"I'm not afraid of her." We reach the blanket and I drop down to sit next to Nicole. "If she does anything too horrible to me, Damian will ground her powers."

"Yeah," Nicole says as she pokes me in the arm, "but by then you'll be smoted."

I shrug and lay back on the blanket, my hands behind my head. "No worries. With all the extra practices and workouts, Coach Lenny will kill me long before she gets the chance."

Nicole lays out next to me. "I can't understand why anyone would run on purpose, anyway. Are you masochistic?"

"Nonrunners don't get it, I guess." I close my eyes and picture myself running. A sense of calm sweeps over me. "There's freedom in running. Escape. Power."

"Insanity," Troy adds.

I pry open one eye to glare at him. He's sitting at the edge of the blanket staring out at the water.

Maybe it is insanity. Every time I hit the wall, when my body screams, *No more of this running crap!* I tell myself this is the last race ever. Am I so stupid that I want to run myself into utter exhaustion for no good reason? I'll just finish this race and then hang up my sneakers. Forever.

Then I push through the wall. And everything becomes clear.

Euphoria sets in—along with a whole boatload of endorphins. I can't remember why I was even thinking about giving it up.

Maybe that is insanity.

Everyone has to find their version of therapy. Running is mine.

I wonder what Troy's is?

"Don't you have something that you just have to do, even though every time you do it you tell yourself you're crazy to even try? But if you don't do it you feel even crazier?"

He keeps staring at the water. He's silent so long I think he's not going to answer. I drop my head back and close my eyes.

"Music," he finally says.

I lift back up on my elbows. "Music?"

"Whenever I play the guitar I feel like it's a colossal waste of time, but I can't stop playing." His voice is almost reverent. "I want to be a musician."

"That's great," I say.

He snorts. "Try telling my parents that."

"The Travatas clan takes their heritage seriously." Nicole exerts enough energy to roll onto her side. "They believe all descendants of Asklepios should pursue the medical profession."

"So because your great-great-something was into medicine they want you to be a doctor, too?" I ask.

"A neurosurgeon." He laughs. "I couldn't even stand to dissect an earthworm in Level 4. How could I cut open a human skull?"

Ew. I shudder, but keep my disgust to myself. This is about Troy and his passions.

"If you want to be a musician—if you *can't* be anything else—then you'll find a way." I lay a reassuring hand on his shoulder. "True callings aren't easy to hide from."

He covers my hand with his own. "Thanks."

"If you two are done with the Hallmark moment, I'd like to watch the fireworks in peace."

I glance up at the empty, silent sky. "What fireworks?"

"Just wait." Troy checks his watch. "In five, four, three, two, one—"

The sky above us explodes in a shimmering burst of color. Red, blue, and green embers flicker through the darkness, raining down around us. Another big sphere of golden sparkles bursts into the sky.

"I didn't even hear the launch," I remark.

"Honey, we don't need to bother with messy explosives," Nicole replies. "All it takes is a little focus and a snap of my fingers."

She snaps her fingers and a little blue spark shoots through the air, landing on Troy's Green Day T-shirt. He quickly pats at the spot where the ember hit—a spot that starts smoking and leaves a little hole above the G.

"Hey," he exclaims. "Watch where you throw the fireworks, Nic."

I laugh out loud at the thought of Troy going up in flames from a single spark. Nicole just shrugs and says, "Sorry. Haven't honed my fireworks skills recently."

"Well don't test them on my clothing."

I settle back into the blanket, feeling the warm sand crunch beneath the blanket, and watch the fireworks while listening to my two friends bickering. It's almost like being home. If not for the whole supernatural-descendants-of-the-gods thing and being thousands of miles away from everything I've ever called home, this island could be bearable.

Almost cool, even.

A sudden outburst sounds down the beach. With lazy heaviness, I loll my head to the side. Griffin and a bunch of other tricksters—armed with a water balloon in each hand—are chasing after Adara and her cheerleader groupies. I recognize a couple of the long distance guys, Christopher and Costas. Christopher is super tall, blond, and actually very sweet—he volunteered to be my training partner at practice when no one else would. Costas, on the other hand, is like a shorter version of Griffin.

While I watch, the boys get the girls surrounded and hold the water balloons menacingly over their heads.

Did I say this island was almost cool? I meant juvenile.

I guess boys are the same everywhere—godly or not.

"Are you sure you want to get in the middle of that?" Nicole asks, drawing my attention away from the chase scene.

"Yeah," I reply, reluctant. "I haven't got a—"

"*Aaack!*" Adara's scream pierces the air as Griffin and Costas trap her between them and pummel her with water balloons.

Now she's cold *and* wet. I don't envy her.

"—choice," I finish.

"All right." Nicole cocks her eyebrows. "But don't say we didn't warn you."

"Consider me warned."

Just then, Griffin—still shaking with laughter at his water balloon strike—looks our way. His eyes stop on me, intense and disapproving. He points at me. The sand next to me glows and a folded piece of paper appears.

Reaching across my chest, I pick up the paper and unfold the note.

Sunday. Noon. Be ready to work.

When I look back up he's gone.

Mom and I stare at the glass display cases filled with shelf after shelf of bakery goodness. There are trays of biscuits, baklava, cakes, pies, and tortes. It seems like they're all drizzled with honey and lit just right to make the reflection hypnotizing. On the wall behind the cases are shelves of baskets, overflowing with dozens of breads. Everything from fist-sized olive rolls to three-foot-long *tsoureki*, a braided festival bread Yia Yia Minta bakes every Greek Independence Day. I bite my lower lip to keep from drooling.

"I've never seen such a variety," Mom says, leaning closer to examine the pies. "No wonder your grandmother is always baking—she could make a different recipe every day of the year and never repeat one."

"Don't tell Yia Yia Minta," I say, "but these look better than hers."

"I hope so." A short, round, middle-aged woman wearing a white chef's coat emerges from the back room, dusting flour off her hands. "We have the Hestia Seal."

"What is the Hestia Seal?" Mom asks.

“Ah, you must be the new *nothos* on the island.” The woman smiles, her fleshy cheeks pushing out into pink apples. “I am Lilika, a descendant of Hestia. My recipes come from the goddess of the hearth herself and are unmatched in all the world.”

“So nice to meet you, Lilika,” Mom says. She wraps her fingers around my T-shirt sleeve and jerks my attention away from the baklava. “I’m Valerie Petrolas, and this is my daughter, Phoebe.”

I’m so captivated by the display of treats that I barely register the fact that Mom introduced herself as a Petrolas. “Holy crap!” I drop to my knees, pressing my face closer to the glass. Closer to the treat to end all treats. “Is that . . . *bougatsa*?”

“The young lady has a favorite, no?” Lilika moves around behind the case, sliding open the panel in the back. “This is my favorite as well.”

“We have to get some, Mom.” I look up at her, pleading. She doesn’t answer, so I crawl closer until I’m at her feet. The bell over the front door rings but I don’t care. I’m focused on begging. Nothing but that sweet custard and cheese pastry could reduce me to begging—well, that and the new Nike+ with built-in iPod sensor. “Please, please, please.”

Mom laughs.

Lilika, who is busy pulling the *bougatsa* out of the case, glances up to see who walked in. “*Moro mou!*” she squeals. She slides the tray back into the case. “*Pou sas echei ontas*, Griffin?”

I only understand one word of what she says, but that name is all I need to know that mortification is in my future. My very near future.

“I’m sorry I haven’t been by in a while, Aunt Lili,” the voice that I dread hearing says. “I’ve been busy.”

Maybe it’s my imagination, but I can feel him staring at me.

Who wouldn't stare at a girl on her knees in the middle of a bakery, pleading with her mom for some stupid pastry. Even if it is the most delicious, custardy pastry she's ever eaten.

Carefully, so I don't draw attention to myself in the off chance that he *hasn't* noticed me, I push off the floor. Still, I can't turn around. Having Griffin laugh at me at school in front of a ton of kids I don't even know was bad enough, but I don't think I'd survive him laughing at me in front of Mom. The kids at the Academy won't even exist on my radar in nine months. Mom is my mom forever.

"Silly boy," Lilika says. Then she gasps. "Of course, you must meet Phoebe. She is new to the Academy. Sweetheart," she says and I can tell she's turned her attention back to me, "I'd like you to meet my nephew, Griffin."

"Phoebe," he says, his voice low and steady. No emotion.

Against my better judgment I turn around to face him. I clasp my hands behind my back so I'm not tempted to wave like a total dork. "Griffin."

He looks adorable, as always. Droplets of water hang off his dark curls, like he just took a shower, and the red cotton of his T-shirt clings in a few choice places. He's watching me with a fixed, unreadable gaze. I can't tell if he's furious or completely unaffected by my presence.

"Wonderful." Lilika claps her hands. "You have already met."

"We're on the cross-country team together, Aunt."

I expect him to add something jerky like, "For now." Or, "Until she loses that first race." When he doesn't, I tilt my head, wondering if I'm looking at the real Griffin Blake. Sure looks like him.

"You must be Mrs. Petrolas," he says, stepping forward and holding out his hand to Mom. "Griffin Blake."

“Valerie, please,” she says. As she shakes his hand she gives me a look that clearly says, *Cute one!* “I’m always pleased to meet Phoebe’s teammates. Though she might not say it, she’s very excited to be on the team.”

Thanks, Mom.

Griffin smiles politely. He flicks his eyes over at me as he says, “We’re excited to have her on the team. She is the most challenging runner I’ve ever practiced with.”

What was that? Sarcasm? Mockery? It didn’t sound fake, but it had to be. Well, I’m not going to stick around to be laughed at with backhanded compliments.

“Speaking of practicing,” I say, grabbing Mom by the hand, “I have tons of homework to finish before my afternoon session.”

Mom frowns, like she doesn’t understand what’s gotten into me, but lets me lead her out of the store. “Phoebe, honey,” she says when we get out onto the cobblestone street, “is everything okay?”

“Sure,” I say. “Why wouldn’t it be?”

“One minute you’re begging for *bougatsa*, the next you’re dragging me out the door.”

Darn! I totally forgot the *bougatsa*. For a second I think about going back, but decide that even custardy goodness isn’t worth facing Griffin’s thinly veiled ridicule again.

“Yeah, well, the sugar would mess up my training diet.” Which is a total lie.

Mom doesn’t let it go. “This has something to do with that boy, doesn’t it—”

“Phoebe, wait!”

I turn to see Griffin jogging down the street toward us, a brown paper bag in his left hand. My heart rate speeds up and I know it's because I'm hoping he's running after me to apologize. To say he wasn't teasing and that he really is glad to have me on the team.

Ha!

"Here," he says, handing me the paper bag. "Aunt Lili didn't want you to leave without your *bougatsa*."

I stare at the bag. Why did my heart have to get its hopes up?

"Thanks," I mumble. "But we didn't pay for this."

When I try to give the bag back he waves me off. "Lili wants you to have it." He dips his head a little so he's looking into my eyes. "She says you have excellent taste in pastry."

"Really?"

He nods, smiling just a tiny bit. I almost miss it.

"Tell her thank you," Mom says, breaking that momentary connection between me and Griffin.

He looks up at her, his eyes wide like he'd forgotten she was even here. "Sure," he says. That polite smile returns. "No problem."

Without another word, he turns and runs back up the street.

"He seems like a nice young man," Mom says, watching him retreat.

"Yeah," I say. "If you catch him on a good day."

Too bad he doesn't have many.

"You're not wearing that," Nicole says the second she walks in my room. "Fuzzy gray sweats will send Griffin into Adara's arms—not yours."

She is wearing a dark denim miniskirt and layered red and white tanks and more bangle bracelets than I ever thought a person's arm could hold. Her look is more back-off than boy-attracting, but I'm not about to argue. Dressing for boys is not in my repertoire.

"Fine," I say, stepping out of my Nikes and heading to my dresser. "What should I wear?"

"Let me see." She pushes me out of the way and begins digging through my drawers, tossing pants and tees over her shoulder. "No." Throws item. "Nope." Throws item. "Nuh-uh."

I catch my baby blue velour track pants before they can land on the floor. "Do you have to throw everything?"

She keeps rummaging, ignoring my question. "Ah-ha!" Pulling a pair of shorts triumphantly from the pile, she waves them over her head. "Put these on."

They're the gray shorts with pink pinstripes I bought for the Race for the Cure last year. Pink is *so* not my color—except for the occasional furry pillow, of course.

"Nicole, these aren't really—"

"Don't you have anything besides T-shirts?"

"Um, no. Not—"

"Here then." She pulls her arms inside her tank top, wiggles around for a second, then emerges with the white under tank in hand. "Put this on."

"I don't—"

"Hurry up." She flings the tank at me. "You shouldn't be late for your first meeting."

I catch the tank, think about arguing, then decide it's futile. Tank and shorts in hand, I head to the bathroom and change out of my comfy gray sweats. I feel practically naked with my legs and arms fully exposed. I'm not used to showing so much skin except on competition days.

When I get back to my room, Nicole is sprawled on my bed, flipping through an old issue of *Runner's World*.

"You actually read this stuff?" she asks, lifting her head. "Holy *dolmades*!"

She sounds shocked.

"What?"

"You," she says, dropping the magazine to the floor, "look hot."

I can feel my cheeks burning red.

Not just because of the compliment. The shorts hug my hips closer than I'm used to, and the tank stretches tight across my breasts, even in my chest-flattening jog bra.

"I had no idea you had curves under those T-shirts." She circles me, gauging my appearance from every angle, I guess. "We can definitely use those to your advantage. And your legs are great—lean and toned and shapely."

"Th-thanks," I stammer. "Do you really think I can . . ."

I can't make myself ask the question.

Nicole looks at me for a long time before saying, "If you want him, we'll get him. Don't worry. And those . . ." She gestures at my chest. ". . . will just make the bait more appealing."

I'm not sure how good I'll be at using *those* at all, but if they'll help me, then I'm all for it.

"Now that your appearance is set—though you might want to try something other than a ponytail for your hair," she waves a hand at my apparently inadequate hairstyle. "Let's discuss strategy."

I reach up and tighten my ponytail. My hair only has two styles: ponytail and down. Ponytail for running. Down for school.

Not even the great Griffin Blake can induce anything more elaborate from me.

"Before we get to, um, strategy," I say, knowing that this is a question I need answered before this goes any further, "I want to ask about your history with Griffin. It seems like you have some bad blood and I don't want to—"

"There's no history," she snaps. "Not the romantic kind, anyway. It's just a personal disagreement. Don't worry about it."

Keep your nose out of my business. I hear the unspoken caution as clearly as if she'd said it aloud.

"Okay." I can take a blatant hint to move on.

She runs her hands through her spiky blonde hair, sending it in all different directions. "Listen," she says, taking a seat on my bed. "I don't really like to talk about this. I mean, I never *have* talked about this with anyone."

"I get it." I sit down next to her. "You don't have to tell me anything."

"No." She shakes her head. "You should know." Taking a deep breath, she says, "Griffin and I used to be friends. Best friends."

Wow, I did *not* see that one coming.

"When we were young we got into trouble. Big trouble." Her eyes shine bright with unshed tears. "My parents wound up exiled from Serfopoula. That's why I didn't start at the Academy until Level 9."

"Oh, Nicole, I'm so sorry."

"The worst of it was," she says, wiping at her tears, "they were punished because of what Griffin and I did. Because he wouldn't accept responsibility for his actions. He let the gods ruin my parents' lives to save his own skin."

"I can't believe that." I know Griffin can be jerky, but the boy I met on the beach—the one I'm going through all this for—has a good heart. "He wouldn't do something that would knowingly hurt—"

"He went in to testify," she snaps. "When he came out, my parents were banished."

Tears stream down her cheeks. Wrapping my arms around her, I squeeze tight. This is what Mom would call the release of repressed emotion. I think it's just good for her to let it all out. I can't believe she never talked to anyone about this before. Then again, everyone else probably already knows the whole story. I'm just glad I could be here for her.

For several minutes we sit there, Nicole crying and me hugging her. Eventually, the tears stop and she begins to sniff.

"So," I say to alleviate the post-traumatic release silence, "you said something about strategy?"

"Yes," she says matter-of-factly, jumping to her feet and pretending like she was never crying. "You can't go in without a game plan. It'd be like . . ." She thinks for a second. ". . . running a race without knowing the course."

Why do I have a feeling I'm not going to like this?

"Okay," I relent. "Strategy."

"I recommend one part helpless girl, one part ample cleavage, and three parts ego-petting." She must see the blank look on my face because she adds, "Do I need to write this down?"

"No," I reply. "But you'll have to explain it."

With a whole body sigh, she sits on the bed. "To get Griffin's attention—in a good way—you need to appeal to his weaknesses. Those would be playing the hero, ogling breasts, and colossal arrogance that could fill the Parthenon."

I nod, but am still not really sure what she means.

Nicole rolls her eyes at my continued confusion. "He's a chauvinistic, hormone-driven, egotistical jerk."

Oh. Is that all? I already knew that.

"The real question," she continues, "is how to use that against him."

"I bet you have a plan."

"As a matter of fact—" She grins wickedly. "I do."

I *know* I'm not going to like this.

"Are you ready for pain?" Griffin asks as I walk up to the starting line.

Nicole suggested I play it weak—no arguing, no witty retorts, nothing but sweetness and sugar. The second I see Griffin's smug smile I know I can't play that part.

"I can take anything you dish out, Blake."

He looks me up and down, hovering over my chest and thighs on the way back up. I'm filled with a little bubble of satisfaction that my clothing is worth the embarrassment. If nothing else, I know that he likes what he sees.

"Let's get started," I say when he doesn't seem to be in any hurry.

“Right,” he says, his eyes snapping back up to my face. “You warmed up?”

“On fire.”

He smirks. “Then on my count.”

We line up at the starting line.

Griffin counts down, “Three, two, one—”

I take off before he says go, speeding down the trail, knowing he’s at least one pace behind. A quarter-mile into the course he catches up with me.

“You cheated.”

“No,” I say casually. “I was just evening the score.”

He has no comeback for that. He knows he cheated last time and I’m confident he’s not going to cheat again. There’s no one here but the two of us to see who wins.

Besides, I bet he’s dying to find out for real who’s faster.

Right then I know I can’t go through with Nicole’s plan. It feels too good to be in a real race for victory—I can’t *not* compete. I’m going to run this race until my feet bleed. And I’m going to win.

I see a blaze of red out of the corner of my eye.

Turning, I see Nicole’s spiky blonde hair amidst the shrubby trees and undergrowth. What is she doing h—

A flash of light glows at my feet and next thing I know I’m pitching to the ground, face-first. Even as I tumble, I feel my feet fly out from under me and I know it’s not another case of knotted shoelaces.

No, Nicole just sprained my ankle for me.

"ARE YOU ALL RIGHT?" Griffin is leaning over me, his brows pinched together in concern.

"Yes," I say, rolling onto my back. "Just peachy."

"What happened?" He looks really anxious, like I'm going to accuse him of zapping me like last time.

No, I know better.

"I'm not sure. I just tr—*aaaack*!" I try to stand, but my right ankle buckles under me. Arms flailing, I collapse forward against Griffin's chest.

Seems like Nicole didn't just knock me down. My ankle doesn't hurt or anything, but it won't support my weight. As I clutch Griffin's shoulders and claw my way upright, I throw a scowl in the direction of the bushes where I glimpsed her. She's long gone, I'm sure.

"You must have really twisted that ankle," Griffin says, placing his hands on my back for support. "Can you walk?"

"Of course I ca—*aaaack*!"

Another step forward—and another tumble immediately into Griffin's arms. What did Nicole do, zap away my ankle muscles?

"Here." Griffin comes up behind me, scoops down, and lifts me into his arms. "I'll carry you."

“No, really, that’s not nec—”

“Yes,” he interrupts. “It is.”

While it is not totally unappealing to be in his arms, this is not how I’d always imagined it would be. Wait—I mean this is not how I’d fleetingly thought it would be when we came up with this plan.

I never wasted my time imagining Griffin and me doing anything. Promise.

Anyway, here I am, cradled in his arms as he makes his way back through the woods. I feel like some fairy-tale damsel in distress being rescued from a dark forest full of ogres and trolls.

But Griffin Blake only acts like a fairy-tale hero when it suits him.

“Why are you being so nice?” I ask.

His blue eyes glance down at me. “I’m not.”

I give him a look that says, “Um, hello!”

“All right,” he relents, then mumbles, “I hrmphoo.”

“What?” I know he’s weird, but I am sure he is capable of intelligible speech.

“I said . . .” He closes his eyes—I glance ahead on the trail to make sure he’s not going to trip over a tree root or anything—and clenches his jaw. “. . . I *have* to.”

“What do you mean you have to?”

I stomp down on the little part of me that wants him to say, *I can’t help myself because I love you, Phoebe.* Talk about delusional.

“It’s in my blood,” he explains. And leaves it at that.

Like that clears everything up.

“I don’t get it.”

He growls and I can feel it in his chest.

"Listen, if you're going to do the silent thing the whole way then just—"

"Hercules is my ancestor."

"Isn't Hercules Roman?"

"The name is," Griffin says. "But most people have never heard of Heracles. Even the gods stopped using that name centuries ago."

"I thought you were descended from Ares."

"I am," he grumbles. "On my great-grandmother's side. Hercules is on my father's line."

"And . . ."

"Descendants of Hercules are compelled to act heroic when someone is in need."

I can't help it—I burst out laughing. That's the funniest thing I've ever heard. He really is helping me because he can't stop himself. This is priceless.

I can see this definitely working to my advantage.

"You can't, however," he says when I can't stop laughing, "abuse the privilege. Only genuine situations of need qualify."

"What?" I ask, suppressing my giggles. "Is there some kind of contract? Qualifications and exceptions to your heroics?"

His jaw clenches again and he doesn't answer.

In fact, he stares straight forward and doesn't even look down at me. I must have touched a nerve or something. Great, now I feel guilty for teasing him—the guy who tried to zap me off the cross-country team in the first place. I have no reason to feel bad for him.

But I do.

"I'm sorry," I hear myself say. "I shouldn't make fun of stuff I don't understand. This hero thing is pretty serious, huh?"

He nods once.

"How many of you are there?"

Grim faced, he keeps staring off ahead—we've made it out of the woods and are now crossing the lawn below the school. Thinking he's so mad he's not going to answer, I drop my head back against his arm and relax. Might as well enjoy the ride.

"One." His blue eyes glow as they meet my brown ones. "Just one."

"You're the only descendant of Hercules?" Wow. That must be a major burden. "How is that possible?"

"There is only one child born to the Herculean line each generation."

"Then what about your parents?"

The glow in his eyes disappears. "They're . . . not around."

"Not around? Are they traveling or something?"

"No."

"Oh." Okay. I have no idea what he's saying—what I'm supposed to get from his cryptic responses—but I get the feeling he's not going to elaborate.

"So, um . . ." I try to think of something to talk about, to break this tense silence. ". . . where are you—"

"You're friends with Nicole."

I'm not sure if I'm more shocked that he's actually speaking or that he's speaking about Nicole. Especially after what she told me about their past.

"Yes," I answer carefully.

"She and I—" He shakes his head. "I don't know if she told you, but—"

"She told me."

I expect him to ask what exactly she said, to deny her accusations and defend himself. Instead, he surprises the crap out of me by asking, "How's she doing?"

"Um, she's . . . okay, I think." Thinking back to her teary revelation this morning, maybe she's not completely fine. At this point I don't think I can lose any points by being completely honest. "She doesn't like you very much."

Griffin snickers in a way that makes it clear that he doesn't think this is funny. "Tell me something I don't know."

Going for broke, I say, "She thinks you got her parents banished."

His jaw clamps shut.

"I don't know why she thinks so, but she—"

"It's true."

My mouth drops open. "It's what? Why would you do that?"

He sighs and rolls his eyes, but somehow I get the feeling he's rolling them at himself and not me. "Not on purpose," he says sadly. "I promise you that."

How do you get someone banished accidentally?

"What happened?" I ask, but he doesn't answer. "She said you testified at Mount Olympus and—"

"Drop it."

"But it doesn't make any sense," I insist. "How can *you* not taking responsibility for something get her parents—"

"I said *drop* it!"

I jerk back at his outburst—though I can't get far since I'm still cradled in his arms. Even though he sounds even angrier than when

I was taunting him in the qualifying race, his grip on me remains relaxed. From the way he's clenching his jaw and staring straight ahead I'm pretty sure I'm not getting any more conversation out of him.

I can't stand the tension-rich silence.

"Do you know where you're going to college?" I ask, hoping he'll go for the change of subject.

No response. Shocking.

"I'm going to USC next year," I say, filling the silence with my own voice. "Hopefully, I'll get a cross-country scholarship. I just have to make a B average and do well in our meets and the coach says he'll give me a full ride, which I'll really need since Mom's not working anymore and I don't expect Damian to pay for *anything* because—"

"Oxford," Griffin blurts. "I'm going to Oxford."

Apparently he's no match for babbling girls. I'll have to keep that in mind in the future.

Remembering that Stella has the same plan, I ask, "Does everyone at the Academy go to Oxford?"

"The school has an . . . arrangement with the university administration."

"What are you going to study?"

It's on the tip of my tongue to add, "Mythology?" but I decide against the sarcasm. At the moment he's being heroic, but tomorrow at school is fair game and I don't want to end up zapped to the ceiling in my underwear or anything.

"Economics."

That's it. One word response.

Not that I expect more.

"I'm going to study sports medicine. I want to be an athletic trainer, maybe for a college or the Olympic team or something."

He grunts, which I take to be his confirmation that he heard what I said but doesn't plan on replying. Which is fine, because I can keep on talking.

"I know I can't run forever—even though I know there are always old guys in the Boston Marathon and stuff like that—but I have to make a living somehow. And this way I still get to be involved in sports without worrying when my knees are going to give out and—"

"We're here."

Lost in my one-sided conversation, I didn't even realize we'd crossed the lawn, passed the school, and made it to the front steps of Damian's house.

I do notice, however, that Griffin does not immediately drop me on my behind and run away as fast as he can.

Maybe it's the hero contract.

"Well, thanks," I say, even though he didn't help me purely out of the goodness of his heart.

Still, he doesn't put me down.

He does look at me, though, his bright blue eyes intent on mine.

It is a frozen moment—I can't move or speak or react at all.

Helpless in his arms, silence ringing in my ears, I notice for the first time all the sensations. The feel of his heart pounding in his chest. His radiating heat. His arms against the bare skin of my legs and shoulder—

Oh. My. God.

I totally forgot the skimpy little running outfit Nicole made me wear. This whole time I've been half-naked in his arms—all right, I know all the important parts are covered and by MTV standards my clothes are practically dowdy, but for me this is exposed.

I'm not sure what to do. Should I kick and scream, demanding he put me down right now? Leap out of his arms—and likely fall flat on my face again thanks to Nicole's amazing disappearing ankle trick? Enjoy the sensation of being held while his head dips down, inching closer and closer to mine—

"Ah-hem."

Startled, I look up to see Stella standing in our open doorway. She has her hands on her hips and looks like she caught us making out on the front steps.

Griffin's ears are red with embarrassment.

Without saying a word he drops me on the steps, nods to Stella, and jogs off across the yard.

"Just keep in mind," Stella snaps, "that you are supposed to be stealing Griffin away *for* me, not *from* me."

I nod absently, not focused on her but on the spot where Griffin had just disappeared over the hill. Holding onto the doorjamb so I don't fall over, I can't waste energy worrying about her being mad at me.

Griffin Blake had been about to kiss me!

And stupid Stella had to interrupt.

PrincessCesca: did he wet his lips?

LostPhoebe: no

PrincessCesca: did he close his eyes?

LostPhoebe: no

PrincessCesca: did he lay his palm on your cheek?

LostPhoebe: no

LostPhoebe: he was kinda busy holding me

PrincessCesca: are you sure he was going to kiss you?

LostPhoebe: for the millionth time . . . yes!

PrincessCesca: you're in trouble

LostPhoebe: tell me about it

PrincessCesca: ES will kill you if you catch him before she can

ES is our shorthand for Evil Stepsister. AKA Stella.

After Griffin dropped me—and I found out that Nicole's ankle zap had worn off and I could walk just fine—I had endured Stella's inquisition about the whole thing.

As soon as she was satisfied, I ran to my room—to the new laptop and Internet connection that will be my salvation for these next few months—and called up Cesca on IM.

LostPhoebe: she won't find out

PrincessCesca: it's a small island

LostPhoebe: Justinian never found out they'd moved the school

PrincessCesca: what?

Oops. Not supposed to let that cat out of the bag. Well, at least I didn't say *who* had moved the school. That would be worse.

LostPhoebe: just some junk about school history

LostPhoebe: we had a pep assembly on Friday

LostPhoebe: they're big on tradition here

The cursor blinks at me for a long time. I can practically hear Cesca thinking from thousands of miles away. Great. If anyone can uncover the big secret, Cesca can. She's the one who knew Justin was cheating on me weeks before the rest of the school found out.

PrincessCesca: yeah, Europeans are all serious about history

LostPhoebe: you're not kidding

LostPhoebe: one of my teachers wears a toga to class

PrincessCesca: talk about your fashion faux pas

Another IM conversation pops up.

NaughtyNic: how's your ankle

LostPhoebe: fine, no thanks to you

NaughtyNic: you were going to back out

LostPhoebe: that didn't mean you had to

PrincessCesca: you still there?

LostPhoebe: yes

LostPhoebe: zap my ankle

NaughtyNic: what's the harm?

NaughtyNic: it didn't hurt

LostPhoebe: no, but

PrincessCesca: you're talking to someone else, aren't you?

LostPhoebe: of course not

LostPhoebe: you're not talking either

LostPhoebe: I could have hurt myself falling

NaughtyNic: but you didn't

NaughtyNic: it all worked out in the end

LostPhoebe: how would you know?

NaughtyNic: I saw him carry you home

PrincessCesca: if you're going to ignore me I'm leaving

LostPhoebe: don't go

PrincessCesca: then tell me who you're talking to

LostPhoebe: a friend from school

LostPhoebe: she has a question about homework

I feel horrible lying to Cesca, but it's easier than answering questions. Most of them aren't even questions I'm allowed to answer.

LostPhoebe: him carrying me home doesn't mean anything

NaughtyNic: what happened?

LostPhoebe: he almost kissed me

NaughtyNic: oh my gods!

NaughtyNic: why didn't he?

LostPhoebe: Stella interrupted

PrincessCesca: Phoebe?

NaughtyNic: did she freak out?

LostPhoebe: no, she doesn't know it was about to happen

PrincessCesca: hello???

LostPhoebe: hold on a sec

PrincessCesca: fine

NaughtyNic: see!!! it all worked out in the end

NaughtyNic: I zapped you for a good cause

LostPhoebe: I don't care if he wound up groveling at my feet

LostPhoebe: that's no excuse to use your supernatural powers on me!

Blink, blink, blink.

NaughtyNic: are you there?

Blink, blink, blink.

NaughtyNic: Phoebe?

I glance back and forth at the two IM windows. Back and forth. Cesca and Nicole. L.A. and Serfopoula.

My heart starts racing.

PrincessCesca: supernatural powers?

Crap!

LostPhoebe: have to go

NaughtyNic: something wrong

LostPhoebe: no, of course not

LostPhoebe: just have to go

LostPhoebe: now

LostPhoebe: bye

I quickly close the conversation with Nicole without waiting for her to reply. I am in so much crap it's not even funny.

PrincessCesca: Phoebe, what's going on?

Quick, think of a plausible explanation.

LostPhoebe: we're doing this fantasy role-playing game

LostPhoebe: every character has special powers

LostPhoebe: they can use them against other characters

LostPhoebe: she used hers against me

LostPhoebe: in the game

Great, now I'm babbling in IM.

Cesca's going to know something's up. In her wildest dreams she wouldn't guess exactly what, but Cesca's like a bulldog—she doesn't let go of something until she's ready.

PrincessCesca: you hate computer games

LostPhoebe: um, not anymore

PrincessCesca: stop lying to me

LostPhoebe: I'm not

PrincessCesca: what's really going on

PrincessCesca: what aren't you telling me?

LostPhoebe: Cesca, I

Tears fill my eyes as I tell my best friend since kindergarten—the girl I've shared every deep, dark secret I've ever had with—that I can't tell her this.

LostPhoebe: I can't

LostPhoebe: I'm sorry

PrincessCesca: fine

I wait for her to say something more, to ask why or to make me tell her. But the stupid cursor just blinks at me. After staring at the unmoving conversation for fifteen minutes I accept the fact that she's gone.

Add one more thing to the list of stuff moving to this stupid island has ruined for me.

"To build a stronger team dynamic," Coach Z says to everyone gathered in the weight room, "we are going to partner you across events for strength training today."

Oh no. This can only end in pain.

Christopher, the big blond who volunteered to be my training partner, is the only person on the team who seems even inclined to be nice—Griffin hasn't so much as spoken to me since Sunday—so pairing me with anyone else is going to be a nightmare.

Coach Z starts going through the roster, pairing up throwers with hurdlers, jumpers with sprinters, mixing everything up.

"Phoebe Castro," he says, tracing his finger across the page on his clipboard, "and Adara Spencer."

My shoulders slump. Of all the people I could be paired with, this is the worst. Even spending the hour-long session in silence with Griffin—who got paired with Vesna Gorgopoulo, a discus thrower who makes the Rock look like a weakling—would be infinitely better.

I glance at Adara, standing in the center of her group of blondes. She is positively fuming. While she stalks over to Coach Z—presumably to demand a different partner—her blondes glare at me. The only one I know by name is Zoe. She's in my World History class and spends all her time flirting with Mr. Sakola. I used to think she was harmless, but the look she's giving me right now could sear a steak.

Adara stomps back to her group, the angry look on her face a clear indication that Coach Z refused to bow down to her wishes. If they weren't my wishes, too, at the moment, then I'd enjoy her defeat.

"Everyone select a machine to start on," Coach Z explains. "When you hear one whistle switch with your partner, when you hear two rotate stations."

While everyone moves to a machine, Adara and I stand glaring at each other.

"Get moving, girls," Coach Z shouts. "You start on the bench."

He points to the bench press in the far corner of the weight room, the only station not taken. Deciding that my training is more important than my animosity, I turn and head for the machine.

I'm just settling in on the bench when Adara joins me.

The first whistle blows and I reach up to take the bar.

"Well, well," Adara says, making no move to spot me. "If it isn't the happy home-wrecker."

Ignoring her, I lift the bar off the brackets and start counting.

One. Two.

"Don't think you can just steal my boyfriend without consequences, *kako*."

"I didn't—" Six. "Steal—" Seven. "Anything."

"What?" She peers down at me. "Did you think I wouldn't hear about what happened on Saturday?"

"I don't—" Twelve. "Really—" Thirteen. "Care."

"It was quite funny, actually," she says, her voice mocking. "Griffin could hardly stop laughing long enough to tell me."

"What?" I let the bar clatter back into place on the brackets.

Sitting up, I look around the room, finding Griffin and Vesna at the lateral pull station. He is watching Vesna pull like three hundred pounds. For a second he turns and glances at me, but then quickly looks away.

Then again, he might have been looking at Adara.

"Castro," Coach Z shouts, "you're still on the—"

Coach Lenny blows the whistle, then winks at me, ignoring the scowl Coach Z throws his way.

I climb off the bench and move behind the bar.

"What exactly did he tell you?" I ask, furious.

"Everything, of course."

We continue in silence, Adara doing bench presses and me thinking of how many ways I could destroy Griffin without getting caught, until Coach Lenny blows the whistle twice and we change stations. Up next on our circuit is the butterfly press. This allows Adara to stand facing me—and blocking my view—the whole time.

"Back off from my boyfriend," she snarls as I start my presses.

"Don't worry," I reply, concentrating on the burn in my pecs so I don't think about Griffin. The betrayer. "I want nothing to do with your boyfriend."

"Oh, I'm not worried." She glances over her shoulder to where Griffin and Vesna are working on triceps curls. "I just want to save you the embarrassment of being the laughingstock of the school."

"Gee," I say, just as the whistle blows. I release the weights with a thud. "Thanks for your concern."

Adara smoothly begins her presses as she talks. "If you don't believe me, ask your friend Nutty Nic. She knows all about being the laughingstock."

"Watch what you say about my friends," I warn. She is dangerously close to crossing a line.

"And if I recall," Adara snickers, "that was Griffin's doing, as well."

My fury should be directed at Griffin, but Adara is right in front of me and all my rage focuses on her.

I'm just about to tell her what she can do with her concern and friendly advice when suddenly her arms snap back, the weights slamming down with an echoing crash. Adara looks stunned, her eyes wide open like they're stuck that way.

Everything in the weight room stops.

"Castro!"

Why is Coach Z yelling at me? "I didn't do anything."

"Precisely," he says. "As the spotter, when your partner is in trouble it is your job to assist her."

"But she wasn't—"

"I begged for help," Adara coos, apparently recovering from her shock. "My arms were all quivery and shaky, like they were going to give out. But she refused. She said she wouldn't lift a finger to help anyone on this team."

"That's a lie," I shout. "I never—"

"In my office," Coach Z says, his voice low and serious. "Now."

Great, there goes cross-country. I'm about to get kicked off the team, and lose any chance at getting that scholarship.

"I saw it happen, Coach."

Everyone turns to look at Griffin. He's looking right at Coach Z—not at me, not at Adara.

"Adara didn't ask for help," he continues. "She just let the weight drop."

I dare a glance at Adara, who is turning an unflattering shade of red.

"Right then," Coach Z stammers. "Everyone back to work."

The weight room returns to the bustle of the workout. Except for Adara, who is glaring at me, me, staring at Griffin, and Griffin, staring at the floor.

"Oh, and Blake," Coach Z says. "Switch places with Spencer."

Stomping across the weight room, Adara takes her place with Vesna—who is now bench-pressing a small car. I walk slowly to the biceps curls station and pick up a pair of dumbbells. Without saying a word, Griffin takes his place at my side, holding his hand beneath mine to spot my movement.

He doesn't say a single word to me the entire workout, and by the time practice is over I'm more confused than ever.

"This Plato is kicking my ass," I grumble, staring blankly at the pages full of philosophical words.

Mr. Dorcas wants us to read *The Republic* and write a ten-page response paper when I don't even understand what the book is about. Like I don't have enough going on in my life.

"You'll get through it," Nicole promises.

"I'm not so sure." I flip the book over to the back cover—something I can actually understand—and read the two sentence bio on Plato. "Too bad he died twenty-three hundred years ago."

She laughs, then goes back to reading.

"You've got powers, Nic." I sigh, slamming the book down on our table. "Can't you summon him back to life so I can ask him to clarify?"

"We can't bring people back from the dead," she says. "Big no-no. In the sixties someone tried to bring back Clytemnestra to star in the school's production of *Agamemnon*. Everyone in the cast aged fifty years in a day." Then, pursing her lips and looking thoughtful, adds, "But hey, Hades is my great-uncle. We could take a field trip to the underworld to find Plato."

"Really?" I ask, brightening.

Maybe there are benefits to going to school with the relatives of Greek gods. Something to offset all the unfortunate zapping.

"Sure." She frowns. "Of course, there's always the chance we won't come back. People get lost down there all the time. And it smells like rotten eggs."

"Great." I flop back in my chair. "My options are: fail the class or spend eternity in the stinky underworld. I'm not sure which one is worse."

Nicole leans across the table and places a hand on my arm. "Don't worry," she says. "You won't fail."

I am just about to let her know what I think of her reassurance by snorting when Mr. Dorcas walks up to our table.

"Miss Castro," he says. "Headmaster Petrolas wants to see you in his office."

Everyone in the class starts *ooh*ing like I'm in big trouble.

Considering recent history, maybe I am.

"He asked you to bring your things."

Maybe I've been expelled?

Hey, a girl can dream.

I quickly gather my stuff and head for the big dog's office.

Damian is pacing behind his massive desk when I get there.

"What's u—"

"Who have you told?" he roars.

I jerk back a little at his harsh tone. "Told about what?"

"The school. Who have you told about the school?"

He's speaking quickly, with an urgency he hasn't shown before.

"If you mean the Big Secret, I haven't told anybody."

I may have let half a detail slip to Cesca the other night, but that in no way constitutes telling the secret.

Damian runs a hand through his salt-and-pepper hair as he sinks into his chair. "Phoebe, please. This is no time for playing games. The safety of the school and everyone on the island is at stake."

If he sounded even a little melodramatic I might have dismissed this line of questioning as paranoid. But he doesn't. So I don't.

"All right." I take a seat across from him. "In an IM chat on Sunday night I accidentally sent my best friend a line about using supernatural powers. I meant to send it to Nicole—I got the windows confused is all. But Cesca won't tell anyone. I'm one hundred percent certain."

Except for maybe Nola—but she wouldn't tell anyone, either.

Only, if Cesca didn't tell anyone, how did Damian find out?

"What happened?" I ask, afraid of the answer.

Rubbing his eyes with one hand, Damian sighs. Loudly.

"The island itself is safe, protected by the gods. The shield, however, only prevents *nothos* from accidentally witnessing something supernatural. If they know what they're looking for the gods cannot stop them." He runs his hand through his hair, messing it up. "If even one untrustworthy *nothos* knows the truth, we are vulnerable to discovery."

Suddenly I feel awful for even the accidental slip-up. Even

though I didn't mean to do it, it still had the same result. From the way Damian looks things must be really bad, too.

"Our web scanners flagged a search from a southern California IP address." He pushes a piece of paper across his desk.

Search string: supernatural powers Serfopoula Greece

Results: suppress

Location: Los Angeles County

"Oh." It has to be Cesca. No one else would even have a clue. But I know she did it with the best intentions. "She must have been worried after I told her I couldn't tell her anything. We haven't kept secrets. Ever. It probably freaked her out."

That makes me feel better about her not responding to the millions of e-mails and IMs I've been sending. Even though she's hurt that I can't confide she's still trying to find out what's going on with me.

She's a true friend.

"We cannot undo your accident," Damian says. He sounds resigned, which makes me feel worse. "There might not be anything to worry about. We shall wait and see if there are any more incidents."

"And if there are?"

"We will have to take countermeasures."

"Countermeasures?" I picture Cesca, her feet encased in concrete blocks, sinking slowly to the floor of the Pacific. Maybe the Greek gods operate like the mafia.

“Nothing so dramatic,” Damian says, smiling and proving once again that he can read emotions fluently, “I assure you.”

I’m not fully appeased, but I guess I have to take his word for it at the moment. If the time comes to enact “countermeasures” I’ll warn Cesca ahead of time so she can flee the country or whatever.

For now, I just smile and nod as I gather up my backpack to leave.

“Oh, Phoebe,” Damian calls as I walk to the door. When I turn around, he adds, “Try not to accidentally reveal any more of our secrets. If you do, I just might have to try the concrete blocks method.”

My jaw drops. “Hey, you said you could only read emotions!”

Damian, cryptic as ever, just smiles and returns his attention to work. How like him.

I’m lucky I don’t keep a diary for him to read.

As I close the door behind me I hear, “Everything I need to know is stored in your hippocampus anyway.”

Because I can’t think of any better response I slam his door.

Believe it or not, I’m starting to feel sympathy for Stella. She’s had to live with him her whole life.

I only have to endure him for nine months.

“Damian and I have been talking, Phoebola,” Mom says. She’s sitting in my room, watching me try to do homework.

“Yeah,” I answer absently, wondering what Plato meant when

he said, *We can easily forgive a child who is afraid of the dark; the real tragedy of life is when men are afraid of the light.* "I would think you two do that a lot."

Sure, I used to be afraid of the dark, but who ever heard of someone being afraid of the light? Maybe he's being metaphorical. Light must be a symbol for something else. How about success? That would be like being afraid to win a race. It would be beyond sad if someone was afraid of winning. I start scribbling down my answer.

I can practically feel her giving me the Mom look.

"You know what I mean." Mom clears her throat before continuing. Uh-oh. "This is all such a big change—for both of us. All of us. It's going to get even harder when you go away to college."

I sit up straight in my chair, the hairs on the back of my neck standing up.

"We think it might be better for you to stay on at the Academy for another year. Maybe even attend college in the U.K. after graduation. That will give you another year to adjust and—"

"What!"

I think my scream can be heard in Athens.

"Now calm down, after everything that's—"

"Calm down? Are you crazy?" I jump up from my desk and start pacing. "You're trying to ruin my entire future and you want me to calm down?"

"We are not trying to ruin your future." She sits on my bed, the picture of calm and collected. "You could really benefit from another year of challenging academics."

My pacing speeds up—if I had a rug I would probably burn a

hole in it. I already know Damian wants this—Stella told me, after all—but my own mother?

"Nola, Cesca, and I have been planning on going to USC together since junior high." I stop pacing long enough to throw my hands in the air. "How can you ask me to just throw all those years of planning—not to mention my friendships—away?"

I resume pacing, my mind racing just as fast.

"I'm not asking you to do anything more than think about it," she says calmly.

I hate it when she does the whole calm-Mom-therapy thing on me. It makes me so mad I do things I might regret.

"It's bad enough you marry a complete stranger," I shout, "and you make me move halfway around the world without telling me I'll be going to school with a bunch of kids with superpowers who can zap me whenever they want. But now, *now* after all this, you want me to stay even longer than absolutely necessary? This is all his idea, isn't it?"

"Of course not," she says, sounding all defensive. "He may be my husband, but I am still your mother."

"Then why?" I demand. "Why this? Why now?"

"Because if you are—" She stops mid-sentence. Standing up slowly, she says, "All I ask is that you think about it."

Aargh! She can't even come up with a bogus excuse.

"Fine," I spit out as she walks to my door. "I'll think about it—and every time I do I'll think about how much I hate you."

Without another word she walks out, closing the door quietly behind her. Not satisfied, I march over to the door, pull it open wide, and sling it shut with a powerful slam.

Somehow that's more appropriate for the end of my relationship with my mother.

Before the echo dies down I burst into tears.

I don't even have Cesca and Nola's shoulders to cry on.

How could my life possibly get any worse?

CHAPTER 8

"PLEASE PUT AWAY YOUR BOOKS and take out several sheets of blank paper." Mr. Dorcas's voice is monotone. "We are having a pop quiz on *The Republic*."

The whole class groans.

Me? I just carry out his instructions with the resignation of a beaten dog. Since the moment I thought my life couldn't get worse, the world, this school, and everyone on this island have conspired to prove me monumentally wrong.

No one but Nicole and Troy are talking to me, though Troy hasn't even been at lunch because he's getting extra tutoring in Chemistry. I keep e-mailing and IMing Cesca and Nola every night in the hope that I'll eventually wear them down. Mom is giving me my distance, not that I mind, and Damian has been so busy with school business that I haven't even seen him in days. And, though I'm not mourning the fact that Stella's stopped speaking to me, I'm starting to miss our sparring sessions. They're better than no human contact at all.

My running times have not improved, despite the millions of hours of extra practice. Coach Lenny assures me I'm just at a plateau and any day now I'm going to see major improvement. I don't believe him.

I still haven't figured out Plato and have given up all hope of ever understanding his concept of justice. Ironically enough, Physics II and Art History—the classes Nicole switched me to—are the only classes I'm actually doing well in. Everything else will be lucky to see a passing grade.

So, of course Mr. Dorcas is giving us a pop quiz on a Friday. It's just the way my life is going.

"Answer the following question." He tugs on the projection screen, sending it rolling into its case and revealing the pop quiz.

An essay question.

Hardly shocking.

> *Plato ends* The Republic *with the myth of Er, a story about the fate of men, both good and bad, in the afterlife. Why do you think he, a believer in reincarnation, chooses this tale with which to end his discourse on justice?*

The first thing that jumps out at me is the word *myth*. After what Troy told me, I don't think some story Plato made up about a guy visiting the afterlife qualifies as "explaining the unexplainable." This is more like a fairy tale, a story that Plato wanted to be true. He wanted to believe that good men would be rewarded and bad men punished because that would mean the world made sense.

Clearly, he'd been burned by the success of some undeserving people.

Half an hour later I turn in my "quiz," my hand cramped from writing a mini-thesis in response. I sink back into my seat. I can't even look forward to a mental break because I was the last person done.

Mr. Dorcas jumps right into his lecture.

He starts writing on the board, his back to the room.

"*Pssst.*" Nicole tosses a note on my desk.

I open the elaborately folded piece of paper.

Troy says he passed his Chem test. No more lunch tutoring.

I write, *Good. I missed him.* Then I toss the note back on Nicole's desk. She opens the note, smiles, then glances to the front of the room and frowns.

Following the direction of her gaze, I see Mr. Dorcas scowling in our direction.

"The note, Miss Matios." He holds out his hand expectantly.

Nicole rises slowly from her seat, leaning closer to me as she whispers, "Distract him."

I nod, wondering what I can do to get Mr. Dorcas's attention.

Not knowing what else to do, I scream, "Ouch!"

"What is it, Miss Castro?"

"I, uh, think something bit me." Twisting around in my seat, I search the floor like I'm looking for the offending creature. "I think it was a scorpion."

"Miss Castro," Mr. Dorcas admonishes as he stalks to my desk, "we don't have scorpions on this island."

Eyes wide, I ask, "Really?"

From the corner of my eye I see the note paper in Nicole's hand glow. She nods at me.

"You must be right," I say to Mr. Dorcas, who eyes me skeptically. "It must have been the elastic in my underpants."

He gives me a solid glare before returning to the front of the room to take the note from Nicole. He then proceeds to read the note out loud.

"I can't wait to read *Aristotle*. No, me either. It will be so much fun." Mr. Dorcas stares at the note, like he can't believe what he read. Then, with a scowl, he crumples up the note and tosses it in the trash. "Return to your seat, Miss Matios."

As she slides back into her chair, Nicole winks at me.

I breathe a sigh of relief. Thank goodness for Nicole—she's the best thing I've got going for me right now.

"Ha ha!" Coach Lenny, waving the stopwatch around like a flag, shouts as I cross the finish line. "I told you."

"Wh-what?" I ask between gasps.

This is the last timed run of our training schedule before next Friday's meet—and our last Saturday session—and I pushed myself as hard as I could go. The rest of our practices are going to be light days, so I can conserve energy for the big race.

"You didn't believe me," he taunts. "You thought I was full of sh—"

"What!" I demand. Hands on my hips, I'm pacing around the starting area trying to regain my breath.

“You dropped a full three minutes.”

I stop moving and my knees buckle beneath me. Bending at the waist, I brace my hands on my thighs to keep from falling to the ground.

“You’re kidding?” Then I wonder if maybe he is—just to keep me motivated. “You better not be kidding or I’ll beat you up as soon I can feel my legs again.”

“Three minutes,” he repeats. “Honest.”

He holds the stopwatch in front of my face. He isn’t joking—the digital numbers read a full three minutes faster than my previous best.

Forgetting my exhaustion, I rush Coach Lenny, flinging my arms around him. “You rock! I can’t believe it.”

“I hate to say I told you so, but—”

“You were right.” I start jumping in a circle around him. “The training actually worked.”

I’m making so much noise I don’t hear anyone walk up.

“Am I missing the celebration?” Griffin asks.

“Griffin,” I cry. “I dropped my time.”

Then, without thinking, I rush him and throw my arms around his neck. He gently wraps his arms around my waist. “Congratulations.”

“Oh,” I say when I realize I’m hugging Griffin, who hasn’t spoken to me in days. “Sorry.”

I release him and step away.

“I’m going back to my office to wrap up,” Coach Lenny says. “If I can trust you to do a solid cooldown, I’ll let you go early.”

“Absolutely,” I insist.

Griffin adds, "I'll make sure she does it, Coach."

Coach Lenny gives me a questioning look. I smile—knowing he wants to know if I'll be okay with Griffin. Then, stopwatch and clipboard in hand, he heads back up to the school, calling over his shoulder, "We're still practicing at eight A.M."

"I wouldn't dream of sleeping in."

I still can't believe it—a whole three minutes. With that time, I could win any race in the world.

"So, the training paid off," Griffin says.

"Yeah," I say. "I can't believe it."

We fall into a silence, even though I'm humming with enough energy to power the school for a month.

"What do you usually do for cooldown?"

"Oh," I say, having totally forgotten my promise. "I walk eight laps."

I'm not eager to leave Griffin—I really want to know why he showed up at my practice on a Saturday morning—but I can't let Coach Lenny or myself down. I'm just about to tell him I have to go when he says, "I'll walk with you."

"Great."

We walk to the stadium in silence, the question of why he's here is killing me. I restrain myself. I wasn't the one who didn't speak for over a week for no reason.

It's definitely up to him to explain himself.

As we emerge from the tunnel, he asks, "So, are you ready for the race on Friday?"

"I think so."

"Good."

We make a full lap before he speaks again.

"Coach Lenny has been working you hard, huh?"

"Yes."

If he's not going to apologize, I'm not going to be more than barely civil. I realize he is a boy and predisposed to abhor admitting he's wrong. He, however, has given me no reason to stick my neck out.

Besides, it's not like he's treated me with respect from day one.

I really shouldn't even expect common courtesy—

"Nice morning."

Okay, so he's making an effort at small talk.

I'm not giving in. "Yup."

That was apparently the extent of his chitchat repertoire because we keep walking in silence, with only the sound of our sneakers crunching on the cinder track. The sun is rising—must be late morning by now—and I'm all sweaty. With the sweat comes irritation.

Why did he come to my practice session? Or better yet, why did he drop off the face of the earth after the whole ankle incident last weekend? Or best of all, why did he act like such an ass when I first got to the Academy?

"Look," I finally say two laps later, fed up. "What's your problem?"

"Nothing."

One word responses are not going to cut it.

"Nothing? You show up here hours before normal people wake up on a Saturday, seem content to not say a word more than absolutely necessary, and I want to know why."

Silence.

“Fine.” I turn off the track, heading for the stadium exit. “Finish my cooldown for me, will ya?”

“Wait,” he calls after me. “Phoebe, wait.”

I am halfway to the exit when he reaches me. His fingers close around my upper arm. I’m not sure if he would physically stop me if I keep going because I stop the second he touches me.

Wheeling around, I jab my index finger in his face. “I have better things to do than finish my session in tension-heavy silence, so unless you’re ready to spill about whatever you came here for, I’m going home.”

His grip on my arm tightens just a little when I start to turn away.

“Okay,” he says, his voice low. “I’ll explain. Let’s get back to your cooldown and I’ll tell you why I’m here.”

I nod my head and follow him back to the track.

“I should—” His pace is brisk, and I walk faster to keep up. “I’m sorry for not talking to you all week. That wasn’t fair.”

“No,” I say as we walk even faster, “it wasn’t. But by now I’m pretty much used to your unfair treatment.”

I’ve had lots of practice.

“I just . . .” He kicks our pace up to a jog. “. . . get uncomfortable when people know my weaknesses.”

“Weaknesses? What are you talking about?”

“My being related to Hercules.”

“Surely other people know about th—”

“Only Headmaster Petrolas,” he says quietly. “And you.”

“What about Nicole?” I ask. They’d been friends when they were kids, she had to know.

“No. Even I didn’t know until I was thirteen.” He stares straight ahead. “By then we weren’t speaking.”

Wow. Instinctively, I inch a little closer so our arms almost brush with each step. “Still, I don’t understand how that’s a weakness.”

“Sometimes his blood controls me. Like last week when I had to carry you home—”

“I didn’t ask you to do that.”

“I know. That’s what I’m saying. I *had* to. I couldn’t help it. It’s not your fault—or mine.” His fists clench. “I hate being weak.”

“Weak?” I give him a sideways glare. “You’re crazy. Any compulsion to help people—voluntary or not—is a strength. It’s noble.”

“You don’t under—”

“There’s nothing to understand, Griffin. You help people. That’s the bottom line. There are a lot of people in the world who don’t help anyone but themselves. And a lot more who wish they could do something—anything—to help someone in need, but can’t or won’t. The fact that you *have* to help people doesn’t diminish the fact that you do help them.”

We walk quietly for a few seconds. I give him time to let what I’m saying sink it—if he’s felt this way his whole life then it might be hard to accept. And it might explain why he’s such a jerk half the time. A little rebellion against his heroic blood.

Not that this excuses his behavior.

As we pass the finish line of our sixth lap, he says, “I guess I never looked at it that way.”

“Well,” I say, speeding up to a full run, “you should.”

He falls silent for a few seconds before blurting, “I broke up with Adara yesterday.”

“Oh really?” I ask, trying for cool, disinterested calm when my insides are jumping for joy. “That’s too bad.”

“No, it’s not,” he says, not looking at me but smiling just the same. “I never realized what an awful person she could be until I saw how she treated you.”

Though my heart is pounding like a bongo, I don’t say anything else. I just let the excitement over the possibilities crackle in the silence.

Together, we half-race around the track a few times before doing another cooldown. Racing Griffin in a good-natured competition feels good—like a kind of freedom I haven’t felt before. I want to win, but at the same time I’m just having fun. And if the big smile on his face is any sign, he’s having fun, too.

When we finish our last lap, he teases, “Race you to the water fountain.”

“No,” I reply, swatting him on the arm. “Then we’d have to cool down again.”

“Afraid you’ll lose?”

I look him straight in the eyes. “I won’t lose.”

Then I take off for the water fountain in the tunnel at full speed. Griffin is fast on my heels as I skid to a stop, bending to take my victory drink.

“Well, well, well,” a girl’s voice echoes through the tunnel. “Aren’t you two having fun.”

“Quite the pair of running buddies,” another girl—the voice sounds like Stella, but I can’t be sure with the echo—says.

Griffin moves closer to my side, like he has to protect me from something. Must be that hero instinct in him. Seconds later, Adara and Stella step out of the shadows at the top of the tunnel, heading straight for us. They come to a stop, posing with hands on hips, directly in front of me.

"Looks like you won the bet," Adara says, looking right at me.

"What bet?" I ask, genuinely confused.

If she's talking about my deal with Stella there was no bet involved. That must mean—

"Dara, don't," Griffin says.

"Sure does." Stella looks me up and down like I'm something stuck to the bottom of her ballet flats. "I believe you owe me a latte."

"What bet?" I repeat.

"It's nothing," Griffin says—not that I believe him.

"Nothing?" Adara looks at Griffin, shocked. "I think this was a major coup."

"And I thank you for it." Stella gives Griffin the most evil looking smile I have ever seen.

"What bet!?"

Adara answers, "It's quite simple, really."

"Griffin said he could get you to fall for him," Stella says, "even though he treated you like trash when you first got here."

"I didn't think he could," Adara says. "I thought you had more self-respect than that."

"But I knew he could." Stella winks at him. "He's charming and you're weak. I was right."

Griffin stands there, stiff and silent.

"We made a bet." Adara links her arm through his. "A latte at Kaldi's coffee shop to whoever was right."

I stare at Griffin. "You knew about this? You started this?"

He makes no indication he even hears me.

"I must confess," Stella coos, turning her attention to Adara. "I did cheat a little. I gave Phoebe some motivation to spend time with him—to befriend him. If you want to call the bet, I understand."

"No," Adara assures her. "You were right. Whether you urged her along or not, she still fell for him like a lead anchor."

My head is spinning.

It was all because of a bet. He spent time with me, treated me like a friend, all because of some stupid bet. The whole Hercules thing was probably a total lie. And that garbage about breaking up with Adara.

Before I can stop myself, I take two steps toward Griffin, pull back my hand, and slap him as hard as I can. I don't wait around to see if I leave a mark.

"Nicole was right about you. You're a selfish bastard." I barely have control of the tears trying to fill my eyes. "Stay away from me."

Then I run all the way home.

Mom tries to get me to talk when I won't even leave my room for dinner, but I tell her it's just hormones and she leaves me alone. Even if she doesn't believe me.

Spending an entire day locked in my room, avoiding all social interaction, gives me a lot of time to think. I go back over all the moments with Griffin, analyzing each one, and decide that I can't tell when he was being straight and when he was playing me. Which only reinforces my decision to stay as far away from him as possible. I can't trust myself to tell which Griffin I'm talking to.

Around ten o'clock I decide to check my e-mail.

I have been avoiding it all day—just in case there's another drama/crisis/problem waiting for me in my inbox. After deleting all the spam—you would think the gods could develop some sort of supernatural spam-blocker—I have three new messages. I decide to open in the order of most likely to make me feel better—or rather, least likely to make me feel like worse crap.

The first is from Coach Jack at USC.

To: lostphoebe@theacademy.gr

From: coachjack@usc.edu

Subject: Cross-Country Scholarships

Miss Phoebe Castro,

I am pleased to announce that you are being considered for the Helen Rawlins Memorial Scholarship. Pending your successful admission to the University of Southern California, you will compete with three other candidates for this prestigious scholarship that will cover your tuition, books, fees, room and board for up to four years of undergraduate education.

Annual renewal of the scholarship is dependent upon maintaining an above-average academic record and participation in the USC cross-country team.

Best of luck,

Coach Jack Farley

This isn't anything I didn't already know. Coach Jack told me at camp that I was up for the scholarship, even though the official announcement wouldn't be made until the fall. He also said that if I get through senior year with a B average and do well in cross-country meets then the scholarship is mine.

Six months ago that didn't seem like a difficult task.

Today it seems impossible.

I move that message into my USC folder and go on to the message from Cesca.

To: lostphoebe@theacademy.gr

From: princesscesca@pacificpark.us

Subject: Jerk Alert

I'm sorry I've been acting like such a jerk, Phoebe. There has been so much going on and I don't have you here to talk to about any of it. When you said you couldn't tell me what that IM was about I guess I just took out all my frustrations on you.

Forgive me?

Cesca

I saved her message for second because I couldn't tell what it was going to be like from the subject line. She could just as easily have been calling me the jerk.

I am massively relieved that she's apologizing—not that she needs to. I'm the one with the secret. I should be apologizing, too.

To: princesscesca@pacificpark.us

From: lostphoebe@theacademy.gr

Subject: Just As Jerky

Forgiven.

Now do you forgive me? I really, really, really wish I could tell you what I meant, but it's not my secret to tell and it affects a lot of other people. Just know that there aren't any important secrets between us and there never will be.

Love and kisses,

Phoebe

After clicking send I stare at my inbox, wondering whether I want to open the third message. It's from Griffin.

Curiosity gets the better of me.

To: lostphoebe@theacademy.gr

From: gblake@theacademy.gr

Subject: If I could do it over . . .

. . . I wouldn't treat you so badly.

I'm sorry.

Today wasn't about the bet.

Give me another chance.

G

Just like him: brief, cryptic, and full of crap.

I'm tempted to delete the message—he certainly has no place taking up bytes in my mailbox—but can't bring myself to do it. Instead, I make a folder named "Liars" and move his message there.

For the first time since running out of the tunnel this morning I actually smile.

All this introspection time today makes me realize that I have to stay focused on my goal. I can't let USC out of my sights for even a second. No matter what Mom, Damian, Griffin, or anybody else on this stupid island thinks or does, I have to get that B average, stay on the cross-country team, and count down the days until I go back to California.

I don't want to be away from Cesca and Nola any longer than absolutely necessary. I've only been gone a few weeks and look what a mess my life has become.

No, from now on I'm single-focus-Phoebe.

Nothing can deter me.

"Mom, I've made my decision," I say when I find her in Damian's office, scanning wedding websites. "I'm going to USC and that's final."

She turns away from the computer, a surprisingly neutral look on her face. I expect her to yell and scream and ground me until I'm twenty-five. Instead, she smiles and says, "If you've considered this carefully as I asked, then I support your decision."

Wow. Where did that trust in my decision-making abilities come from? What happened to nothing but dictates and unilateral decisions?

I'm not going to question my good fortune.

Who knows when the rug will be pulled out from under me.

"Yes, I have," I explain. "I don't fit in here and I am only making things difficult and uncomfortable for myself and everyone else."

She steeples her hands over Damian's desk. Uh-oh, therapist mode.

“That sounds like you’re running away from your problems.”

“No,” I insist as I drop into one of the chairs in front of the desk. “It’s more than that, really. I miss Cesca and Nola and Southern California. I even miss . . .” I pull out the surefire family card. “. . . Yia Yia Minta. I bet she misses me, too.”

Mom smiles. “Nice try.”

Can’t I get anything past the adults in this house? Mom might as well read minds like Damian.

“Fine, it’s not about Yia Yia Minta. It’s about me.” I cross my arms over my chest. “I’m not happy here. I’m not going to be happy here. I’m counting the days until I can go home—something this place will never be for me.”

She watches me for a long time, like she’s evaluating me for a psych report. I’m used to this. She’s been shrinking my head since I was a baby—and it’s not going to work any better now than it did then.

I just lie back and relax until she reaches her conclusion.

What she says surprises the crap out of me.

“I’m sorry for putting you through this.” She actually looks sad. “If there had been any other way—I feel so selfish for turning your world upside-down, just so I could be happy.”

Her voice kinda cracks at the end, and I see tears form in her eyes. Can she really be this heartbroken? After all, she’s the one who brought me here. I tried to tell her I didn’t want to—

She sobs. A big gasping sob backed up by a whole lot of tears.

As she reaches for a tissue from the nearest bookshelf, I feel super guilty for making her feel so rotten.

“Don’t be ridiculous, Mom,” I soothe. “You deserve happiness as much as anybody. More, on most days.”

“I should have waited,” she says, shaking her head. “Damian and I could have married next summer.”

I wince as she blows her nose with a big honk.

“I’m over that,” I say, handing her the box of tissues.

“I’m going to miss you so much when you go off to college.” The tears start again with more force. “After your father died you were the only thing that kept me going. I want to hold on to you for a little longer, is that so wrong?”

“Aw, Mom.” I jump out of my chair and hurry around to her side. Pulling her into a big bear hug, I promise, “I’ll still come back on holidays and maybe even summer vacation. I’ll be the only kid on campus who gets to spend all her off time on a Greek island. Everyone will be so jealous.”

She laughs through her sniffles and squeezes me back.

We are still clutched in a tight hug when Damian walks in.

“We have a problem,” he says, his voice tight and flat. “A big problem.”

CHAPTER 9

"OUR WEB SCANNERS flagged another search," Damian says.

I can practically hear his teeth grinding. Letting go of Mom, I stand up straight to defend my friend.

"It wasn't Cesca this time," I say. "I'm certain."

Mom looks back and forth between us like she has no clue what's going on. Maybe Damian hasn't told her anything.

"The scanners also caught a blog post titled *Secrets of Serfopoula*." A muscle just below his left eye starts twitching. "We suppressed the post, but the entry was . . . imaginative."

"How?" I ask.

"What's going on here?" Mom asks.

Damian answers my question. "The author proposes that Serfopoula is the secret base of operations for an elite force of superheroes."

"Well," I say, relieved, "at least it isn't accurate."

"No," Damian replies, "but it suggests that the origins of the superheroes date back to ancient mythology."

"Oh." That's a little closer to home. "Well, I know it's not Cesca, because she doesn't have a blog. Besides, that's a huge leap of imagination from supernatural powers to Greek mythology. Maybe this is completely unrelated to my slip-up."

Mom stands up and smacks her hand on the desk. "Will someone please tell me what's going on?"

Damian raises his brows at me—a clear indication that I should be the one to tell her. Taking a deep breath, I explain, "I let half a detail slip in an IM chat with Cesca last week." Turning to Damian, I add, "Not enough for her to jump to this conclusion. Besides, Cesca wouldn't do this. She couldn't. Her computer literacy does not extend far beyond turning it on and opening IM."

"The fact remains," he says, "that someone is looking into the island and that is jeopardizing our security."

Mom gasps. "Are the children in danger?"

"Not yet," he assures her. "But if the perpetrator outwits our web scanners, they could be. We all could be."

"Well," I insist, "it's not Cesca."

"I know that." Damian unfolds a piece of paper from his pocket. "The author of the blog is using the name *JAM Freak*."

Oh no! I gasp and both Mom and Damian turn to look at me.

"Do you know who that is?" he asks.

My mind racing, I can only nod.

"Who is it?" Mom asks.

I shake my head, not believing it.

He wouldn't.

He couldn't.

Damian hands me the paper.

Blog entry: Secrets of Serfopoula

Results: suppress

Location: Los Angeles County

Author: JAM Freak

He did.

Crumpling up the paper, I drop it on Damian's desk. I can feel my ears overheating and I see red all around the edges of my vision.

"If we know who the author is," I ask, "can we, like, erase his memory, or something?"

"His?" Mom parrots.

Damian takes a step closer. "Yes."

My lips spread into a Stella-worthy evil grin. This boy is going to regret ever messing with me, my family, and this stupid island. I feel excitement bubbling up inside. I've been waiting two years to say, *Payback ain't pretty*. "Justin Mars."

Damian writes down Justin's name on a sticky note.

"I'll dispatch someone immediately to shroud his memory of the island and anything peripherally related." He looks at me, questioning. "He might forget you, as well, Phoebe."

I smile bigger. "Good."

That dark stain on my dating record is going to pay for trying to harass me from two thousand miles away.

The only question is: How did he find out about my IM slip-up?

Remembering some of the strange phrasing in Cesca's last e-mail, I'm afraid I know the answer.

"Mom," I say, "I need to make a phone call."

She looks confused, but nods. "All right."

When she and Damian make no move to leave, I add, "In private."

Damian seems to understand what I'm about to do. He takes Mom by the shoulders and leads her out. "Come, Valerie. Let's leave Phoebe to her phone call."

He waggles his eyebrows at her. She giggles in return and they hurry out of the office—headed for their bedroom, no doubt.

I wait until my gag reflex relaxes before dialing Cesca's number—burned into my memory since she got her private line in sixth grade—careful to add the international dialing code first.

She answers on the third ring.

"Hi, Cesca."

"Phoebe?" She sounds shocked. "Is that you?"

"Yeah, it's me. Mom felt sorry for me," I say. "She approved an international phone call for therapy purposes."

Which would be partly true, if I had asked for a therapy call.

The other part is my having to find out if my suspicions of who she told about my "immortal powers" comment are right. And if my suspicions about why are way off base—which I hope they are.

"What's wrong?" Now she sounds more nervous than shocked.

"Nothing's wrong," I say. "I just wanted to talk to you. To ask you a question."

"Oh." Nervous, nervous, nervous. "What's that?"

I take a deep breath, hoping I'm wrong. "Who did you tell what I said about immortal powers?"

Silence from the other end.

Then, "I thought you couldn't talk about that."

"I'm talking about it now."

"Oh." More silence.

"Cesca?"

"No one," she whispers into the phone. "I didn't tell anyone."

Now, I can tell when Cesca's lying—not that she does it very often—and she isn't lying to me now. She honestly didn't tell anyone about my comment.

"Are you sure?" I ask, just in case I missed something.

"Yes," she whispers.

Why is she whispering, I wonder—

"Who you talking to?" a male voice asks in the background.

A male voice I recognize.

"Just, um . . ." Cesca's voice is muffled, like she's holding her hand over the receiver. ". . . a friend."

"Who?" he repeats.

"A fr—"

"He's there," I demand, "isn't he?"

"What?" She's talking to me again. "Who?"

Now she's lying. To me. Her best friend.

"Justin." I had so hoped it wasn't true. "Why is he in your room?"

"He, uh . . ." She sounds resigned. "Phoebe, I wanted to tell you. Really I did."

"But?" I ask.

"There just never seemed a good time."

"For what, Cesca?"

"To tell you that Justin and I have been seeing each other."

My last hope that this was all some big misunderstanding—that I was totally wrong—vanishes. My best friend and my worst ex are dating.

“You’re right,” I say. “There is no good time to tell me that.”

“Phoebe, I’m sorry.”

“You’re sorry?” I say, stunned. “I’m sorry you didn’t learn from my mistake. You’re too good for him, Cesca.”

“I . . .” Her voices drops to a whisper again. “. . . I know. I just don’t know how to end it.”

“If it’s already over for you why did you tell him what I said?”

“I didn’t.”

“He found out somehow,” I explain. “He tried to post about it in his blog.”

“Well, I didn’t—” She gasps, then shouts—thankfully not at me—“Why you rotten, sneaky bast—”

“What?” I interrupt.

“Hold on,” she says into the phone. Then I hear the click of the receiver being set down on her desk. “How *dare* you read my private IM chat? You went on my computer and read my personal files, didn’t you?”

“I, uh,” Justin stammers in the background. “No?”

Bad move, Justin. If you’re going to lie, at least do it with conviction.

“Get your privacy-invading stinky ass out of my room.” Cesca is screaming so loud it sounds like she is talking directly into the receiver. “I never want to see you again. When you see me walking down the hall you’d better step out of my way!”

Two seconds later a loud *thwack* echoes through the phone.

That, I think, is the sound of Cesca slamming the door after kicking Justin out of her room.

"You still there, Phoebe?"

"I'm here." I'm relieved she sounds back to normal. "You all right?"

"Ugh, yes." She sighs into the phone. "Can you believe how stupid I was? It's not like I thought he would change. Can you still be friends with someone so stupid?"

"Hey," I say, trying to rally her spirits, "you forget you're talking to the girl who went out with him first. I think I get the stupidity crown."

We laugh and I'm just thankful that our friendship is back on track. I don't know what I'd do without Cesca to go to when I have a problem. I can always count on Cesca to set me straight. I mean, I love Nola, but she's not the most grounded cookie in the jar.

"So," she says hesitantly, "did he cause major problems for you?"

"No, not major."

"Oh."

"Look, Cesca. I really, really, really wish I could tell you what this is all about, but—"

"I understand. Just like I wouldn't expect you to break my confidence if I had a secret, so I wouldn't ask you to break someone else's, either."

Huge sigh of relief. It's so much better to talk through things like this on the phone. E-mail is so impersonal—and so open to interpretation. We chat awhile longer—not too long because I know international calls can be astronomically expensive—before hanging up, promising to e-mail at least every other day. And to not keep any more secrets unless they're somebody else's.

Mom is waiting for me when I emerge.

“Is everything all right?” she asks.

“Yeah,” I say. “We just had some stuff to talk through.”

“I know how much you miss your friends.” She wraps an arm around my shoulder. “I’m sure you’ll see them again soon.”

Not soon enough.

“At least they’re flying out for the wedding,” she adds.

I force a grin. “Only three months away.”

“Don’t worry.” She gives me a good squeeze before releasing me. “Your friendships will survive the hurdles of time and space.”

“Thanks, Mom,” I say, not meaning it.

Three months and seven thousand miles is more than I’m willing to put between my friendships.

“Nervous?” Nicole asks as she slides in next to me at our lunch table. “The big race is only days away.”

“Nah.” I shrug.

On the inside, I’m boiling with nerves at the mere mention of the race. Sure, I’ve competed in dozens, maybe hundreds of races in my lifetime. This one is different.

There is more riding on the outcome. I’m used to racing for myself, trying to beat my time or beat my opponent. This time I’m racing for my racing future. Not just my slot on the team is at stake. If I don’t race well this year then no scholarship. No scholarship, no USC.

Talk about pressure.

But there’s more to this race than staying on the team. In all my years of running I’ve had a pretty easy time. Make a little effort and win the race. This time I'm going to have to exert myself—run all-out. I'm racing against some of the best high school athletes in the world, grounded powers or not. This is my first real opportunity to see what I'm made of on the racecourse.

I'm afraid to find out I'm made of nothing more than some talent and very little grit and determination.

Like my T-shirt says, NO GUTS, NO GLORY.

Still, I'm not about to let anyone know how nervous I am.

"No big deal," I say, then take an I'm-totally-calm bite of my hamburger.

Troy walks up while my mouth is full and drops into the seat across from me. Ever since he finished Chemistry tutoring he's been in the dumps.

"Hi," he says.

I try to say, "Hi," around my hamburger, but it sounds more like, "Mrff," so I add a wave.

"I can't stand this vortex of gloom anymore, Travatas," Nicole blurts. "What's your problem?"

"Yeah," I say after taking a big gulp of pineapple Fanta to wash down the hamburger. "You seem so, well, not you."

He shrugs, "I don't know. I guess it's just that, ever since I passed that test my dad has been pressuring me to apply for the Level 13 pre-med program."

It kills me to see Troy so torn up. He obviously doesn't want to be a doctor, so I don't know why his parents are forcing him to try. Music is his passion and they should support that. Just like Mom supports my running.

"You have to tell them," I venture.

“Tell them what?” he asks.

“About your dreams,” I explain. “That you want to be a musician.”

He laughs out loud. “Yeah right. I like my powers, thank you very much, and I'd prefer to keep them.”

“They can take them away?” I ask. Maybe, if I push Stella enough, Damian will strip her powers.

“No,” Nicole answers, rolling her eyes at Troy. “Only the gods can revoke powers.”

“But my parents could ground them until I'm twenty-one.”

“Come on, Travatas,” Nicole says. “Grow some courage and confess. I hear it's good for the soul.”

“I appreciate that you guys care,” he says in a way that suggests he doesn't appreciate it at all, “but I have to handle this my way.”

“Fine,” Nicole says with a shrug. “Don't say we didn't try. Now, can we talk about how we're going to get back at Blake and the evil twins?”

I knew this was going to come up again. Ever since I told her what happened she's been pressing me to go after revenge—a revenge that I know wouldn't be just about me.

But revenge is hollow. I'd prefer amnesia.

“I don't want revenge,” I tell Nicole for like the fiftieth time. “I just want to forget about it and never talk about them again.”

Just because I live in the same house as Stella doesn't mean I have to talk to her. The last few dinners have been blissfully silent. It doesn't hurt that I threatened to tell Damian what she did. The thought of another week without her powers is apparently enough to keep her quiet.

Though she did leave an empty latte cup outside my door.

"I can understand not bothering with Stella and Adara. . . ." Nicole lifts up her hamburger bun and gives the contents a wary look. ". . . they've been hideous harpies since the day I got here."

She drops the bun and pushes her plate away.

"Longer," Troy adds. "Those two have been up to no good since they were five. We can't expect them to change now."

"But Griffin," Nicole says.

"Yeah." Troy's eyes light up. "Blake deserves to be taken down a notch or two."

"I could do a few heinous things to him without losing sleep." Nicole clearly harbors serious feelings of resentment over whatever happened between her and Griffin in the past. I'm not about to let her thirst for revenge push me into action.

"No," I say definitively. "I don't want to do anything to any of them. No revenge. Got it?"

Humiliation is bad enough. I just want to forget about it and move on.

I look at each of them, waiting for verbal consent.

Reluctantly, Troy nods his head. "Fine."

Nicole, on the other hand, is cagier. "No promises." When I stare her down, she adds, "But I'll leave you out of whatever I do. Okay?"

I say, "Okay."

Still, I'm a little worried.

Nicole can be unpredictable—if she can zap away my ankle without a second thought, who knows what revenge she's going to exact on Griffin. If he weren't the scum of the earth—and I didn't know she couldn't actually *kill* him—I might feel inclined to warn him.

I manage to steer clear of Stella until dinner on Tuesday before the race. Since she finally decides to dine with the rest of us and I'm focused on properly fueling my body for the week, I guess there's no way to avoid sharing the meal with her.

"Evening, Daddy." She plants a big kiss on his cheek. "Valerie." She nods to Mom. Then sits down, not acknowledging me.

Damian glances at each of us over a spoonful of bean soup.

"No greeting for your sister?" he asks before finishing his bite.

"Good evening, Phoebe." She smiles falsely. "I'm not sure I can eat a bite—I had a big latte for lunch."

That's it. Pushing back from the table, I knock my chair over as I lunge across the table. "You little—"

"Phoebe!" Mom shouts, jumping up and clearly prepared to stop me.

I freeze, my knee poised over the table, ready to launch into Stella's smirking lap. Knowing they'll never let me actually get away with throttling her at the dinner table I lower back into my seat.

"What is this about?" Mom asks once I've calmed down.

"Why don't you ask the ice queen over there?" I snap.

Stella schools her features into a look of pure innocence. "I'm sure I have no idea what you're talking about."

"Listen, girls," Mom begins. "Whatever's bothering you, it will be better if you talk it out. We will all be living in the same house for the next year, and—"

"Nine months." I think it's important to be clear when it comes to details.

That earns me a mom look. "There is always a period of adjustment when families combine."

"Her face could use an adjustment."

"Phoebe," Mom gasps.

Stella crosses her arms across her chest and raises one eyebrow. "I'd like to see you try."

"Stella," Damian warns, "do not make the situation worse."

"Damian," Mom says, moving behind him and placing her hands on his shoulders. "Why don't we leave the girls alone for a few minutes," she suggests. "I'm sure they would rather discuss their problem without an audience."

Damian looks like he wants to argue, but lets Mom lead him to the kitchen anyway. Just before they disappear out the back door, he looks over his shoulder and gives Stella a stern look that clearly says, "Work this out. Now."

Hey, I was willing to forgive and—well, not forgive, but forget anyway. But she has to keep throwing it in my face with the whole I'm-so-full-on-my-latte thing.

"I have no idea what your problem is," she says, casually taking a sip of her water. "Your attitude is really quite awful."

"My attitude?" I gasp. "You're the one who—"

"Still crying the same old song, Phoebe? Let it go."

"Let it go?" She is so full of—

I stand up slowly and calmly and say in as steady a voice as possible, "Listen. *You* made that awful bet with Adara. *You* tricked me into helping you win that awful bet. *You* let me believe—"

Oh no, I can feel the tears tightening up my throat. Not good. I take a calming breath. I've decided on brutal honesty at this point, there's no stopping now.

"I actually started to believe that Griffin liked me—*me*, the lowly little *nothos*—when no one else in your high and mighty cliques would do more than look at me with scorn." I blink against the tears now filling my eyes. "And the worst part is that I was actually starting to like him, the real him. Or at least what I thought was the real him. And come to find out he was only playing a part, too."

That's what hurts the most. Not the bet or the deal or any of that. It's that they're right about me. I really am so weak that I would fall for a guy who'd done nothing but treat me like scum since I got to this stupid school without even putting up much of a fight.

I'm pathetic, and that's what really hurts.

"Phoebe," Stella says, an unnatural softness to her usually icy voice.

I'm prepared for a scathing comment.

Instead, she walks around the table to stand right in front of me, and says, "I'm sorry. I didn't realize how much—" She shakes her head and starts again. "I know how much unrequited love can hurt. If I had known you had any real feeling for him . . ."

I am floored beyond belief. Stella is exhibiting real honest-to-goodness sympathy, an emotion I believed her incapable of.

That, and she's apologized.

I almost feel like checking out the windows for flying pigs.

"If it helps any," she says quietly, "it wasn't my idea."

"It doesn't," I say, mostly because I'm not surprised. Sure Stella's right up there with the evil bi'atches in history, but she doesn't hold a candle to Adara.

"And I don't think Griffin—"

"No," I interrupt, not wanting to even hear his name. I'd rather forgive Stella. I still have to live with her. "Look, I—I accept your apology. Just don't mention him again, okay?"

Then, to my total shock and amazement, Stella pulls me into a big hug. At first I'm kinda startled and I just stand there, awkward. Eventually I realize she's waiting for me to participate, so I lift up my arms and pat her gently on the back.

Apparently that's enough because she releases me and steps back.

"Just don't think this is going to change our relationship. I still don't like you." Her eyes are shining a little brighter than usual.

"Right back at ya."

I'm blinking in astonishment at the fact that she's wiping away tears when Damian and Mom walk back in.

"Everything okay?" he asks.

"Yes," Stella says, moving back to her chair.

Mom looks at me, her eyes questioning. I shrug and take my seat. I don't have any more of a clue about what happened than she does. I have a feeling, though, there won't be any more bets made on my anticipated behavior in the near future. And I guess that's all any girl can ask for.

"This is our last practice before the big meet. No practice tomorrow, so I expect you all to rest up and eat complex carbs. On Friday we compete for the Cycladian Cup. The victors get to display the coveted trophy at their school for the next year." Coach Z gives us all a stern scowl. "The losers get nothing but dust in their teeth."

This is apparently the big pep speech for the meet.

I've heard so many of these in my lifetime I just tune out.

Instead, I glance over the crowd of teammates listening avidly to Coach Z's threats and promises. Adara and her blondes, Zoe included, are right up front, watching Coach Z with rapt attention. There must be some sort of gender war going on because there's not a single guy sitting with them. My gaze flicks briefly to Griffin, surrounded by Christopher, Costas, and the rest of the Ares jockheads. He looks up, like he feels my eyes on him, and I immediately look the other way.

Eye contact is too much contact as far as I'm concerned.

He doesn't take the hint.

No, he stands up, weaves his way through the crowd while Coach Z is still speaking, and sits down next to me on the grass.

"Phoebe, I—"

I get up and move away.

He follows me.

"We haven't seen the trophy at this school in five years," Coach Z says, scowling at Griffin's disregard. "I want that trophy back in our front hall this year."

Everyone cheers.

I keep evading Griffin, who is shadowing my every step.

"Now break up into your events and get in a good practice," Coach Z says, dismissing the group to our individual coaches.

I head for Coach Lenny, hoping our workouts will separate us.

"Today we'll be working out in pairs," Coach Lenny explains. "I want you to push each other to perform at your highest level. The pairs are as follows—"

He starts reading names from his clipboard. As he works through the roster, I'm starting to get worried—he hasn't read my name or Griffin's yet.

No, I tell myself. Coach Lenny wouldn't do this to me.

Then he does. "Phoebe Castro and Griffin Blake."

He gives us a brief rundown of our workouts then turns to walk out of the stadium. I jog up and tap him on the shoulder. Griffin, of course, is right behind me.

"Something wrong?" Coach Lenny asks when he sees the sour look on my face.

"No, sir," Griffin answers.

I glare at him. "Pair me with someone else, Coach."

"He's the only one capable of pushing you, Phoebe." Coach Lenny gives me an apologetic look. "Work with him."

"No. He's an a—"

"For the sake of your running," Coach Lenny says. "It's just for one day." Then he gives Griffin a threatening look. "Follow the workout, push her to do her best, or you'll answer to me on race day."

"Yes, sir," Griffin replies, the picture of a perfect gentleman.

Ha. What a put on.

The second Coach Lenny walks away he starts in. "Phoebe, I know you're mad, and you have every right to be—"

"Thanks for the permission," I say.

I stalk across the inner lawn, find an empty spot with lots of room, and settle in to do my stretches. Griffin, right on my tail, sits down next to me, mimicking my actions.

“Hey, how is my being part of that bet,” he asks, “any worse than you making that deal with Stella?”

I clamp my jaw and don’t say a word.

“I’m sorry, Phoebe, that wasn’t how I wanted to start.”

I reach for my other foot, leaning away from him.

“I’m not going to let you shut me out,” he says, reaching for his toes. “You have the right to be mad, but I have the right to explain myself.”

I exhale deeply into my stretch. “I don’t have to listen.”

“No, you don’t have to.” He leans out over his left leg, stretching his quads. “But you will.”

He’s right. Purely driven by curiosity I at least want to hear whatever lame excuse he’s come up with. Then I can file it away under too-stupid-to-believe and move on with my life.

My time is too precious to waste on the likes of Griffin Blake.

“It started out as a bet,” he has the nerve to admit. “Not my bet, but a bet nonetheless.”

I give him a look that says I know this much already.

“That’s why I agreed to meet you that Sunday.”

“Thanks,” I say. “Glad to know I’m such a prize you need extra motivation just to go for a run—”

“I’m sorry, all right.” He reaches so abruptly for his right foot I’m surprised he doesn’t tear a tendon. “How many times do I have to say it?”

“About a million more times would be a good start.”

He sits back, giving up all pretense of stretching. “It started out as a bet,” he bites out, “but it didn’t end up that way.”

What a load of hooey.

"If I had been honest with myself—" He starts tugging up little clumps of grass. "I would have realized that the bet was just an excuse. A reason for me to spend time with you. One I didn't have to explain to anyone."

I continue with my stretches, working through all my leg muscles and ignoring his little heartfelt speech. Ignoring the fact that my deal with Stella served pretty much the same purpose—a reason to go after Griffin without guilt over how Nicole felt about him.

"Even though I was a total jerk, you still gave me a chance."

"Stupid me."

"Second chances are a rare thing around here." He inches closer on the grass. "When I was seven my parents got on Hera's bad side. No one has seen them since."

That makes me pause. That would have been about the same time Nicole's parents got banished.

He'd said his folks weren't around—and I remember thinking how vague he was. I hadn't even considered they might be dead. I'd just thought they left him with his aunt while they traveled the world or something.

I never thought his parents being gone had anything to do with Nicole's.

My heart melts. Just a little.

"Here I was, carrying you in my arms because I had to, and you were trying to get me to open up. You wanted to know me. Despite how horrible I had been to you." He leans in and whispers, "That's when the bet ended for me."

Another few drops of ice melt away.

Not ready to get burned twice in one week, I tell myself not to fall for his lies. He could be making every last word of this up, too.

And even if my initial motives for meeting him that Sunday were barely better than his—though I think a deal is way less offensive than a bet—at least I admitted to myself early on that I was really going after Griffin for myself.

Rising, I start twisting at the waist to warm up my upper body.

Griffin scrambles to his feet.

"Last Saturday after your practice," he says, pleading. "That was real. The rest doesn't matter."

"It matters to me."

I stop moving long enough to meet his sad stare.

Clearly, he's not sure what to say. Which is fine with me because I've heard enough lies to last a lifetime.

"Let's just get this workout over with," I snap, fed up and thinking of all the homework I have waiting for me.

Our first segment is a two mile run at moderate pace.

I walk toward the regular starting line, but Griffin has other ideas.

"Why don't we run a different course today?"

I eye him suspiciously. Certain he has something underhanded up his sleeve—even if he's wearing a short-sleeved shirt—I want to argue, but honestly it will be a relief to see anything other than that shrubby course.

"Fine," I relent. "But if you try to pull anything I'm telling Coach Lenny about the shoelaces."

He just rolls his eyes at me and says, "Come on."

Griffin heads out of the stadium and circles around to the right. Not wanting to follow behind him like a second-place dog I settle in at his side, matching him step for step. He must be pulling his stride because his legs are like twice as long as mine.

Neither of us speaks or looks at the other while he leads us down a steep path behind the far stadium wall. It looks like just another wooded cross-country course until we break through the trees. We're on the beach.

"I figured that with all your extra training," he says, "you haven't had time for many beach runs. Which I think you love as much as I do."

I shrug, secretly loving the way the sand squishes beneath my feet. With every stride I have to work harder to push myself forward. This is my personal heaven.

Now, I love the L.A. beaches—especially when I get permission to drive up to Malibu and watch the surfers while I run—but nothing compares to the beach on Serfopoula. The sand is pristine. Gleaming white.

Glancing over my shoulder, I see the footprints we made disappearing as the sand pours back in on itself.

The sand in California is so full of gunk it keeps your footprint until the tides wash in.

"Was I right?" Griffin asks.

I scowl at him for interrupting my daydream. I'm still mad at him, after all. "About what?"

"The beach."

"It's okay," I lie.

He grins with that cocky smile. "Considering how pissed you are at me, I'll take that as a hell yes."

"Whatever." I roll my eyes.

But he's right.

We run half a mile in silence. My eyes trained on the horizon, my mind trained on the rhythm. Step, step, step, breathe. Our footfalls are perfectly timed. Step, step, step, breathe. From the corner of my eye I see his chest rise and fall in time with my every breath. Step, step, step--

"You'll get over being mad at me."

"Not likely."

Step, step, step—

"I promise not to gloat about it when you do."

"I won't."

Step, step, step—

"Because I want to be with you so badly I don't care if you're screaming at me the whole time as long as I'm with you."

I stop dead in my tracks.

Two steps later, Griffin notices I've stopped and jogs back to me.

"We have another mile to go," he says, as if I've stopped because I think we're done. Then his face wrinkles up in concern. "Did you hurt your ankle again? I thought you said it was completely . . ."

"Did you mean that?"

". . . healed. What?"

"Did you mean what you just said?"

"Of course I did." He kneels down and inspects my ankle. "Now tell me—"

I grab him by the arm and pull him back up. "My ankle is fine."

He looks at me funny for a second before that cocky smile comes back. "Oh. Good."

"Yeah," I say. "Good."

"I am sorrier than you can imagine," he says.

"Yeah—" I take a deep breath. "I know."

"Does that mean I'm—"

"Forgiven? No." I smile when his face falls. "Not yet."

His smile returns.

"But you will be."

With one small step he closes the distance between us. My heart starts racing as he lifts his hand to my cheek. His fingertips hover over my temple. I can feel his heat even though he isn't actually touching me.

Then he leans forward—like in slow motion—until his face is micrometers from mine.

The smile in his bright blue eyes vanishes. My eyes flutter closed—the anticipation is killing me. I haven't kissed anyone since that jerk I used to date—what was his name?—and I feel like I've never wanted to kiss anyone more than I want to kiss Griffin Blake right now.

His lips brush mine. Barely. Just a tickle, really.

But it's more than enough.

My entire body sparks like the fireworks from bonfire night.

It takes me a few seconds to realize he's not kissing me anymore. I reluctantly open my eyes to find him inches away. His smile is back.

"Come on," he says, taking me by the hand. "I promised Coach I'd give you a good workout." He tugs and I stumble after him.

“We’ve got another mile left on our warm-up. Then the real work begins.”

Hand in hand—okay, so it’s not the best training technique—we finish our run. And the rest of the workout.

All I can think the whole time is, “When did my life get so good?”

chapter 10

"MORNING," GRIFFIN SAYS when he appears at my locker. "Want an escort to Tyrant's class?"

He leans in and kisses me, really briefly, on the lips.

"I thought you'd never ask," I say, still marveling at how much my life has changed since yesterday. "Do you want to go into the village after school?"

I grab my copy of *Ulysses* and throw it in my bag.

When Griffin doesn't answer, I add, "Maybe we could go for ice cream."

After zipping up my backpack, I slam my locker shut and turn to take my place at Griffin's side. That's when I see why he stopped talking.

Nicole and Troy are standing a few feet away, looking like they're contemplating murder. Great, I wanted the chance to tell them about this before they saw us together. To explain before they jump to conclusions.

Then Griffin shows up at my locker and I forget all my good intentions.

"Hey guys," I say, trying to sound like everything's perfectly normal. "What's up?"

ℯ❀ℯ❀ℯ❀ℯ❀

"What are you doing with him?" Nicole demands.

Troy doesn't say anything, just crosses his arms over his blink-182 tee and glares.

"I should go," Griffin says as he starts to back away.

"No," I say, grabbing his arm. "Don't go." If he and I are going to be together, then Nicole and Troy come with the package. It'll be better for everyone if we air things out now.

He moves to my side and I slip my arm around his. Nicole's scowl deepens.

"As of yesterday," she says, sneering, "you hated his guts."

"I know." I squeeze his arm tighter so he knows that's all changed. "But we talked things through."

"You were nothing but a bet to him," Troy finally says.

"No!" Griffin shouts. "That's not true. It was never just about the bet."

Nicole snorts. "Right, as if we'd ever trust anything you say."

There's a sudden tension in the air, an electricity that's about something much more deep-rooted than my fight with Griffin. Nicole looks ready to unleash her powers on him, regardless of the consequences.

They've kept their feelings about the past—about whatever ended their friendship and disrupted their parents' lives—long enough. I know that Troy is mainly upset out of loyalty to me, for the heart-ache Griffin had caused, and to Nicole, for whatever she believes Griffin did to her. If we work through the problem with Nicole . . . well, at least it will be a start.

"I think it's time to confront the past." Boy, do I sound like therapist Mom, or what? "Both of you have been avoiding this for too long."

“I’m not avoiding anything,” Nicole snaps, “except a lying, two-faced traitor.” She spits on the ground before turning and stalking away.

I nudge Griffin in the ribs and he steps forward.

“Nicole, wait,” he says. “Phoebe is right.”

She doesn’t turn around or say anything, but she stops walking away.

“We were friends once,” Griffin continues. “Can’t we put the past behind us? I know that things ended badly with us—”

“Badly?” She spins around. “Badly!? Considering everything that happened, I think ‘badly’ is an understatement.”

Griffin steps back from her outrage. I grab his hand and lace our fingers together—for support . . . and to keep him from running. He squeezes tight and I can feel his pulse racing. He is just as skilled at hiding his emotions as Nicole, and they are not going to work through this without help.

“He wasn’t trying to diminish the past,” I say. “He just wants to talk about—”

“Forget it, she doesn’t want to talk,” Griffin interrupts. “I’m sorry for whatever you think I did back then and for whatever harm you think I caused, but I think you’re exaggerating the situation.”

Nicole looks like she’s trying to burn a hole right through his skull. “My father lost his job and my parents got exiled from the island.”

“And mine got banished from the face of the Earth.”

“It’s nothing more than they deserved,” she says, her entire body shaking with rage.

Griffin jerks back like he’s been slapped in the face. So that’s what happened to his parents. Wrapping my free hand around our laced fingers, I concentrate on sending every ounce of compassion and sympathy I can to him. His hand relaxes and I can tell that he's calming down.

Nicole keeps going. "If you hadn't been so self-centered, if you had only told the council where we were—"

"I did," he whispers, his words echoing through the ancient halls.

Nicole stares at him, blinking. "You—what?"

"I did tell them," he says, his voice steady. "I told the high council that we were the ones that stole the nectar of the gods and fed it to Hera's son."

"Oh my gods," Troy gasps. He'd been silent and huddled against the lockers up to this point, so what Griffin just said must have been really bad.

"What?" I ask.

"If a god consumes ambrosia before the age of two, it steals his immortality," Griffin, not taking his eyes off Nicole, explains. "I told them that we didn't know. We were only seven, for Zeus's sake."

"Y-you did?" Nicole stammers, as if she can't believe what Griffin said. "You told them?"

"I did."

"Then why—"

"My parents insisted I was lying to protect them." The muscles of his jaw clench and I can tell he's boiling with emotion—he has been holding on to this since his parents disappeared more than ten years ago.

I lift our joined hands and kiss his palm.

He adds, "They took the punishment that should have been mine."

For the longest time, Nicole just stares at him. My heart breaks for her. She has been holding on to this resentment for such a long time, too. It must be hard to realize that all those years of resentment were misplaced.

Finally, eyes glistening, she says, "And mine." She wipes roughly at the tears. "It was my idea."

Then she does the most surprising thing. She rushes forward and pulls Griffin into a hug. Now, I haven't known Nicole for all that long, but I think it's safe to say that public displays of affection—or any display of affection—is not really her thing.

"All these years," she says, her voice tight. "You were my best friend and I blamed you—"

"Shhh," Griffin says, squeezing my hand tighter and using his other to stroke Nicole's back. "I came to grips with my guilt a long time ago. Don't you pick up where I left off."

It could be his hero instinct compelling him to make her feel better, but something tells me that this is as much about Griffin healing as it is about Nicole. That's a lot of anguish for them to carry. Hercules has nothing to do with this.

In that moment, I feel a connection to him like I've never felt with anyone before. Like I can feel what he's feeling. Little tingles—like a whole bunch of static shocks—prick at my palm where it meets Griffin's. He lays his cheek against Nicole's head and our eyes meet over her spiky blonde hair. A spark flashes in his eyes. He can feel the connection, too.

I glance at Troy, who looks totally stunned.

He's such a good friend I know he resented Griffin on Nicole's behalf. I bet he's just as shocked as she is to hear Griffin's side of the story. When I give him a look that says, "What do you think?" he just shakes his head in disbelief.

When Nicole finally steps back, her eyes are red but dry.

"Well," she says, pulling on her tough girl attitude, "we'd better get to class. One more tardy and Tyrant's making me clean the blackboards with my tongue."

Without another word, she turns and heads off down the hall. Troy stares for a second, then shrugs and trails after her.

Griffin slips his arm around my waist as we follow, hugging me close to his side. "Thanks," he whispers in my ear. "That would never have happened without you."

"But I didn't—"

"I know," he says. "You didn't *do* anything. It just seems like good things have been happening for me since you got here."

Wow. I'm trying to think up a suitable response when Nicole glances back over her shoulder and shouts, "Hurry up, Blake. I may have forgiven you, but I'm not licking chalk dust for anyone."

We all laugh, and I feel like things are finally starting to come together.

My life in Serfopoula may not be perfect, but it seems to be getting better every day.

The next morning I nearly throw up.

This isn't out of the ordinary. I nearly throw up before every race.

But this morning is so bad I can't even eat my customary oatmeal with brown sugar and raisins pre-race breakfast.

I try not to take this as a bad omen.

Then again, at a school full of descendants it's highly possible someone—Adara—has bribed the Fates to ruin my life today. Stella has been so . . . well, not nice exactly, but not horrid, lately that when Damian threatened to ground her powers for a year if she interfered with the race she actually laughed at him. It's not like we're friends, but I think we have an understanding.

Somehow I make it through the school day. Not without a lot of help from Nicole in Algebra and Physics and meeting Griffin between every class. He's a wonder at calming my nerves, but every time he leaves they come back.

At least my nerves keep me from paying attention to all the whispers. I hear the occasional "Blake," "*kako,*" and "outsider," but mostly my nerves block it all out. I know the entire school must be humming with gossip about us and if not for the race I would probably be embarrassed that everyone from the Hades harem to the Zeus set is hungrily gossiping about us. Right now, the race consumes all my attention.

And when I'm with Griffin, everything else fades away.

Too bad we can't race together.

By the time I walk to the locker room to change and get the pep talk from the coaches I'm all nerves. I've never been this nervous before a race. Nothing I've tried seems to help—not even the aromatherapy sachet Nicole gave me during lunch. I'm pretty sure it's full of dead flowers that can't help me from the grave.

I'm on my way through the door when I hear Troy.

"Phoebe!"

He runs down the hall—pretty fast for a guy who claims to hate running more than Brussels sprouts—and slides to a stop in front of me.

"Hey." I wave. "What's up?"

"I just . . ." He smiles wryly. ". . . wanted to wish you luck."

"Thanks," I say. "That means a lot."

"I have something for you," he says, stepping back. After fishing around in his pocket, he produces a long braided string. "It's a—"

"Friendship bracelet," I say. Just like the one Nola gave me in kindergarten—the one that finally wore off in third grade after more than three years of continual wear.

Sticking out my wrist, I let him tie on the bracelet.

Looking at Troy with thoughts of Nola in my head I wonder what she would think of him. With his tie-dyed Grateful Dead T-shirt, well-worn blue jeans, and leather-free Vans he's like her male mirror image.

Maybe they will meet at the wedding.

"It's not just a friendship bracelet," he says as he finishes tying off the ends. "It doubles as a super-duty good luck charm. With this . . ." He lets go of my arm and grins. ". . . you can't lose."

"Thanks, I—"

Coach Lenny sticks his head out in the hall. "Hurry up, Castro."

I tell Troy, "I gotta get changed. Thanks." I give him one more hug. "Really."

"Good luck," Troy says. "See you at the finish line."

ꝏꝏꝏꝏꝏ

I turn and run into the locker room wondering how my nerves just disappeared. Then again, I don't need to know why. They're gone and I'm ready to race.

ꝏꝏꝏ

There are three other schools in the meet today. The team from Lyceum Olympia is the strongest. Coach Lenny told me their lead runner—Jackie Lavaris—is going to be on the Greek team next Olympics. She's my stiffest competition.

But the racers from Academia Athena—an all-girls military school—look pretty tough. Their camo uniforms might have something to do with that impression. Some of the Hestia School girls look like their preppy softness could be a veneer. I've learned to never underestimate a runner based on appearances—the pink shorts could be a disguise.

I'm standing in our starting block—the painted square where all the runners from the Academy will start—taking deep, calming breaths and shaking out my legs.

Under the light blue shorts of my uniform I'm wearing my lucky underwear. Since I can't wear any of my running t-shirts on race day I always wear my *DON'T WORRY--YOU'LL PASS OUT BEFORE YOU DIE* undies. They are just a reminder not to leave anything on the course. Running won't kill me, but losing might.

"Oh no!" Zoe cries.

"What?" I ask. "What's wrong?"

She points at her foot and the broken lace on her left shoe. After a quick glance around to see if anyone's watching she points her finger at the offending lace.

Nothing happens.

She frowns and points again.

Again, nothing.

"What the—"

"Surprise," Coach Lenny says as he walks up.

"Coach," Zoe whines. "My powers are—"

"Grounded," he says.

"B-but—" Her lower lip pouts out and starts to quiver. Totally fake and totally not working on Coach Lenny.

"We just finished going through the roster. Everyone on the team is grounded for today," he explains. Then, looking at me, adds, "We want this to be a fair race."

Zoe scowls at me but doesn't say anything.

I watch her stalk off to find the supply box to get a replacement lace. Why does everyone have to blame me for everything? I didn't ask them to do this. Sure, I knew they were talking about it, but it's not like I could do anything either way.

Besides, if anyone's to blame it's Griffin. He's the one who zapped me in tryouts. He's really, really sorry now, but that doesn't change the fact that he did it.

But does anyone blame him? Nooo. Why would they? He's one of their own.

That's when it hits me. No matter what I do—no matter how hard I race, how much Griffin likes me, how much I try just to stay out of everyone's way—I'll never fit in here. There's only one requirement to belonging at the Academy and I can't fill it.

That realization could throw me into a deep, dark depression that I can't afford to wallow in today. So, drawing on years of pre-race psychology experience, I shove those thoughts into the back of my mind.

And just in time, too.

"Racers, to your positions," Coach Lenny—referee of the day—calls.

The five girls from the Academy and I line up in our box. The girls from Lyceum Olympia, Academia Athena, and Hestia School line up in theirs.

Coach Lenny holds up the starting pistol and my heart jumps.

Then he fires the go shot and everything else fades away.

Halfway through the eight kilometer—five mile—race I'm in the lead pack with four other girls. Jackie Lavaris is a few paces ahead of me.

My eyes are trained on her back. I've read her number—thirty-seven—about a million times. At least once for every step since we left the starting line.

I turn it into my mantra.

Thir-ty-sev-en.

Over and over and over again.

Thir-ty-sev-en. Thir-ty-sev-en. Thir-ty-sev-en.

If someone asked me my age right now I'd tell them thirty-seven.

I wish I could know what Jackie is focusing on. She's like a machine. Same rhythm, same pace over every terrain. Every slope. Every turn.

I'm starting to wonder if I'll be able to catch her.

One mile from the finish line I hit the wall.

My legs feel like melted Jell-O. Every breath I manage to suck in sends sharp pain through my lungs and radiating out to the rest of my body. I can't feel my feet anymore.

But my eyes are glued to number thirty-seven.

Thir-ty-sev-en.

Jackie is only two paces in front of me now. The other girls from the lead pack faded half a mile ago, so we are alone in the lead. In the four miles I have been watching her, Jackie hasn't shown a single sign of weakness. No slip or stumble. No surreptitious glance over her shoulder to see who's close.

Nothing.

The only sign that she's actually exerting herself is the sweat soaking her shorts and tank top. That keeps me going—at least she's working hard.

But I can feel myself weakening.

Like I'm using the very last of my energy reserves and am not going to have anything left for a strong finish. In fact, I might not have anything left at all.

Suddenly, Jackie moves ahead three paces.

No, she doesn't move ahead. I drop back.

I'm fading.

Crap! I've worked too hard the last three weeks—my entire life—to lose now. All those extra hours and lack of sleep weren't in vain. I won't let it be for nothing.

And I'm not letting four miles worth of thir-ty-sev-ens go to waste.

Digging deeper than I've ever dug before, I scrape up the last shreds of my energy from the furthest reaches of my soul and—just as I pass the four-and-a-half-mile mark—step up my pace a notch. I close in two paces.

I feel myself burst through the wall, demolishing it with a mental sledgehammer. Energy—or adrenaline or endorphins—flows through me and all my pain fades away.

My leg muscles tighten for a second to let me know they're back in action. I feel my feet pound the dirt path. My lungs fill with oxygen and I'm not racked with crippling pain anymore. It's like I'm just starting the race instead of almost finishing.

I've pushed through the wall before, but it's never felt like this. Like I'm racing fresh. Fully recovered.

We pass the four-and-three-quarter-mile mark.

I close in another pace.

Only one pace separates me from victory.

I can see the finish line—and the small sea of people waiting—in the distance. It's a straightaway from here.

The onlookers catch sight of Jackie and send up a cheer.

Spurred on, I close in another pace. We're neck-and-neck. For the first time in the entire race, she glances to the side. I grin at the shocked look on her face—until she speeds up and I have to match her pace to catch her.

The finish line is closing in, so I turn up the fire and try to take the lead. Jackie keeps my pace easily. I give it more. So does Jackie. I can't get ahead.

I take a deep breath and—for a split-second—close my eyes. I think of my dad, wanting to win this race, like every other one, for him.

When I open my eyes I'm ahead.

I don't look to see where Jackie is. I'm ahead and I'm not going to lose the lead.

Thinking of Dad, I put every ounce of my being into closing the last hundred yards. I see everyone cheering for me—Coach Lenny, Mom, Damian, Stella (yes, even Stella), Troy, Griffin, Nicole, and—

Oh my god!

Nola and Cesca are standing at the finish line.

A bright glow surrounds me as I pound the dirt. Something's not right, but my mind is mush and all I can think about is getting to the finish line—first—before collapsing. My best friends and my new friends are all there waiting for me and I have to get there or die trying.

Then, all of a sudden, I'm across the line.

The crowd around me is cheering.

Everyone rushes me, surrounding me, hugging me. I struggle to breathe and remain upright. The endorphins are failing me now.

The last thing I remember before collapsing is Troy's smiling face and that's when I know. I didn't win this race without help.

Which means I didn't win at all.

CHAPTER 11

"I CAN'T BELIEVE you guys are here," I repeat for, like, the millionth time, as we walk back across campus. After my race, we had stayed to watch the boys run. Griffin won by nearly two minutes and, even though he was a sweaty mess when he met Nola and Cesca, they were suitably impressed. It feels so good to have my girls at my side.

"We thought you needed a little . . ." Cesca grins. ". . . extra support."

Nola hugs me. Again.

"Damian and I made the arrangements with their parents," Mom says. "They have to return on the ferry tomorrow, so they don't miss any more days of school."

"Only one day," I cry. It's not enough. But it's way better than nothing.

Damian walks up next to me. "We also thought it might be easier for you to . . . explain your situation in person."

"Explain my—" I stop cold. Is Damian saying what I think he's saying? "You mean?"

He nods.

I'm floored by how much trust he just put in me. He doesn't

know Nola and Cesca from anyone, but he trusts me enough to trust them.

"Thanks," I say. Then, I can't help it, I fling my arms around him and give him a big hug.

"You are more than welcome," he says in his typical, formal voice. But there is a warmth in there that I never noticed before.

I can't believe he's really letting me tell Nola and Cesca about the school, the island, everything.

Now, all I have to do is figure out *how* to tell them.

"First, however," he says in full on principal mode, "we need to have a discussion."

Right. I knew this trust thing was too good to be true. My shoulders slump. I glance ahead at Mom and the girls who are getting ahead of us.

"Phoebe," he says, laying a hand on my shoulder, "this has nothing to do with your friends."

"Oh," I say, surprised. "All right."

"Why don't we go to the school and your friends can look around while we talk?"

I nod, sensing that what he wants to tell me is a pretty big deal. Considering all the major life-flipping news I've gotten lately, I'm a little nervous about what more he could possibly have to talk to me about. Maybe he knows that Troy cheated to help me win.

"Hey girls," I shout, running to catch up with them. "Wanna see my new school?"

We detour across the central lawn toward the front steps.

"Pacific Park hasn't been the same without you," Cesca says.

"Did she tell you what she did to Justin?" Nola asks.

“No,” I say, grinning at my girls. “What?”

“It’s nothing,” Cesca says with a wink. “Really.”

Nola rolls her eyes at the understatement. “She pantsed him in front of the whole school at the homecoming assembly.”

I’m so not surprised. Cesca is not the sort of person whose bad side you want to be on. She’s vindictive as—well, as Stella, I guess. I never really noticed it before, but Cesca can be a real bi’atch to people who cross her. Or who cross her friends. If I were on the other side of her anger I might feel the same way about her as I do about Stella.

And if I were on the other side of Stella’s anger, I might feel the same for her that I do for Cesca.

Huh. Stella as my best friend. Not likely. But still, I feel like maybe I understand where she’s coming from a little better.

“Suffice it to say I think he’ll have a hard time finding a date anytime soon.” Cesca checks her nails likes it’s no big deal. “Power Rangers boxers aren’t exactly *en vogue* right now.”

I laugh at the thought of Justin exposed to the entire student body.

“How old is this school, anyway?” Cesca asks, staring up at the massive templelike façade of the Academy. “This building looks ancient.”

“It is,” I say. “It’s fifteen hundred years old.”

“Holy hot tamale,” Cesca gasps.

“They have excellent landscaping,” Nola says. “I can’t believe the grass is so healthy in such an arid climate.”

“Yeah, well . . .” I glance back over my shoulder at Mom and

Damian, following us across the lawn. "There's a very good reason for that."

"Phoebe!"

I spin around, looking up to see Troy standing at the top of the steps. He's grinning like a crazy person. Maybe he is.

"You!" I shout.

"Where'd you go?" he asks, standing with his fists on his hips. "You took off so fast I didn't get a chance to congratulate you."

I turn to the girls. "Give me a minute?"

"Sure," Cesca says.

Nola nods. "No problem."

Leaving them at the base of the steps, I stomp up to meet Troy. "I can't imagine why I'd want to get away quickly, can you?"

"What?" He looks genuinely confused. "You're not making any sense."

"What? What!" I jab my finger into his chest. "After what you did, you have the nerve to ask what?"

"What I did? What are you talking about?"

"I know what your 'good luck charm' did, Troy." I cross my arms across my chest. "I saw the glow."

"The glow?" He frowns. "I saw it too, but I have no idea what you're talking about."

"Look, I know you were just trying to help. But cheating is cheating. You humiliated me. I can't even face the team, let alone look at myself in the mirror."

"Cheating? You cheated?" He shakes his head, as if he doesn't understand. "You're not making any sense."

In all my years of running I've never cheated. When other racers were trying anabolic steroids, synthetic hormones, and amphetamines I just trained harder. I focused on perfecting my technique, improving my endurance, and obsessing about my nutrition.

Now, after all those years of hard work and integrity, in just one race on this island, I'm a cheater. Someone—and I have a pretty good idea who that powers-charmed-bracelet-giving someone is—used godly powers to help me win. I won a race that I didn't deserve to win.

Winning by cheating isn't winning at all.

"*I* didn't cheat," I say, barely keeping my volume under control because I am so irritated that he keeps playing dumb, "but it feels like I did. When you gave me your powers, I—"

"Whoa!" He jumps back, waving his hands in front of his chest defensively. "When I *gave* you my powers? I couldn't even do that if I wanted to."

Holding up my hand, I pluck at the friendship bracelet. "Then what do you call this?"

"A friendship bracelet."

"Ha," I snort.

"We can't just *give* our powers to someone else." He steps closer, his voice calm and certain. "Besides the fact that it would probably kill the person on the receiving end, your stepdad would expel me in a heartbeat. I like you a lot Phoebe, but I'm not about to throw away my future for anyone."

"If you're just going to lie to me, then I'd like you to leave." I turn my back to him and head down the steps.

He doesn't say a word, so I think he's gone.

When I glance back he's still there. Staring at me. He looks like I've kicked him in the guts. With that wounded look in his eyes, he turns and walks into the school. I shrug it off, telling myself I don't care about the feelings of a cheater, no matter how cute and sincere he seems. No matter how good of a friend I thought he was.

Damian smiles oddly. "I wouldn't be too hard on the boy," he says. "Shall we go inside and have our talk?"

I nod and we all head up the broad stone steps. Now I'm even more confused. Either Damian doesn't know about the cheating, or he doesn't care.

Coach Lenny is waiting in Damian's office. For a second I stare at him, shocked that he's there. This *must* be about my cheating. I drop my gaze to the floor. I can't face him. I can't stand to see the look of betrayal in his eyes. After we worked so hard, so many extra hours, for it all to just not count because of Troy's misplaced desire to help.

But I know it's Coach's right to confront me. He put in as much extra time and effort as I did, and he deserves to grill me about why I've quit the team.

"I'm so sorry, Coach," I say, dropping into the chair next to his. "I didn't know what he did."

Coach frowns. "What who did? And why in Hades are you sorry? You're my superstar. You won the race."

Damian moves around behind his desk, lowering into his big leather chair. "Phoebe thinks she cheated," he says as he pulls open a desk drawer. "She thinks Travatas gave her a power-granting charm."

Lenny gapes at him. "But that's not even—"

"I know." Damian lays the folder on the desk.

"I quit the team," I say, trying to at least save myself the embarrassment of getting kicked off. But even as I say the words my eyes fill with tears—I've never felt as close to a coach as I do to Coach Lenny. It breaks my heart to know I can't run for him anymore. "I'll send you an official e-mail of resignation when I get home."

Mom comes up behind me and places her hands on my shoulders, softly massaging my tension. "Listen to what they have to say, Phoebe."

"You're still on the team," he says. "And you didn't cheat."

I stare at him blankly. He's clearly in denial.

"Even if you had wanted to, you couldn't have," he explains. "Everyone's powers were grounded for this race. Even yours."

"I don't know how he did it, Coach—" I wipe away a stray tear. "But I know you saw the glow."

"Of course I saw it," he says. "Everyone saw it."

"You can't tell me that wasn't someone's powers."

"No, Phoebe, I can't tell you that."

"I'm telling you, it w—" His words register. "What?"

"You're right," he says. "That glow that surrounded you at the end of the race was the glow of immortal powers."

"Then, why—"

"You're missing his point, Phoebola." Mom squeezes my shoulders tighter.

Coach looks at me expectantly. I shake my head. I don't understand what he's saying. It's like I know something's not sinking in, but I just can't figure out what. He says I'm right and I'm wrong. How can I be both? Either someone helped me cheat or they didn't.

Damian slides the file folder across the desk; Coach picks it up, opens it, and shuffles through the stack of papers inside. "Have you ever done something you thought yourself physically incapable of doing?" he asks.

Startled by the abrupt change of subject, I snap, "Other than winning the race?"

"Yes," Damian says, patiently. "Other than that."

"No," I say flatly. Then I remember the time I sent Adara flying across the locker room. "I mean, I suppose so. Who hasn't?"

"We've done some investigating, Phoebe." Coach pulls out what looks like a computer printout of run times. "Ever since you kept up with me in the first warm-up session I had my suspicions. I mean, I'm a descendant of Hermes. No *nothos* should be able to keep my pace. But you did."

"So?" I read upside-down that the title of the printout is "Castro Results."

"And, like you said, your performance in the race was . . ." He reads over the report. ". . . Supernatural."

"Listen," I say, sniffling, "I appreciate whatever you're trying to do to make me feel better, but I know I didn't win the race fairly, so if you could get to the point—"

"Phoebe, you're a descendant of Nike," Mom says. "You have godly blood."

I feel my jaw drop and I think I make a sound like, "Gah ung," but everything else blanks out.

For about twelve seconds.

Then I'm fully conscious, mind racing. "What do you mean 'a descendant of Nike'?" I twist around, staring up at Mom and trying to capture the thoughts jumbled around in my head. "Nike like the running shoe."

"Not exactly," she says with a huge grin. "Nike like the goddess. The goddess of victory."

"What!?"

"Here," Coach says, handing me the folder. "Read this."

I look down at a newspaper article. The familiar headline reads, "Football Star Mysteriously Dies on the Field." It's an article about my dad's death. I don't have to read it—I have it memorized.

At last night's playoff game between the Chargers and the Broncos, San Diego star running back Nicholas Castro collapsed on the three yard line, ball in hand. The former USC all-star was only nine feet from the winning touchdown. Though he was rushed to Cedars-Sinai hospital for treatment he was declared dead on arrival. Doctors could find no obvious cause of death and have ruled it undetermined.

"So?" I shove the article back at him.

Why is he bringing Dad into this?

"Your father did not die of natural causes." Mom's voice is whisper soft.

"What?" I gasp.

Damian leans across the desk and takes my hand. "The gods smote him because he broke the rules."

ℴ

"What rules?" I stare at him, furious that they're saying all this stuff about my dad. "What are you talking about?"

"The primary rule among descendants choosing to live in the *nothos* world is they may not use their powers overtly to succeed in that world. The risk of exposure is too great." Damian's face is full of sympathy. "Your father used his powers to further his football career. On national television. He knew he would be punished."

None of this makes sense.

Dad was part god?

I'm part god?

Dad died for football?

"Oh honey," Mom soothes, squeezing me tightly. "As soon as Damian told me I knew you'd be upset. Hell, I was upset. The fact that your father never—"

"Did you just swear?" I asked between threatening tears.

"Did I?" she repeated. "I suppose so. I'm just so mad that in all the years we were married, you father kept this secret from me. That he kept it from you."

"Wait?" I interrupt. "When Damian told you?" This is déjà vu all over again. "How long have you known?"

I'm having flashbacks to the whole you're-going-to-a-school-for-the-relatives-of-Greek-gods thing. A sharp pain starts at the base of my skull and slowly spreads across my entire head. Why do people keep withholding major details of my life from me? Do I seem incapable of handling astonishing news? I would think that by now I've proven myself pretty rational in the face of unbelievable information.

I glare at Mom, daring her to lie to me.

“Damian told me his suspicions a few days after we arrived,” she admits. “Until he received a genealogical report on your father a few days ago we weren’t sure.”

“And you didn’t tell me about his ‘suspicions’ earlier—why?”

“Damian wanted to. But I stopped him.” She brushes my hair out of my eyes. “Once I knew what this world would be like, I wanted you to have a chance to find your own home at the school. If you had known—if others had known—you would have been judged solely on your association with Nike.”

“Instead I was judged as the only *nothos*. As a *kako* with bad blood.” No. Even as I say this, though, I realize it’s not true.

Sure, at first that’s what happened. But Nicole never thought any less of me for not being godly—in fact, I think she liked me better for being *nothos*. I may go down in her estimation now. Troy never cared, either. Oh crap, I have to apologize to him. And Griffin . . . well, he was a little more work. No matter what he thought of me, though, he never called me *kako*. I smile—Griffin liked me before he even knew it.

Plus, all my hard work paid off. I won the race. Even before the whole glowing incident I was leagues ahead of every last racer from the Academy.

“Wait a second,” I say, realizing something. “Coach, you said I didn’t cheat—that I couldn’t have because my powers were grounded. If that glow was my powers, how is that possible?”

Coach shifts uncomfortably in his chair.

“That was certainly a surprise,” Damian says. “Even with your heritage.”

“From what Damian told me,” Mom says, moving around to his

side of the desk and leaning her hip against his chair, "this is the most exciting part."

More exciting than the whole I'm-a-descendant-of-Nike thing?

"A general grounding of powers is usually sufficient to prevent any adolescent descendant from using them," Damian explains.

"I didn't think I'd need to use something more powerful," Coach mutters.

"I believe the glow we all saw was your powers *trying* to manifest." Damian leans forward and rests his elbows on the desk. "The fact that yours—latent and dormant as they were—managed to appear at all suggests that they are quite potent."

I stare at him. "How is that possible?"

"Like any other talent, powers strength vary greatly from person to person," Damian says. "There is a correlation between strength and the concentration of godly blood you carry. In short, the closer your proximity to a deity, the stronger your powers."

"Which is a complicated way of saying . . .?"

Mom beams. "That your father was Nike's grandson."

It's a good thing I'm sitting down, because otherwise I think I'd fall over. I'm only one "great" away from a goddess?

"Your powers," Damian says, "have phenomenal potential."

Coach pumps his fist. "We are so going to win the Mediterranean Cup this year!" When Mom, Damian, and I all glare at him, he hurries to say, "Not that we'd use her powers to win, of course. Phoebe doesn't need powers to kick tail on the course."

Powers? My powers? I have phenomenal powers? Now that is a strange thought.

Yet somehow it makes sense. When I think about how easy running has always come for me, and how sometimes I can almost sense what other people are feeling (not to mention my almost unnatural obsession with Nike shoes) it seems almost logical that I'm descended from the goddess of victory herself. Being here, on Serfopoula, has made these things even more apparent. I dropped my already exceptional running time. I connect with Griffin and—I will never, ever admit this to Mom—I feel even closer to Dad. Maybe it was my godly blood coming home?

Another thought occurs. If I have godly blood then I must be able to zap stuff like everyone else. I know Nicole said you have to learn how to use powers, but I wonder if I can . . .

As soon as the thought enters my mind I get a tingling feeling in my hands. I look down and they're glowing.

Mom gasps.

Coach's jaw drops.

Damian smiles. Until the collection of framed diplomas and stuff hanging on the wall suddenly crash to the floor.

Maybe there's more to this whole zapping thing than I thought.

"Powers are not something to be toyed with." Damian waves his hand and the frames all zip back up onto the wall. "You will need to train. Extensively. Other students have had years to learn how to control their powers. If you can tap into yours this easily—and unintentionally—then you must take great care in your thoughts and actions until you have mastered them."

I hang my head. "Sorry."

Suddenly, the enormity of what I've just learned about myself hits me. I'm part god. I have supernatural powers. Powers I have no idea how to control.

“This is the other reason, besides your being my baby girl . . .” Mom gives me a watery smile. “. . . that I think you need to stay on at the Academy for an additional year.”

She’s right. Who knows what kind of damage I can do? I could probably destroy this entire island without even—

No, I probably shouldn’t even *think* that.

“Hey girls,” I say as I walk out of Damian’s office in a daze.

They’re standing in front of the trophy case with the golden apple, and when I speak they jump like they got caught watching the neighbor boy undress. I know this, because that’s just how we looked when we got caught spying on jerky Justin in eighth grade.

“Hi, Phoebes.” Cesca recovers first. “Have a good chat with the stepdad?”

Nola looks guiltily over her shoulder at the apple. I guess Damian is right: that apple is dangerous.

“Um, actually,” I say, knowing the time has come to tell them the truth about the island, “I have some pretty heavy stuff to tell you guys.” Nola still hasn’t looked away from the trophy case, so I suggest, “Why don’t we go out into the courtyard?”

Cesca and I each grab Nola by a shoulder and drag her around the corner and out through the double doors that open onto the courtyard. There is a line of stone benches circling the perimeter, so we head for one of those.

Nola elects to sit on the ground, pretzel-style, and turns her face up to absorb the sun.

Cesca checks the bench for dust. When it passes inspection, she sits and carefully crosses her legs.

I'm too wound up to sit. Instead, I start pacing. "I have something to tell you."

"Sounds serious," Nola says.

"Well . . ." I stalk three steps before spinning around. "It is."

Nola and Cesca look at each other. Knowing from years of experience that I mean it, they settle in for whatever I have to say.

"Cesca," I begin. "I don't know if you told Nola about my IM slip-up—"

"I didn't." She looks offended that I would even ask.

"But," I continue, indicating she shouldn't interrupt, "I want to explain to both of you the secret of Serfopoula."

"Aha!" Nola jumps up and points at me. "I knew there was something fishy about this island."

"Nola, please," I say.

Cesca smacks her on the leg. "Sit down and let her finish."

Nola sinks reluctantly back to the ground, but I can tell she's still gloating. And this time she's right.

"It's not a secret military testing ground or a witness protection hideout for the Kennedy conspirators."

Her lower lip pouts out and I can tell she's vastly disappointed.

"It is," I say, drawing it out with a sense of the dramatic, "more mythology than conspiracy." At their confused looks I continue. "Serfopoula is protected because the Academy is a private school for the descendants of Greek gods."

"For the what?" Nola asks.

Cesca uncrosses her legs and leans forward. "Get out."

“Really,” I say. “Everyone at the school is descended from a Greek god. Even my stepdad.”

I can’t quite bring myself to say it out loud—to say that I’m a descendant, too. It’s not that I’m afraid of how they’ll react—they’re my best friends and they love me—but somehow, saying it makes it undeniable. My freak status in the normal world will be irrevocable.

“Wow,” Cesca says, her voice full of awe.

Nola is silent. She looks like she’s in one of those meditative trances she goes into when she’s deep in yoga. That’s her way of dealing with major shocks.

“That is . . .” Cesca shakes her head. “. . . flipping awesome. So, like, these kids are related to Zeus and Apollo and Aphrodite and all of them?”

“Yup.”

“I don’t believe it,” Nola finally says.

“Do they have powers and stuff?” Cesca asks.

“More than you want to know about,” I say, speaking from experience.

“I don’t believe it,” Nola says again.

“Like what?” Cesca asks. “What can they do?”

“Whatever they want, as far as I can tell.”

“I don’t believe it!”

We both stare at Nola, shocked by her vehement outburst. She’s usually so calm and balanced, it’s a major shock when she gets upset.

“Nola, it’s true,” I say.

“That explains it,” Cesca says.

“Explains what?” I ask.

“That glow around you at the end of the race.”

I freeze.

“Come on, Nola,” Cesca says as she pokes the unmoving Nola in the ribs. “You saw that glow. What else could it have been?”

“No,” Nola insists. “I don’t believe it. Nothing you can do or say—”

Nola suddenly floats three feet off the ground before plopping back down on a giant cushion that wasn’t there a few seconds ago. I’m pretty sure I didn’t do that—wouldn’t know how to even if I wanted to. I look over my shoulder and see Troy standing in the doorway.

He winks.

I owe him one whopper of an apology.

Turning back to the girls, I say, “One second,” before running across the courtyard.

“She looked like she could use a little undeniable proof,” he says as I hurry over to him.

“Oh, Troy,” I say, hoping he’ll forgive me. “I’m so sorry. I shouldn’t have accused you when I didn’t have any proof. I shouldn’t have jumped to accusations at all, no matter what happened—”

“Hey,” he interrupts. “Don’t worry about it. It’s no big deal.”

“It is,” I insist. “Especially since it wasn’t you . . . it was me.”

He smiles like I’m totally dense. “Well, yeah. I could have told you that weeks ago.”

“You could have—” I shake my head. “How did you know?”

“A guy doesn’t come from a two-thousand-year line of doctors without being able to tell a little about a person’s physiology.”

“Then why didn’t you . . .?”

He raises his hands in surrender. “I didn’t want to be the messenger. You scare me." When I act appalled, he adds, "I figured you'd find out in your own time. Besides, I don't want to be on Petrolas's bad side. I'm the creative type—I'd never survive detention."

"You," I say, leaning forward and giving him a peck on the cheek, "are a rock star in coward's clothing."

"Was that supposed to be a compliment?"

"Of course," I insist.

He waves good-bye and I head back over to my girls.

"Who's the yumsicle?" Cesca asks.

"That's Troy," I say. "He's just a friend."

"I suppose," she says, "with a boy like Griffin around, Troy *can* be just a friend. Too bad there aren't boys like that at Pacific Park."

"If there were boys like that at Pacific Park, Southern California would be in for a world of trouble," I say with a laugh.

Nola is staring at the ground, muttering silently to herself. If I could read lips I'd probably hear a whole vocabulary I've never heard from Nola before.

When she finally manages to speak, all she says is, "Okay. I believe it."

"I can't believe you went this long without telling us," Cesca says.

And I feel horrible about that. "Like I said, it wasn't my secret to tell. If Mom and Damian hadn't given me the go-ahead I wouldn't be telling you now. It kills me to keep secrets from you guys, but I swear this is the only one." I bite my lip. "Only there's one last part of it."

They both look up at me eagerly.

Closing my eyes, I exhale fully. "I just found out . . . like five minutes ago . . . that well, I'm . . ." I suck in a quick breath—better to rip the bandage off in one quick pull—and blurt, "I'm part-god, too."

Cesca's mouth falls open. "Get out!"

"Omigod," Nola gasps, her eyes bulging wide with shock.

For what feels like hours they stare at me. Great, I'm a freak show. How can I expect to go out into the real world again when even my best friends think I'm a total abnormality?

Finally, Cesca speaks. "Oh, honey," she says, smiling. "We've always known you were a goddess. This just makes it legit."

Have I mentioned how much I love my best friends? In a heartbeat, they're both on their feet and we're in a massive group hug, complete with tears of joy.

"But that's the last secret, I promise," I say when I recover the ability to speak. "You know absolutely everything else."

I step back so I can wipe away my tears.

Cesca gets a weird look on her face as she turns to look at Nola. Nola looks just as strange. I recognize the looks. Guilt.

"Um, Phoebe," Cesca begins.

I know something's up because she sounds hesitant. Cesca is never hesitant.

"There's something we've been meaning to tell you," Nola says, having found her voice.

"What?" I'm getting scared, they are both acting strange.

Cesca clasps her hands together behind her back. "I know we've been planning on going to USC together since, like, forever."

"But," Nola says, wrapping an arm around my shoulders, "sometimes plans change."

"What are you guys talking about?"

"Well . . ." Cesca looks around me to Nola, then nods. "I'm not going to USC next year. Parsons accepted me early admission. If I want to go into couture fashion I can't be in L.A."

Parsons? That's on the whole other side of the country. "You're going to school in New York?"

She nods and looks apologetic.

I turn as Nola says, "And I'm going to Berkeley." She reaches out and tucks a stray lock of hair behind my ear. "It has the best Environmental Sciences program in the country."

I know they're right—about studying fashion in New York and environmental science at Berkeley—but I feel like they've betrayed me. We've been planning this for years now, and all of a sudden they change their minds at the last minute. How is that fair?

But as I look at them—both looking totally guilty for going separate ways—I realize how selfish I'm being. How could I ask them to give up their futures just so we can go to school together?

"You know," I say, putting my arms around them and pulling them back into a big hug, "I think this is great."

They both look at me like I've lost my mind. Maybe I have. But if I've learned anything from moving halfway around the world, it's that a change of plans can be a good thing. Sometimes it can even be a great thing. Right now, I can't imagine what my life would be like if Mom and I were still in L.A. No Greek gods. No Griffin. No Nicole and Troy. No learning that I'm part-goddess. All those things feel like a natural part of my life now. Who knows what the next set of changes might bring?

"We're best friends, no matter how far apart we are," I say. "Just because we have to go after life in different directions doesn't mean we're not still sisters on the inside."

When Damian leaves to take Nola and Cesca back to Athens and their plane, Mom goes with him. I go running.

As I lace up my Nikes I stop and stare at that perfect little swish. For years it's meant so much to me—a symbol of my running, my passion, and my connection to my dad. Now I know that all those things are part of me that can't be contained by a scrap of colorful leather.

Quickly knotting my laces, I head out the front door and toward the beach.

As my adrenaline flows, my mind clears and it's like every moment of my life leading to this moment makes perfect sense. Nike is in my soul. In my blood. And so is my dad. Maybe I feel so close to him when I run because that's when he's closest to me—that's when my Nike genes kick into full gear, and that's my dad.

I smile and shake my head. I'm a descendant of Nike!

Maybe Mom was right—about not telling me sooner about my heritage. I mean, if I'd been labeled as a Nike I'd have been tossed in with the Ares crowd in a flash. Nicole and Troy and I might never have become friends. They would have been off-limits to me. And the truce I have with Stella would have been completely fake. We might not be best friends, but at least I know how to read her bullcrap and that she is genuinely starting to like me—even if it's against her will.

Reaching the rocky cliffs at the far end of the beach, I sink down into the powder-soft sand. Sure, Griffin and I could have still ended up together since we'd have been in the same clique, but nothing else about my life would be—

“I figured I’d find you here.”

I look up as Griffin sits down on the sand next to me.

“I was just thinking about you,” I say.

“I would hope so,” he says, smiling, “I’ve been trailing you since you hit the beach.”

“Couldn’t keep up, huh?”

He shrugs. “Thought you needed some time.”

He sits there, arms resting on his knees as he stares out over the water, looking at me with those breathtaking blue eyes. Though he doesn’t say anything, I know he knows.

“Who told you?” I ask.

“About your heritage?” He focuses on the water. “Travatas.”

Suddenly there’s a distance between us, and not the physical kind. Griffin is miles away on the inside and I’m not sure what that means. What if that means there’s some kind of Olympic law against our dating? Maybe Ares’s and Nike’s aren’t allowed to—

“There was a prophecy,” he says, interrupting my increasingly panicked thoughts.

“A prophecy?” This could be even worse. I remember that prophecy from *Oedipus*—what if Griffin is supposed to kill me, or, *ew,* what if we’re related or something.

“Before I was born, my mother visited the oracle and requested a reading.” There’s a hint of sadness in his eyes. My panic vanishes as I realize that he’s thinking about his mom.

“What did the oracle say?”

He smiles sadly and shakes his head. “She told my mother that her son would find his match in a daughter of victory.”

“Oh,” I say. Then, “Ohhh! Wow.”

Daughter of victory. That's *me.*

Turning to look at me—a few stray curls falling across his forehead—he says, "Yeah, *wow.*"

I tuck one of the curls behind his ear. "Well, I am the only one who beat your tail on the racecourse."

He throws back his head and laughs. "Oh Phoebe," he says—I still get shivers when he says my name—and hugs me close to his side. "That's the least of it. You just found out you're Nike's great-granddaughter. You can do—almost—whatever you want in the entire world."

I close my eyes. It's the *almost* that brings sudden tears to my eyes.

All I can think is why did Dad choose football over staying with us? He loved us, I know he did. I have enough memories of him to know that without a doubt. Was football worth more than that? More than us?

For six years I've thought he died in a freak accident, in some bizarre act of nature. That if he had known about it beforehand, he would have never played in that game. If he had only known, he would still be with us.

But now I know he *did* know. Maybe not that he would be smoted at that particular game, but eventually.

Everything I ever thought about my dad is wrong.

Like I never knew him at all.

Then again, when I'm running I can't imagine giving that up for anything. I don't think I would ever cheat, but maybe the temptation of greatness was more powerful than questionable ethics for Dad. Or maybe, like how mine tried to come out during the race, he hadn't meant to use his powers.

~~~

"I didn't mean to try to cheat," I say, wanting Griffin to know I would never cheat on purpose. "I know if Coach hadn't grounded everyone's powers, mine would have come out, but that's not me. That's not how I—"

"Come on, Phoebe." He levels an exasperated stare at me. "You've just realized you have powers. Of course it's going to take some training to learn how to control them." His lips creep into a small smile. "When I first got my powers I was eight. I zapped my nanny to the Amazon."

"But see . . ." I turn to face him. ". . . you've had ten years to practice. How can I expect to control them like you—"

"You won't," he says, squeezing me closer. "Not at first."

I shake my head, overwhelmed by the idea of having powers and having to learn to control them.

"For a while—maybe even a long while—they'll be controlled by your emotions." He places his hand over mine, lacing our fingers together. "Like today."

I turn to face him. "That's what I'm worried about. I didn't even know what I was doing. What if I—"

"You wouldn't have been driven to using your powers by the need to prove yourself if I hadn't let my emotions get the better of me at tryouts." He looks out at the water, his cheeks red. "I didn't consciously knot your shoelaces, you know."

"What do you mean?"

He takes my hand and starts rubbing his thumb in little circles against my palm.

He sighs. "I was so conflicted about my feelings for you—feeling like I should scare you off because I thought you were a *nothos* and
~~~

at the same time feeling overwhelmingly attracted to you . . . to something inside you. Since that first morning on the beach. Even though I knew who—what—you were, I couldn't stop feeling this way. I just—" His cheeks turn redder. "My powers responded to my emotions and—"

"Sent me tumbling face-first into the dirt?" I say, joking. "Yeah, I remember that part."

"I'm sorry," he says, squeezing my hand tighter. "I wish I could go back and—"

"So you're saying even you can't fully control your powers?"

With his free hand, he rubs his palm against the knee of his jeans. "It takes a lifetime to have complete control. We all have to work at it." Looking up at me from beneath his lids, he adds, "The teachers at the Academy can help you learn control faster than you ever could on your own."

Is he right? Would it be better if I stayed on Serfopoula through next year and learned how to use—I mean control my powers?

"Who knows what havoc you might wreak on the poor, unsuspecting citizens of Los Angeles?" He leans over and nudges me with his shoulder. "You'd be endangering the safety of millions of people."

"Really?" I ask with feigned awe. "Am I that powerful?"

He looks like he wants to lie, but thinks better of it—and a good thing, too, because I've had enough lies and half-truths to last me a lifetime.

"No," he admits. "Probably not. But you could level a house or two."

"Well, then. For the safety of Los Angeles," I say in mock severity, leaning into his shoulder, "I should learn to control my powers before I return."

"So you're staying?" he asks, his voice full of anticipation. "Through Level 13?"

"Maybe . . ." I hedge. "If you'll teach me one trick."

"Anything."

"Teach me how to turn water green."

He frowns at me. "What have you got planned?"

"Nothing," I promise innocently. "I just want to help my mom with her wedding color scheme."

"All right," he says, laying back and pulling me down next to him. "I'll teach you on one condition."

Smiling, I nudge closer until my mouth is inches from his. "What's that?"

"You never . . ." He leans forward to peck a kiss on my cheek. ". . . ever . . ." On my other cheek. ". . . use that trick . . ." On the tip of my nose. ". . . on me."

Instead of answering, I kiss him.

I wonder if he realizes that no answer means no promise. Then he reaches up and cradles my cheek in his hand and I stop wondering anything.

I'm kissing a boy with godly powers and movie-star-worthy looks. I'm part god myself. I'm surrounded by the turquoise Aegean, and stretched out on the pristine beach of Serfopoula, a tiny island I'm suddenly glad no one has ever even heard of.

EPILOGUE

WHEN THE ACADEMY'S string quartet plays the opening strains of Handel's *Water Music* the flower girl—Damian's four-year-old niece—starts down the aisle, throwing white rose petals everywhere.

Beside me I can feel Stella fuming, and not because I get to walk with Damian's only attendant, his best man, and she has to walk alone.

The wedding planner points to her and motions down the aisle. Stella shakes her head vehemently, backing up like she wants to leave the church.

"Huh-uh," I say, pushing her back into the doorway. "Don't want to ruin the wedding."

Her stare could melt glass. And if Damian hadn't grounded her powers this morning, I'd probably be a puddle on the floor right now. With one last snarl in my direction, she turns and walks toward the altar.

I don't know why she's so upset.

The green tint of her hair really brings out her eyes. And coordinates perfectly with her blue-green bridesmaid dress. I think after all the crap she put me through those first few weeks of school, I deserve a little good-natured retribution. Besides, it's not like it'll be documented for all eternity—Griffin taught me how to make sure it doesn't show up in the photos.

Some people are never happy.

I, on the other hand, have never been happier.

I managed to make it through the first semester of Level 12 with my B average—my C in Literature balanced out by an A in Art History. I've even decided to stay on another year at the Academy—only partly so I can go to Oxford with Griffin next year. I'm having a blast—sometimes literally—learning how to use my powers. Another year of instruction and my Nikes might actually stop spontaneously combusting every time I'm in a close race.

As I pass the pews, I glance at Cesca and Nola and smile. Nola nudges Troy, who hasn't noticed that the wedding started two minutes ago. He looks up and waves. Thankfully he was very forgiving of a certain ignorant girl who didn't believe he didn't use his powers to help her cheat.

Cesca is arguing with the boy next to her—he was in my Physics class but I can never remember his name.

Leave it to Cesca to pick a battle with a complete stranger.

In the pew on the other side of the aisle Nicole and Griffin are sitting with Damian's sister-in-law. Griffin has Damian's youngest niece in his lap. He looks up at me and grins just as the toddler slaps him so loud I hear it.

Griffin scowls like I had something to do with her lashing out. I just smile and let him wonder. It's better if he doesn't know what I'm capable of.

Approaching the altar I look at Damian. He looks handsome in his tuxedo, but he also looks . . . nervous! I can't believe it. I never thought I would live to see Damian Petrolas nervous, but here he is.

Grinning like a fool, he looks at me. I smile softly and nod. He has nothing to be nervous about. Mom's as in love with him as he is with her. He relaxes a little and I sigh with relief. We'd probably have to do this whole ceremony again if he passes out.

I take my place next to Stella and ignore her fuming.

The quartet switches smoothly over to the wedding march. Everyone in the packed church stands, turning to watch Mom walk down the aisle.

She looks beautiful—a vision in ecru.

I've never seen her happier, either.

As she makes her step-stop way down the aisle, I think about how much has changed in a few short months. And through all the ups and downs, I think the ends definitely justify the means. There isn't a single thing I would go back and change.

Not that I could.

Nicole promises me that any attempts at time travel result in serious punishment—and the possible nullification of all existence.

But I've learned that I do have a few tricks up my sleeve.

Keeping my hand hidden behind my bouquet, I point a finger at the ceiling. The air above the guests glows faintly. Dozens of white rose petals float perfectly to the floor, showering Mom in a floral snowfall. She looks up, letting some of the petals float over her face. When she looks back down the aisle she gives me one of the biggest tear-filled smiles I've ever seen.

She mouths, *Thank you.*

I just smile. I am definitely getting used to this goddess thing.

thank you . . .

. . . Sarah Shumway, goddess of editing, for helping forge my story into something worthy of the Dutton name—and for understanding—or at least not fighting—my excessive use of em dashes.

. . . Jenny Bent, goddess of agenting, for being my perfect agent, keeping the faith, and having my back every step along the sometimes rocky way, and for telling me to call more often.

. . . Sharie Kohler, goddess of critique partnering, for saving me more times and in more ways than I can count, and for inspiring me to be a better writer in every way.

. . . Shane Bolks, goddess of mentoring, for answering my endless stream of questions, and for listening to all my wild ideas with admirable patience and a straight face.

. . . The Buzz Girls, goddesses of booksboysbuzz.com, for being the best cheering section a girl could want, and for sharing their innermost selves without hesitation or reservation.

. . . Don and Jane Childs, god and goddess of parenting, for supporting me unconditionally no matter how many times I say, "Here's my new plan," and for insisting that it's because they love me and not because I'm their only child. I love you, too.

Turn the page for a preview of

goddess boot camp

CHAPTER I

HYDROKINESIS

SOURCE: POSEIDON

The ability to control and move liquids. Density of liquid affects level of control. Water is the easiest liquid to manipulate because, with the exception of dramatically dry environments (i.e. Las Vegas, Sahara Desert, Australian Outback), it is always present in the surrounding air.

DYNAMOTHEOS STUDY GUIDE © Stella Petrolas

I.

Am.

A.

Goddess.

An honest-to-goodness goddess.

With superpowers and everything.

Okay, so I'm just a minor, minor, *minor* goddess. Technically, I'm supposed to say *hematheos*, which means godly blood, or *part* god, but goddess sounds much more impressive (to the like ten people I'm allowed to tell). There's no percentage requirement or anything—all that matters is having a god or goddess somewhere up the line, and my great-grandmother, it turns out, is Nike. The goddess; not the shoe. That makes me a tiny leaf on a narrow branch of the massive and ancient family tree of the gods.

So I can say with only minor hesitation that I, Phoebe Castro, am a goddess. The thing is, I only learned this about myself a few months ago—when my mom married a Greek guy and transplanted me halfway around the world to the tiny island of Serfopoula.

I spent the first seventeen years of my life believing I was a perfectly normal girl from a *semi*functional family with a deceased dad and a workaholic mom. Then *wham-o*, I find out Dad's dead because he disobeyed some supernatural edict and got smoted to Hades and I am, in fact, part of the *fully* dysfunctional family of Greek gods. Talk about your issues.

Being part goddess comes with some serious perks, though. Namely *powers*. I can pretty much do whatever I want whenever I want so long as I don't break any of those aforementioned supernatural edicts. These include, but are not limited to: no bringing people back from the dead (not a problem because, even though I'm dying to see my dad again, I don't actually want to *die* to do it. I have a lot to live for—like my fabulous boyfriend, Griffin Blake), no traveling through time in either direction, and no using your powers to succeed in the *nothos*—the normal human—world.

These seem like no big deal, right? Well, they wouldn't be . . . if I could keep my powers under control. But that is way harder than I ever imagined.

My stepdad, Damian Petrolas—part god himself—says it's going to take time and training. Everyone else at the Academy—the ultra-private school for the descendants of Greek gods where he happens to be the headmaster—has known about their powers almost since birth. They started learning how to use them properly before they could walk. But even they sometimes have trouble keeping their powers under control, like last September when my not-yet-boyfriend Griffin accidentally knotted my Nikes together during cross-country tryouts.

Like I said, I've only *known* about these powers for a few months and these things aren't exactly easy to control. Once, I slept through my alarm and tried to zap myself to class before the bell—my first-period teacher, Ms. "Tyrant" Tyrovolas, has a zero-tolerance tardy policy—and wound up crashing a parent-headmaster conference in Damian's office. Can you say detention?

Clearly it's going to take a while to figure this out.

So I could spend more time on my powers training, Damian banned me from running more than five miles a day until school let out (last week, thank Nike!). Even my cross-country coach at the Academy, Coach Lenny, supported the reduced running time. He says I can never race in the Olympics if there's a chance I might accidentally turn my competitors into molasses or something. Only the lure of the Olympics could convince me to cut back on running. That and the fear of accidentally getting myself smoted by the gods. Eternity in the underworld is a pretty big deterrent.

All the time I used to spend on cross-country I had to spend on learning to control my powers. Not that all the extra training helped much. Countless after-school sessions and weekend lessons—with

Damian, Griffin, my friends Nicole Matios and Troy Travatas, various Academy teachers, or, on days when the Fates were feeling vengeful, my evil stepsister, Stella—and I'm still a menace. No matter how many times I close my eyes and concentrate on moving the book across the table, sensing my instructor du jour's thoughts, or manifesting an apple from thin air, it inevitably backfires. Hideously.

Sure, with Griffin's help I figured out how to turn Stella's hair green for Mom and Damian's wedding, but my attempt at zapping myself some new Nikes ended very, very badly. Let's just say I like my toes and I'm thankful every day that I have all ten of them.

Now it's summer break and I still have only limited control.

I'm back to my regular running schedule, training for the Pythian Games trials, which are just two weeks away, and wondering whether my next powers screwup will be the one that lands me in Hades.

Some days I wish I'd never learned the truth. Life would be so much less complicated if Mom had never met Damian. Right now, I'd be back in L.A. with Nola and Cesca, enjoying my last summer before college by spending hours on the beach. Maybe finally learning how to surf from some hottie surfer boy who would totally fall in love with Nola and—

"Phoebe!"

I shudder at the sound of Damian's voice echoing through the house. He sounds really, really, *really* upset.

"Yes?" I answer as sweetly as possible from the relative safety of my bedroom. Not that walls hinder his ability to read minds—or sense fear.

I watch the door nervously. I know it's a bad sign when I see water streaming under the crack, flowing into the grout lines between each tile and pooling in the depressions of the age-worn ceramic surfaces.

"Trust me," Damian says from the other side of my door, "you do not wish to make me open this door myself."

I leap up from my desk chair and, neatly avoiding the rivulets lacing across my floor, pull open the door. "Damian, I'm—"

My mouth drops open and my apology sticks in my throat.

Normally impeccably-dressed-in-a-suit-and-tie Damian is standing there wearing board shorts, Birkenstocks, and a shark's-tooth necklace. Oh, and he's *soaking* wet.

"Omigods, Damian," I blurt, staring instantly at the floor—I do not need to see my stepdad's bare chest, thank you very much. "I'm so sorry. I didn't mean to, um . . ." I wave my hand up and down in his direction, still averting my eyes. "Sorry, sorry, sorry. I was just thinking about how much I miss L.A. and that I've never learned how to surf and now that school's out I could go if I didn't have the Pythian trials and my stupid powers weren't—"

Damian holds up his hand and takes a deep, *deep* breath. He lets it out super slow, with a little bit of a growl from the back of his throat. And then he takes another. And another.

I've really done it this time. I mean, the palm tree in the living room had been bad enough, but he is clearly beyond furious at the moment.

Instinctively I inch back a step . . . right into a growing puddle. The sloshing sound of me smacking into the water breaks his deep breathing.

“I am not angry with you,” he says, carefully enunciating each word. “Truly.”

I’m not convinced.

He runs a hand through his wet hair, sending a fresh spray of water droplets everywhere.

“Oh, for Hera’s sake,” he mutters. For a second I’m nearly blinded by a bright glow, and when I open my eyes again, Damian is back to his dry, fully clothed self. The puddles are still there. “Let us speak in my office, shall we?”

I hang my head and follow Damian through the house. Why do these things keep happening to me? I mean, you’d think after all these months I’d have improved a little. At least enough so that things wouldn’t go haywire when I’m just randomly thinking about completely non-powers-related stuff.

“Please,” Damian gestures at a chair in front of his desk. “Have a seat.”

Sinking into the soft leather—hard-core-hippie Nola would have a field day with the cruel and unnecessary use of animal hide—I try to clear my mind of all thoughts. It’s thinking that gets me into trouble. If I could go the rest of my life without thinking, then—

“I know you are using your powers neither carelessly nor intentionally,” Damian says as he lowers into his chair. “But in the several months since your powers first manifested, your control has not improved. In fact”—he pinches the bridge of his nose like the idea of my uncontrolled powers gives him a headache—“it may have gotten worse.”

Worse? My heart sinks. I’ve been spending hours upon hours working on controlling my powers. All right, some of those hours—okay, *many* of those hours—were spent with Griffin. And maybe we don't *always* spend every second on my training, but hey, a girl can't focus on work *all* the time when in the presence of such a god. Can she?

"I don't blame you, Phoebe. We both know that, since you are the third generation removed from Nike, your powers are stronger than most. It is not surprising that you are having difficulty controlling them." He smiles kindly and my stomach kind of clenches.

I don't need pity . . . I need help.

"I don't know what else to do," I say, trying not to whine. I am so not a whiner. "I'm sorry. I've been working hard. Maybe I just need a little more time."

"Unfortunately," he says, "we have little time left."

Little time left? What is that supposed to mean? No one ever said anything about a time limit. No learn-to-use-your-powers-by-summer-or-else speech. Suddenly I have an image of myself, chained to the wall in the school dungeon—not that they have one, but this is my nightmare and I can be as creative as I want—being tempted by cheesy, yummy *bougatsa* I'm not allowed to eat until I learn to—

"Phoebe," Damian says, interrupting my fantasy of torture and bringing my attention back to his desk—which is, I realize with sad resignation, now covered in the cheesy pastry treat. Damian waves his hand over the *bougatsa*, erasing it as quickly as it came, and says, "Please, try to restrain your rampant imagination. No one is going to torture you for your lack of control."

“Sorry,” I say for like the millionth time. I don’t mean it any less, but it’s starting to feel like the only thing I know how to say.

I shake off the self-pity. Feeling sorry for myself is not going to solve the problem.

Damian leans forward, resting his elbows on his pastry-free desk. “I was hoping this would not be an issue. That you would harness your powers in your own time without intervention from the gods, but—”

“Whoa!” I jump forward to the edge of my seat and wave my hands in front of me. “The gods?”

Damian smiles tightly and tugs at the knot in his tie.

Oh no. In the nine months since Mom and I moved in, I’ve learned that an uncomfortable Damian is *never* a good sign.

“Since we discovered your heritage, the gods have been closely monitoring your *dynamotheos* progress.”

“My dyno-what?”

“*Dynamotheos,*” he repeats. “The official term for the powers derived from the gods. They’ve been observing you—”

“Observing me?” My teeth clench. “Like how?”

I imagine the sneaky gods spying on me in the shower or the locker room or when I’m “studying” with Griffin.

“Circumspectly, I assure you.”

I am *not* assured.

Damian shuffles papers on his desk. “In any event, they are . . . *ah-hem* . . . concerned about your progress.”

Not the *ah-hem*. I have a feeling I’m in big trouble.

“The gods have decreed that you must . . . *ah-hem* . . . pass a test of their design before the upcoming summer solstice.”

“And what *exactly* does this test entail?” I ask, already fearing the answer. Whenever Damian breaks into *ah-hems* and nervous shuffling, it always spells bad news for me.

My introduction to this nervous Damian was last year when he told me the Greek gods—you know, Zeus, Hermes, Aphrodite . . . those gods—were real, not myth. So there's probably something major—and majorly unpleasant—coming my way.

“I couldn't say, exactly. In my time as headmaster, they have only demanded such a test from one other student.” His mouth tightens a little around the edges. “It will be designed with your personal strengths and weaknesses in mind. I can tell you, however, that it will put your powers—and your control of your powers—to the ultimate test. That is why I would like to accelerate your training.”

“Why?” I shift nervously in my seat. “When exactly is summer solstice?”

“The precise date is . . . *ah-hem* . . . the twenty-first.” He readjusts his tie. Again. “Of June.”

“The twenty-first of June?” I leap out of my chair and start pacing. “That's only . . .” I count down on my fingers. “Sixteen days away.”

“The gods do not prize patience as a great virtue.”

“You think?” I ask, pulling out my best sarcasm.

I am not even pacified by the fact that he looks embarrassed.

He *should* be embarrassed. Even if this isn't his fault.

Why does this stuff happen to me? I mean, I barely make it through what should have been my skate-through senior year with a B average. Now, after deciding to stick around an extra year to work on my powers—and to spend another year with the previously mentioned amazing boyfriend, Griffin—I find out I have to pass a test that proves I know how to control my powers *first*. Talk about a contradiction.

"What happens if I fail?" I ask. "Do I have to repeat Level 12, or what?"

"You will not fail," he says, way too eagerly. "You have my word."

"Okay," I agree. "But what if I *do*?"

"If you do?" More paper shuffling. "You will be placed in a kind of . . . remedial program."

There is something more he's not saying, I can tell. I've learned to read him pretty well since he became my stepdad. But, at this point, I'm not prepared to dwell. I have an extreme imagination for coming up with all kinds of crazy punishment scenarios, but in this world—the world of myths and gods and *dynamotheos* powers—sometimes even my worst fears pale in comparison. Prometheus getting his liver pecked out daily by a giant eagle comes to mind. I don't *want* to know what he's not telling me.

"I will not allow you to fail," he says again.

"How exactly are you going to make sure I don't? Do you have some kind of magical get-out-of-Hades-free card?" I pace back and forth in front of his desk. "You and Mom are leaving in the morning for your honeymoon. You can't exactly work with me from Thailand, can you?"

"Of course not," he answers smoothly. "I have already arranged for an alternative training program."

I silently hope this means even more private lessons from Griffin, but I know I'm not that lucky. And Damian's not that considerate of my love life.

"No, not private lessons," he says, proving again that he can read minds. "I have enrolled you in *Dynamotheos* Development Camp. You begin in the morning."

"Now I have to pass this mysterious test before summer solstice or I'll get held back a year." I flop back next to Nicole on my bed, staring at the white plaster ceiling while my feet dangle off the edge. "Or locked in the school dungeon or chained to a mountainside—"

"You're being melodramatic," Nicole interrupts. "No one's been chained to a mountain in centuries. And those rumors about the torture devices in the dungeon are completely fabricated."

At my panicked look, she relents. "I'm teasing." She grabs a pillow and smacks me over the stomach. "Lighten up, will ya?"

I try to relax with a deep breath and a heavy sigh. It doesn't work.

Nicole is so much better at the whole go-with-the-flow, leave-your-worries-behind thing. Me? I'm like a poster child for stressing about stuff you can't control.

I don't know what I'd do if she weren't staying on Serfopoula for the summer. Of course, she stays on Serfopoula *every* summer—it's one of the contingencies for allowing her back on the island to attend the Academy after her parents were banished by the gods. She can't leave until she graduates.

That sucks for her, but I'm glad she's here.

"Does Petrolas have a plan to boost your training?"

"Yeah." I sigh, wishing I was a little more spiky-blonde-haired extremist girl, instead of long-brown-ponytailed worry girl. "He's sending me to *Dynamotheos* Development Camp for the next two weeks."

"Goddess Boot Camp?" she gasps. "Seriously?"

Goddess Boot Camp? My stomach knots at the thought of a military-style training program. Multimile marches at dawn. Rope climbs in the rain. Instructors standing on my back while I do a million push-ups. A far cry from the cross-country and wilderness camps I've experienced.

"Is there something wrong with that?"

"No." Nicole starts laughing uncontrollably, practically rolling off my bed. "Nothing"—*laugh, laugh, laugh*—"wrong"—*laugh, laugh, laugh*—"with that."

"What?" I demand, shoving her shoulder so she *does* roll off the bed. "I'm going to be turned into a goat, aren't I? How can I train for the Pythian trials with four legs?"

I follow her off the bed and start pacing.

The Pythian Games are a huge deal. Apparently, the Olympics weren't always the only games in town. When the last ancient Olympics were held in the year 393, the Pythian Games became restricted to *hematheos* competitors and went underground. They've been held every four years—except during World Wars I and II—since forever.

Griffin and I were invited by the coach of the Cycladian team—

who also happens to be Coach Lenny—to try out for this summer's games.

We're supposed to start training today. In fact—I check my watch—he's supposed to be here any second.

"Relax," Nicole says as she pulls herself off the floor. "It's not so much scary as . . ." She smiles. "Embarassing."

"Great. That's just what I need." I flop into the giant squishy chair Mom and Damian bought for my birthday, sinking into the turquoise velvet softness. "Another reason for everyone to make fun of me."

Being the new girl at a school full of descendants of the gods is no cakewalk. You'd think once I found out I was a descendant, too, they would let up. But no. Most of them still treat me like a total outsider. An interloper who can't control her powers. An intruder. Especially after I "stole" Griffin—as if you can steal someone who doesn't want to be stolen—away from cheer queen Adara Spencer. And don't think she has ever let me forget it. When we had to give our final speeches in Oral Communications two weeks ago, she made every word I said come out in pig latin.

Partly, Damian says, it's that I'm closer to Nike than most of them are to their gods. They're jealous, he says. Right. And jerky Justin dumped me because I was too good for him.

"Don't worry," Nicole says, trying to be reassuring after laughing herself into hysterics. "Maybe no one will find out you're in boot camp."

"Really?" I ask, hopeful even if she's just trying to make me feel better.

“Sure.” She takes a seat on my bed. “Usually it’s just a couple of upper-class counselors, a faculty director, and about a dozen, um, campers.”

My racing heart calms down. A little.

“Okay,” I say, breathing a sigh of relief. “That should be okay. Maybe the counselors will be friendlies.”

Not that there are many. Besides Nicole, our good friend Troy, Griffin, and a couple of my cross-country teammates, there aren’t many kids at the Academy I could call friendly, let alone friends.

With my luck, they’ll be a couple of Adara’s groupies who can’t wait to expose my embarrassment to the world. It’s not like I can do anything to make them like me since I didn’t do anything to make them hate me in the first place. My existence is reason enough for them.

Besides, the truth is I am a little freaked out about controlling my powers, especially considering how my dad died. I haven’t worked out all the details yet, but he used his powers to improve his football career . . . and wound up smoted by the gods. I don’t think I’ll ever know exactly what happened. The gods frown on the misuse of powers in the *nothos* world and they could just as easily smote me for using them accidentally.

Controlling my powers is a good thing, and I’m looking forward to the day when I can zap myself a Gatorade without worrying that I’ll wind up wrestling an alligator.

“Who knows?” I say. “Going to Goddess Boot Camp could be fun.”